Cash Up Front

Front

Second Edition

Cash Up Front

Second Edition

Mike Faricy

Library of Congress Control Number: 2023915502
paperback ISBN: 978-1-962080-39-2
e-Book ISBN: 978-1-962080-40-8

MJF Publishing books may be purchased for education, Business, or promotional use. For information on bulk purchases,
please contact the author directly at mikefaricyauthor@gmail.com

Published by

MJF Publishing
https://www.mikefaricybooks.com

To Teresa
"We need to talk..."

Acknowledgments

I would like to thank the following people for their help and support:

Special thanks to my editors, Kitty, Donna and Rhonda for their hard work, cheerful patience and positive feedback.

I would like to thank Ann and Julie for their creative talent and not slitting their wrists or jumping off the high bridge when dealing with my Neanderthal computer capabilities.

Special thanks to Ann for her patience.

Last, I would like to thank family and friends for their encouragement and unqualified support. Special thanks to Maggie, Jed, Schatz, Pat, Av, Emily and Pat for not rolling their eyes, at least when I was there, and most of all, to my wife Teresa whose belief, support and inspiration has from day one, never waned.

Prologue

The waiter wore a black tux and latex gloves. He smiled, turned off the gas torch, and handed a white ramekin with crème brûlée to Heidi and one to me. He said something to Heidi in French. She smiled and said, "No, Merci," and he left.

With my spoon, I tapped the melted sugar top he had just torched. It sounded like I was tapping the countertop. Crème brûlée, I loved the stuff." What did the waiter ask you?"

"He wanted to know if I'd go home with him tonight."

My eyes grew wide. I held my spoon in midair, about an inch from my mouth. "What? He really asked that?"

Heidi rolled her eyes and said, "Yeah, right, Dev. Get the hook out of your mouth."

She was wearing an exquisite blue silk dress with spaghetti straps, tight, low cut, and wonderfully short. This week, her hair was dark and gorgeous, straight and curving around her jawline. She looked like she'd just stepped out of a fashion magazine." Well, you are the most beautiful woman in the place."

"Mmm-mmm, aren't you just playing all your cards right tonight."

"Hey, it's your birthday, and by the way, I meant what I said. You are the most beautiful woman in this place." Social distancing was in effect. Tables were about ten feet apart. No tables seated more than four people. The waiters in this top-notch restaurant were wearing tuxedos, latex gloves, and face masks.

She took another spoonful of crème brûlée and got an almost orgasmic look on her face. "Oh, God help me, but I could eat a dozen of these."

"If you want another one, I'll order it."

"Oh, thanks, but I'd better not. I need to behave."

"Behave?"

"Don't worry, Dev. Relax, you'll get your reward before the night is over. This has been the most wonderful night. Thank you for making it so special."

"Like I said, it's your birthday, and you threatened me within an inch of my life if I got you a gift or a card."

"Sorry, but you know how I get about growing a year older."

"Yeah, I know how you get, just like a fine wine, better with every year. Speaking of which, would you like another glass or maybe an after-dinner drink?"

"Oh, thanks, I would, but not here, maybe once we get back to my place."

I smiled and finished my crème brûlée in six quick scoops of my spoon.

"Dev, slow down. I'm going to take my time here, and then we'll go home and attend to your needs, well, and mine too," she said and smiled.

I eventually paid the tab. Keeping my fingers crossed, my credit card wouldn't be denied. We headed out the door fifteen minutes later. I handed the valet our ticket. He nodded and headed back to the parking lot. As he disappeared, a black stretch-limo suddenly pulled out of the parking lot and stopped in front of us.

"You didn't have to do this," Heidi joked.

My first thought was it must be for someone at a groom's dinner or maybe some high-priced out of town business guy, but then the rear door opened and a muscular guy about six-five, with a shaved head and an S-curved nose stepped out and held the door open. He cleared his throat and coughed.

A voice from the back seat called "Heidi Bauer?"

"Oh my God," Heidi said as she bent over to look in. "Yes?"

"If you wouldn't mind joining me, I'd like to talk to you about an investment."

"Dev? Did you do this?"

I shook my head and looked at the guy with the 'S' curved nose. "No, honest. I don't know what this is about."

"Please, Miss Bauer, this shouldn't take more than twenty minutes or so. I'm sure you'll find my offer very much to your liking. We'll drop you off at home, and you can continue your evening."

"I'm sorry, do I know you?"

"No, at least not yet. My name is Tommy Benedetti. Please, if you wouldn't mind, I'm on a bit of a tight schedule."

"Well, I'm… You see I'm with someone and I really can't meet right—"

"Melvin, if you would please," the voice said.

The middle door suddenly opened, and two guys slid out. One of them had a skull tattoo on his right forearm with the numbers 666 on the forehead of the skull. They took three steps toward Heidi as I stepped in front of her and said, "Heidi, get back in the restaurant and call the—"

The thug with the skull tattoo gave me a quick, solid elbow in the solar plexus and a chop to the back of my neck. I collapsed on my knees, attempting to catch my breath. I looked up just in time to see the stretch-limo make a right turn out of the parking lot. I reached in my pocket for my phone only to remember it was sitting exactly where I left it so I wouldn't forget it, on the corner of my dresser.

I slowly stood, cranked my head left and right, and heard my neck crack a couple of times. A pair of headlights came out of the parking lot, Heidi's red Mercedes. The valet hopped out of the car and held the driver's door for me. I pulled a bill from my pocket and shoved it at him as I hopped behind the wheel. As I accelerated, I glanced over and realized I'd handed him a twenty. Too late to correct that mistake, he grinned and gave me a thumbs-up as I shot out of the parking lot and screeched into a right-hand turn. I raced down University Avenue swerving past everyone driving close to the speed limit. After four miles, it was obvious the stretch limo had turned off somewhere along the way. I swore, slapped the steering wheel a couple of times, slowed down, and headed over to Heidi's house.

One

I pulled in behind my car parked in front of Heidi's house. I ran up to the front door and used her keys to unlock the door. "Heidi. Heidi?" I called, hoping she'd answer. Unfortunately, she didn't. The table lamp next to the front window was on and so were the kitchen lights, just the way we'd left them.

I was standing in the living room, looking out the picture window, sipping my second Jameson. I was cursing myself for not packing a gun. The stretch limo suddenly pulled to a stop, and the same thug with the S-curved nose hopped out of the back and held the door open. Heidi slid out of the limo carrying a metal briefcase just as I hurried out the front door with a carving knife.

"Heidi? Heidi? Are you okay? Heidi?"

The thug gave me an unconcerned glance, nodded at Heidi, and slid back into the limo. The door closed as it sped up the street then turned at the corner and disappeared.

"You okay, Heidi?"

"Yeah, I'm fine, I think. I could use a drink, Dev."

"Come on. Let's get you inside. What the hell was with those guys? Did they hurt you? Did they—"

Heidi looked at the carving knife in my right hand and said, "Dev, relax, I'm okay. He just wanted to talk, and he gave me these funds for an investment," she said and held up the metal briefcase. The thing was silver with a black handle, rounded corners, a combination lock, and looked large enough to maybe carry a change of clothes. "Let's just go inside, please," she said and headed across the lawn, picking up her pace the closer she got to the front door.

She made her way into the kitchen and set the brief-case on the counter. She washed her hands with the antibacterial hand wash for two or three minutes. All the while, mumbling, "Crazy. Absolutely crazy. He said he was going to invest. Not that he wanted to, but that he was going to. God, I need a drink. This was crazy. Absolutely crazy."

"You have some wine in the fridge?" I asked, opening the refrigerator door. There were three bottles of white wine and a bottle of prosecco lying on the top shelf.

"I've got vodka in the cabinet," she said and shot another squirt of hand wash into her hand. I went out to the dining room and opened the door to the liquor cabinet. There were three different vodka bottles. I grabbed the bottle of Grey Goose and went back to the kitchen. I took a martini glass out of the cupboard and placed it on the kitchen counter.

"Just a glass and some ice," she said as she did a final rinse of her now sterilized hands.

"Okay, you want some olives or vermouth in—"

"God, never mind, I'll do it myself," she said. She grabbed the bottle out of my hand and poured an inch of vodka into the water glass next to the kitchen sink. She drained the glass and shuddered. "Oh, God," she groaned and cleared her throat. She poured two inches into the glass, grabbed two ice cubes from the freezer, tossed them into the glass then took a somewhat sensible sip.

"Feeling better? Calming down?" I asked.

"I'm not sure."

"What did that guy want? What did he say his name was, Tommy something?"

"Tommy Benedetti. He wanted to invest in Lemax Partners."

"Lemax Partners, isn't that your new fund? The one you were looking for investors?"

She shot me a look. "I'm looking for qualified investors. Not some criminal gangster who throws me into a car, hands me a bunch of cash, and tells me there's more where that came from."

"Well, it sounds like you just got the investment you were looking for. You don't have to like the guy. You just have to take—"

"Don't have to like the guy? Dev, what he's looking for is a fund to launder his illegal profits from whatever criminal enterprise he's involved in. You don't think it's even a little bit strange he obviously followed us and gave me cash as an initial investment?" she raised her chin to indicate the metal briefcase then drained her glass, shuddered, and poured two more inches of vodka into the glass.

"Did you look inside?"

"He showed me. Go ahead and open it. The combination is one, two, three."

"You're kidding," I said, looking at the combination lock. Sure enough, the dials were set in the one, two, three combination mode. I pushed the button, and the lock snapped open. I undid the toggle locks on either end and lifted the lid. The case was filled with bundles of hundred-dollar bills held together with rubber bands, crisp, fresh, hundred-dollar bills. A handwritten, torn piece of paper on each bundle had '$10,000' written on it with a black Sharpie. I counted the bundles. There were twenty. I picked up one of the bundles and fanned it, all hundreds.

"Holy shit. Talk about cash up front. How much is in here, a hundred grand?"

"No, Dev. He said two hundred grand. Two hundred thousand dollars. Remind me not to have you do any accounting for me."

"The guy just gave you two hundred grand?"

"Yes, for an investment in the Lemax Partners fund. I can't think of a faster way to get Federal authorities involved, shut down the fund, and ruin my career and reputation."

"What?"

"Dev, what do you think the odds are he earned this money in some honest way?" she said and drained her vodka glass.

"I guess about zero."

"Yeah, right. I am so screwed."

"Can't you report him or just give it back to him?"

"Oh yeah, sure I can. If I decide to do that, he promised me in no uncertain terms, that I'd be dead within twenty-four hours. He expects to see a ten percent return on his investment."

"Two thousand bucks?"

She rolled her eyes, "No, Dev, ten percent is twenty thousand dollars," she said and shook her head. She took two more ice cubes from the freezer, placed them in the glass, and refilled the glass with vodka, spilling some onto the counter. "Oh, shit," she said, slurring her words slightly.

TWO

I woke up on the couch in Heidi's living room just after three to the sound of Heidi getting sick in the bathroom. I knocked on the bathroom door and asked, "Are you okay, Heidi. Can I get you anything?"

"No. I'll, I'll be okay in a little minute. I just need to… Oh God," she groaned and got sick again. Too bad, Grey Goose is a very good vodka. I went into the kitchen, filled a glass with water, got the aspirin bottle out of the cabinet, brought them into her bedroom, and set them on a bedside table. I turned on the light and picked up her blue silk dress from the floor. The zipper in the back was still zipped up, but the fabric had been pulled away from the zipper. One of the spaghetti straps was torn in half. I placed the dress on the bench at the end of her bed then stood next to the bathroom door listening to her groan and cough for another minute or two. So much for romance.

That was enough for me. I went back to the couch, slipped on my shoes, and grabbed the spare key from the key holder next to the back door. I set the metal briefcase underneath the kitchen table, made sure the place was locked up and drove home.

I made coffee for the morning and headed up to bed. Morton was stretched out on my bed, and I had to move him over so I could climb in. I set my alarm and was sound asleep a minute later.

I woke five minutes before my alarm went off, showered, dressed, and headed downstairs. I was on my computer and sipping coffee when I heard Morton jump off the bed. A couple of minutes later, he appeared in the kitchen and headed over to me for his morning scratch behind the ears. I let him outside, filled his food and water dish, and scrambled some eggs for myself. After breakfast, we got in the car and drove down to the office. I made a fresh pot of coffee, left a message for Louie, and headed over to Heidi's.

Thankfully, the place was still locked up. I quietly opened the door, checked on Heidi sound asleep in bed with an empty saucepan next to her, and went into the kitchen. I made a pot of coffee, plugged in my computer, and went online. I heard Heidi turning on the shower maybe an hour later. I arranged some breakfast items on the kitchen counter while she was in the shower. Nothing fancy, bread for toast and grape jelly. I set some eggs out but didn't think she'd want any. It had been at least a decade since I'd seen her as drunk as she was last night. It had been a forty-eight-hour recovery ten years ago. It would be interesting to see how she would do now.

I grabbed her untouched water glass and the bottle of aspirin from the bedside table and set them on the kitchen counter. Heidi entered the kitchen a half-hour later dressed in a light blue terrycloth bathrobe that was calf-length and cinched tightly around her waist. She sat on a stool at the kitchen counter. I pushed the glass of water and aspirin bottle toward her. She put four aspirin in her hand, tossed them into her mouth, and washed them down with three or four swallows of water.

"How's the head?"

"I was afraid earlier I was going to die; now I'm afraid I won't."

"Okay, that tells me you're going to be fine. When you're ready you should have some toast and grape jelly just to get some sugar in your system and curb that hangover. You give me the word, and I'll cook you up some scrambled eggs and bacon for breakfast.

At the mention of breakfast, she looked like she was about to get sick.

"Or, I could not cook breakfast if that would be better."

"Mmm-mmm," she groaned and casually looked around. "Did you move that briefcase?" she asked, suddenly sounding worried.

"I just set it under the kitchen table, so it was more or less out of sight. You want me to put it somewhere?"

"I want to get it out of my house. I think I should maybe put it in a safety deposit box for the time being."

"You have some bank in mind?"

She nodded. "I've got some contacts down at First National. I can get a safety deposit box today. If Benedetti starts to ask any questions, I can put him off for a couple of days until I figure out exactly what I'm going to do."

"Any idea why he picked you?"

"Probably history, I've given consistently good returns for a number of years."

"I'll say."

She looked at me and shook her head. "Not funny, Dev. And I'm sorry last night didn't exactly work out the way you planned."

"What could be better than dinner and then carrying you to bed while you called me some other guys name."

She grimaced, "Oh, sorry, whose name did I say?"

"Which time?"

"Oh, God."

"Listen, I want you to have some toast and grape jelly just to get some sugar content going in your bloodstream."

"Oh, I don't—"

"Hey, trust me, Heidi. It will cut the length of your hangover time in half."

She closed her eyes and nodded. After three pieces of toast slathered in grape jelly, she actually showed some signs of life.

Two hours later, I drove her down to the First National Bank in her red Mercedes. She had her sunglasses on and more or less stared at the floor for the entire ten-minute trip. I pulled into the parking ramp, and we entered the bank on the second floor.

Dennis Constantine, the guy Heidi knew, was seated behind his desk wearing latex gloves. "Hello, Heidi," he said, ignoring me. "Long time no see. Have a seat, sign on the dotted line and we'll debit your account for the annual fee, two hundred and seventy-five dollars." As he spoke, he set two pairs of latex gloves and two face masks for us on the far side of the desk.

They exchanged pleasantries for a moment, but I had the distinct impression there may have been some personal history in the background. He phoned an underling to show us to the vault. The contents of the metal briefcase fit nicely into the safety deposit box, number 744. We pulled back in front of Heidi's house about ninety minutes after we'd first left.

"Thanks, Dev," she said as I turned off the Mercedes. "I hope you don't mind, but I'm going back to bed. You've really been nice. Sorry to ruin the evening."

"Not a problem. You just lay low and maybe no vodka tonight."

"Oh please, don't even mention that." She actually seemed to grow slightly pale behind her sunglasses.

I handed her the car keys then climbed out of the car. She pushed the fob, locking the Mercedes and headed up her front sidewalk without saying another word. I watched until she closed the door behind her, then hopped in my car and headed back to the office.

Three

Morton was the only one in the office when I returned. Louie had clearly been there because there was no more than a half cup of coffee left in the pot and the burner was still on. I dumped the remnants in the sink, made a fresh pot, and took Morton out for a brief ten-minute walk. My cell-phone rang just as we were about to head back into the office.

"Haskell Investigations"

"Hi, may I speak with Dev Haskell, please?" a woman asked. Her voice wasn't what I would call high-pitched, but the lilt was definitely female.

"Speaking."

"Oh, Mr. Haskell, my name is Tracy Kelly. I got your name from a friend of mine, Gladys Wilson. You did some investigating for her four years ago."

Gladys Wilson had been married to a local state representative, Arnold Wilson. Along with the usual political chicanery, he'd managed to appoint three or four women to various positions and, in return, received some very personal benefits. I'd gotten photographs and hotel receipts for Gladys, which she used to file for divorce.

Arnold entered some sexual rehab facility for a six-week vacation, held onto his senate seat, and, last I heard, was reelected." Yes, I remember the case. Most unfortunate. How is she doing?"

"She's doing very well," Tracy said. "She's started a therapy service for those of us who feel there may be something going on in our relationship besides our partner working long hours."

"How can I help you, Tracy?"

"Unfortunately, I'm afraid I'm dealing with a similar circumstance. I believe my husband is having an affair."

"I'm sorry to hear that, Tracy. There are a number of steps that can be taken. I think it would be best if we met and discussed the various options." Other than taking Morton for a walk, I didn't have anything scheduled for the foreseeable future. "I could clear my calendar and meet with you later today or tomorrow, and we could begin to formulate a plan based on what—"

"Unfortunately, I have a conflict. Here's the problem. I'm getting on a plane this afternoon and flying down to Chicago to attend to some family business. I'll be gone for a week. I fully expect Brandon, that's my husband, I fully expect him to use the opportunity to misbehave. I'd like you to get me the evidence, photos, receipts, hopefully, the name of his participant or, God forbid, participants. Whatever you think would be appropriate to file for divorce."

"I suppose I could do that. I can foresee a couple of, not problems, but difficulties. The more personal information I have on your husband, the better the chances are of confirming your suspicions. Places he may go to socialize, names of individuals you suspect may be involved. Where your husband is employed, things he may enjoy, you know sports, movies, maybe books, woodworking. Really anything you can think of. You said his name was Brandon?"

"Yes, Brandon Lovelace, of all things." She followed with a small laugh. "Here's what I've done. I've enclosed photographs and some fairly detailed personal information on him. I could have this messengered to you today. I'll enclose the funds. Shall we say a down payment of five hundred dollars? I'll be back next Tuesday, and hopefully, you would have some documentable evidence that I would be able to use when I take my next step."

"Your next step being divorce?"

"Unfortunately, yes," she said.

A down payment of five hundred dollars. I hadn't had a client in the past six weeks. Under the circumstances, not a lot of thought was required. "Okay, I can work with that. Would you be kind enough to include your phone number? Hopefully, I won't have to contact you, but in the event I do, I'll have the number. Tracy, please feel free to call me at any time. Let me give you my office address."

"Is your office still on Randolph Avenue?"

"Yes, it is."

"Then I have the address. Gladys was kind enough to give it to me. You should have the information this afternoon."

"All right, Tracy. I'll look for it. Wishing you a safe flight to Chicago. Any questions or concerns, please feel free to call me. My condolences that your marriage has reached this point."

"Thank you, but I already feel better knowing you're involved. Thank you so much," she said and disconnected.

Not bad, a new client who wants to pay in advance. Heidi's sitting on two hundred grand in cash, and it was just a little after the noon hour. Things were looking up.

Four

Louie was seated behind his picnic table desk with his feet up. As I opened the door and Morton headed toward his latest chew toy Louie opened one eye. "Oh, finally. Where have you two been?"

"Just out for a quick walk," I lied. "You in court this morning?"

"Yeah, my client was the woman in detox who hit her neighbor's cars parked on the street."

"She hit two or three, didn't she?"

Louie shook his head. "Four actually, and another one a block away they're still investigating. She's eventually going to get nailed with that one, too."

"Did she get sentenced?"

Louie shook his head. "Not yet. Her license has been revoked. She'll be paying for all repairs. Her car is in the impound lot. She's going to be attending daily AA meetings in the workhouse, which, at the moment, is probably the best place for her. We've got another court date in thirty days, provided she remains on the straight and narrow."

"And if she doesn't?"

"If she doesn't? She'll be looking at some serious time, and not in the workhouse. Hell of a way to meet your new neighbors, smash up their cars. She signed a year's lease on her apartment last month and moved in. I'm guessing the landlord doesn't need the hassle, so she'll most likely be evicted in the next thirty days. Just about the time she's released from the workhouse. You look all happy. You find out the government's going to send you another stimulus check?"

"Even better, I just got off a call from a woman who wants to pay me in advance. Sending the information and a check over by messenger this afternoon."

"What does she want you to do?"

"Cheating husband, wants photos and documentation before she files for divorce."

"God, what is with people? Is he involved with some woman he's working with?"

"I don't really know. She was hopping on a plane this afternoon and couldn't come in to go over the facts personally. Hopefully, the information she sends will give me a little clearer picture. Hey, you ever hear of some guy named Tommy Benedetti?"

"It rings a bell, but I can't recall specifics. Whatever it is, my cloudy memory suggests it's nothing positive."

I went on to tell Louie about last night's event, Tommy Benedetti in the stretch limo with his thugs giving Heidi the briefcase full of cash.

"That sounds beyond crazy. Benedetti, isn't he the guy who did something with online betting? Fixed a number of games or the odds or something?"

"You know, Louie, now that you mention it, that kind of rings a bell. I'm going to have to do a little research on him."

"What's Heidi think about it?"

"She's not too happy. With everything going on in the economy, it's not like there's a line of potential investors waiting to get into this LeMax Fund, and then if the word got out that this character was in on the project, the thing would tank in about twenty-four hours along with her reputation. She's going to have to figure out a way to get that money back to this guy. You wouldn't happen to have any ideas, would you?"

Louie shook his head. "Nope, that's way out of my league. You know who might? And believe me, I know you don't want to hear his name."

"Who?" I asked.

"Your pal, Gustafson."

"Tubby Gustafson? God, I don't want that nutcase or anyone associated with him anywhere near Heidi. Talk about ruining your reputation."

"Yeah, but he just might be the guy who would know up-to-date information on this Benedetti character."

Hmm-mmm, the more I thought about it, the more Louie might have a point.

"What are you thinking?" Louie asked.

"Unfortunately, I'm thinking you're probably right."

"So give him a call."

"It's too easy for him to dodge me. He'll either have one of his idiots answer the phone, provided they know how to do that, or he'll let my call drop into his voicemail and then block any future calls. No, I got a better idea. I'll go see him in person. That way, I've got at least a fifty-fifty chance of actually talking to him."

"Mind if I give you a piece of advice?"

"What is it?"

"Maybe don't mention the cash. He finds out about that and he's liable to strong-arm Heidi or something. Just tell him they had a conversation, Benedetti pressured her, and she doesn't want to get him pissed off."

"Good advice," I said, picking my keys up off the desk. You gonna be here for a while?"

"I'm here for the rest of the afternoon."

"Watch the Bow-wow till I get back."

"Not a problem, safe journey."

"Thanks, oh, and I'm expecting the file from this Tracy Kelly woman to arrive this afternoon. You mind signing for it?"

"Not a problem, good luck, and be careful," Louie said as I headed out the door.

I thought it might be a good idea to check on Heidi since her place was more or less on the way to Tubby Gustafson's house. Thankfully, Tommy Benedetti's stretch limo wasn't parked in front. I pulled in behind her

Mercedes, headed up to the door and rang her doorbell. I rang it a second time and waited. I pulled her spare key from my pocket and was about to unlock the door when it opened.

Heidi stood in front of me, not looking her best. She was still attired in her blue terrycloth bathrobe. She wore fuzzy white slippers on her feet, and as I stepped into the living room, she climbed back onto the couch and pulled a knitted blanket up to her chin. The television had John Travolta disco dancing around, wearing a black, open-collar shirt, and a white three-piece suit, Saturday Night Fever from forty-five years ago.

"How's it going, Heidi?"

"My head is still throbbing."

"Gee, and you're watching this junk? Who knew? Think there might be some tie-in?"

"You're not helping," she said.

"This movie is older than we are, Heidi."

"Ruining the mood, Dev."

"Okay, okay. Anything you need? Have you eaten anything since the toast and jelly this morning?"

"I'm really not hungry."

"I tell you what. I've got to meet with a guy. I'll pick up something for you on the way back. You have to get some food in you."

"Don't bring me McDonalds."

"I'm going to stop at a deli and get you some chicken soup. It'll calm your stomach and start to get you back on the right track. Okay?"

"Thanks, Dev."

"Maybe close your eyes and try to take a little nap."

"Enough with the direction, Dev. Hey, look, now he's wearing clothes like you."

I glanced at the TV. Travolta was in a leather jacket and a black t-shirt.

"That's an improvement," I said. "I'll see you in a bit."

Five

Tubby Gustafson lived and worked from inside his brick mansion. An eight-foot-high brick wall surrounded the place. Security cameras monitored every square inch of the property and armed guards stood outside and inside the entrance. The double iron gates were closed, and I had to get out of my car and push the call button on the intercom attached to the brick pillar. A green light flashed on when I pushed the button, and a voice growled, "Yeah."

It wasn't Tubby speaking, but then it never was. Some thug was checking me out while monitoring a bank of security cameras covering the property. The camera covering the front gate was mounted overhead, and I was tempted to wave.

"I'd like to see Mr. Gustafson, please. My name is Dev Haskell."

He didn't say anything. I just heard a click that indicated he'd turned off the intercom. The green light was still on, which meant I was being monitored. The voice came back maybe two minutes later. "What's this about?"

"I learned some news I thought might be of interest to Mr. Gustafson. But I'll only tell him."

I heard a sigh come across the speaker, and the audio clicked off again. Maybe a minute later, one of the gates scraped and groaned open. I climbed behind the wheel and drove along the circular drive to the parking area just beyond the front door. Two guys lingered on either side of the front door, leaning against the house in the shade of a maple tree. They watched as I parked the car, pulled on my mask, and climbed out. As I turned to face them, they moved off the brick wall and walked in opposite directions, distancing themselves even further from one another. They each had a handgun shoved into their belt.

I was familiar with the drill. As I approached, I kept my hands at my side and stopped about ten feet from the front door.

The heavier of the two approached with a hand-held metal detector. The thing was black with yellow letters that read 'Search Wand,' and he proceeded to wave it over me, checking for weapons. The thing gave off a tone when it went over my pocket.

"Oh, sorry, my car keys," I said and pulled the keys out of my pocket.

"You dumb shit, Haskell."

"I said I was sorry."

He shook his head and said, "Get your ass in there. He's okay, Gary. You can let numb nuts in."

"Thank you," I said, smiled, and headed for the front door. The other guy chuckled as I approached, and he opened the door for me.

I stepped inside, and the door closed behind me. Another thug was sitting just a few feet inside the massive entry. He had on a surgical mask and latex gloves. "Arms out on either side, look straight ahead," he said.

I assumed the position, spreading my legs and stretching my arms out on either side. He patted me down and then said, "You're here to speak to Mr. Gustafson?"

"Yeah, I'm Dev—"

"Believe me. I know who the hell you are, Haskell. Here, put on these gloves and this proper mask before you appear before Mr. Gustafson." I slipped on the pair of blue latex gloves and tied the surgical mask at the back of my head. "Okay, he's in his office. Follow me."

I knew where Tubby's office was. There was a grand staircase in the marble-floored entryway. The staircase rose halfway up to the second floor. After eight or nine steps, it made a right-angle turn and rose another eight or nine steps before connecting with the second floor. Halfway up on the wall was a large gilt-framed painting of Tubby standing in front of a fireplace. He was holding three rolls of documents as if he'd just written a manuscript or maybe some psalms. In the painting, he was trim, almost muscular, with a nose maybe half the size of the baked potato that, in reality, was attached to his face. We walked past the staircase toward the long hall. Tubby's office was the third door on the left at the end of the hall.

But that wasn't where we went. Instead, the thug stopped just before the hall and opened a door that blended in with the paneling that ran up the side of the staircase. A light flashed on in a small room, not much more than a closet really, illuminating a chair, a small desk with a keyboard, and a large computer screen attached to the wall.

"Just press that button on the upper right corner of the keyboard. That turns on the computer, and Mr. Gustafson will join you in a minute. When you're finished, I'll let you out."

I had to lower my head to step in beneath the staircase. I settled into the chair as the door closed behind me, and I heard a lock click into place. I pushed the button to turn on the computer. As the screen illuminated, the computer gave off a musical tone. A moment later, Tubby's fat head appeared across the entire screen, maybe six times larger than in person. He was wearing a blue surgical mask over his mouth. His red, pitted nose, the size of a football on the screen, was obviously too large for the mask to handle and remained uncovered. "Now, what the hell do you want, Haskell? Go ahead. You've got three minutes."

"Oh, umm, nice to see you, sir. Good security here against the virus. I'm glad you're safe and doing well, and—"

"Get to the point, Haskell. I'm busy."

I'll say he was busy. Naked Tubby was stretched out on a massage table that had to have been reinforced with a steel I beam. Two Asian women wearing latex gloves, surgical masks, and black thongs were busy massaging his massive, corpulent body.

Fortunately, Tubby was lying on his stomach, although his flesh oozed over both sides of the massage table. One woman was massaging the calf on his left leg while the other woman appeared to be kneading a pile of hairy bread dough, which was actually Tubby's shoulder.

He peered into the computer screen from what had to be a distance of no more than six inches. His face appeared ten times its actual size on the large screen mounted on the wall. He suddenly shouted, "Well, get to the point, Haskell. Just what, exactly, is so damn important that you've interrupted my daily workout?"

I came back to my senses, attempted to put naked Tubby and his fat face out of my mind, and said, "Oh, umm. Well, sir, I came across some information I thought you might find interesting. Do you know a—"

"Haskell, your three minutes are almost up. I swear to God if you don't get to the point and damn soon, I'm going to—"

"Tommy Benedetti," I half-shouted and focused on the keyboard so I wouldn't have to look at the image of Tubby.

"Benedetti? What do you know about that bastard?"

"Well, sir, my understanding is he has two hundred thousand dollars in cash and has been attempting to invest it in a number of investment funds around town. Thus far, every place he's tried has turned him down. My understanding is, he's becoming a bit desperate, and now he's threatening the fund managers."

"Investment funds? Which ones?"

"I'm sorry, sir, but I don't really know that."

"Oh, for God's sake. Who in the hell told you this?"

"I'm not at liberty to say. I—"

"Not at liberty," Tubby shouted.

The woman massaging his calf said something, stepped over, and began massaging the calf on his right leg. A large black thong suddenly brushed across the screen, and the other woman moved to his left shoulder. I could suddenly only see half of Tubby's face, the left side, and a clear image of the topless woman massaging his left shoulder. Fortunately for her, she was wearing gloves.

"Haskell, I'll expect a full report in forty-eight hours."

"But sir, I don't—"

"Silencio! You half-wit," he shouted then farted. Fortunately, the woman massaging his calf had the mask on, although I wasn't sure it provided enough protection. The portion of his face that I could see was even redder than usual. "You've got forty-eight hours. I want a complete update on exactly what funds he's trying to invest in. Now, get out." With that, the screen went blank.

I sat for a long moment then stood and attempted to turn the doorknob. It was locked and rattled back and forth. I knocked on the door and called, "Hello. Hello. Umm, I'm all finished in here. Mr. Gustafson said I could leave. Hello, are you out there? Hello? Is anybody—"

The lock suddenly snapped, and the door opened. "Everything go all right?" the thug wearing the surgical mask and gloves asked. I couldn't see his mouth, but I could tell by his eyes he was laughing.

"Yeah, fine, just fine. I got my marching orders. I'll be doing some work for Mr. Gustafson."

"Work? Oh, is that what it's called?"

Six

I stopped at Cecil's Deli and got a container of chicken soup, a corned beef sandwich on rye, and a chocolate chip cookie for Heidi. I drove over to her place and let myself in with her spare key. She was still ensconced on the couch watching Saturday Night Fever. Travolta was walking down the street wearing a black leather jacket and a red shirt. His shirt collar was spread out across his shoulders. He wore a gold chain with a medallion around his neck.

"Hey, turn off the movie. I brought you a late lunch."

"Please don't tell me you got a Big Mac."

"No, I didn't. I went to Cecil's and got you some of the best chicken soup in town. I got a corned beef sandwich on Russian rye for when you get your appetite back. How are you feeling?"

"A little better."

I let it go at that. "Turn off that movie and join me in the kitchen."

As I headed into the kitchen, I heard the noise from the tv suddenly stop. I pulled a bowl from the cabinet and a soup spoon from the drawer. I poured the soup into the bowl. It steamed and gave off a wonderful scent.

Heidi settled onto a kitchen stool and I pulled the bowl in front of her. She leaned down and inhaled the steam wafting up from the bowl. "Mmm-mmm, it smells delicious."

"It'll do wonders for you. What would you like to drink?"

"There's 7-Up in the fridge," she said and took a spoonful of soup. "Oh, this is just what the doctor ordered."

"Yeah, you'll feel a lot better," I said, opening the refrigerator and pulling out a 20-ounce bottle of 7-Up that was half-full. "Eat that soup, get back on the couch, and maybe take a nap. I got you that corned beef sandwich and a chocolate chip cookie for dinner," I said, nodding at the box on the counter.

"Thanks, Dev. I probably shouldn't eat that cookie. It'll go right to my waist."

"You sure?"

She nodded, so I took the cookie, and in three quick bites, had it devoured.

"Dev?" Heidi whined.

"You just said you didn't want it."

"Well, at least give me a chance to reconsider. Hey, I'm sorry about last night. I know you had other plans for when we got back here. So did I."

I gave her a kiss on the forehead. "I'm going to take off. Maybe get a nap in this afternoon. You'll feel a lot better. I'll check in with you later."

"Thanks," she called as I stepped out of the kitchen and heard her slurp another spoonful of soup. I glanced at the tv in the living room. Saturday Night Fever had only played for seven minutes, and another hour and fifty-two minutes remained, which meant she was going to watch it a second time. God, no wonder she had a headache. I locked the door behind me and headed back to the office.

Louie was working away on his computer as I stepped in.

"How'd it go with Tubby?" he asked without looking up.

"About like I expected. I will say this, he's playing it safe, wearing a mask and gloves and has his staff, at least inside the house, doing the same thing."

"He give you an update on Benedetti?"

"Not exactly."

"Define, not exactly."

I went on to tell Louie about my brief, high-tech meeting with Tubby. I mentioned the closet beneath the staircase and the two women massaging him.

"They were just wearing gloves and masks?"

"And thongs, Louie. Don't forget that part."

He shook his head and mumbled something about being in the wrong business.

Morton was off his bed and walked over to get his head scratched. When I finished, he walked over and stood in front of the door then looked over his shoulder at me.

"I'd better take him for a walk. Be back in ten minutes."

"I'll be here," Louie said.

Seven

We did a reasonably quick walk through the neighborhood. Morton took his time sniffing every other tree and the front gate on every fence. It was closer to a half-hour before we were back in the office. I unhooked Morton's leash, and he headed for his bed.

Without looking up from his keyboard, Louie said, "Hey, a messenger delivered an envelope addressed to you. I signed for it and set it on your desk chair.

"Oh, yeah. From my new client, Tracy. The information on her husband. Thanks for signing for it. Did you have to pay anything?"

"I gave the guy a dollar tip, only 'cause that was all the cash I had."

"I owe you one at The Spot," I said and picked the envelope off my desk chair. I'd been expecting a standard business envelope. Instead, it was a large manila envelope, and as I picked it up from my chair, it clearly held a number of sheets of paper. I slit the top of the envelope with my letter opener and pulled out a document about twenty pages thick along with three photos and the five hundred-dollar bills paper-clipped to the document. I stuffed the bills in my wallet.

The photos were of a nicely groomed, dark-haired guy, with maybe a four-day growth of beard. He wore an open-collar shirt and suit in one photo and a v-neck sweater in the other two. I pegged his age at mid to late thirties.

The document was double spaced with pages numbered from one to eighteen. The first two pages appeared to be Brandon Lovelace's resume. The next page was a copy of his driver's license and a business card. It turns out he was a real estate developer, aged forty-six. I looked at the photos again. He definitely looked ten years younger than his age. His business card listed him as the CEO of a company called Brace Development. I wondered if 'BRACE' came from **Bra**ndon Lovel**ace**. The fourth page was a copy of their marriage license. Brandon and Tracy had been married for seven years. The rest was an informal biography of Brandon Lovelace. If nothing else, Tracy Kelly was certainly thorough. She didn't include a photograph of herself or her with Brandon, but then, she wasn't paying me to investigate her. I settled into my desk chair and began reading.

Brandon was from Beardsley, Minnesota. A small town about two hundred miles due west of St. Paul on the South Dakota border. I'd been there once as a kid, visiting distant cousins and going pheasant hunting. I was nine at the time, so my hunting activity consisted of acting like a dog, helping to scare up birds in the couple hundred miles of cornfields we traipsed through. My success at the task was questionable and probably one of a number of reasons I wasn't invited back the following year.

Brandon and Tracy met at the University of Minnesota. Brandon was working on his Master of Architecture degree, and Tracy was an undergraduate in the education program. They met at a mutual friends BBQ party in July while taking summer school courses, stayed in touch, and moved in together eighteen months later. They were married in 2013. Brandon was a CEO, Tracy taught at an elementary school. All in all, a fairly typical relationship.

Brandon's hobbies were hunting, fishing, and bridge. Tracy had penned in a note next to the hobbies that read, *'No time to do these in the last four years. Busy running the company. Now fourteen employees.'*

Brandon's office was in downtown St. Paul in the Northwestern Building, located on Fourth Street. The building was home to artists, entrepreneurs, and architects. Which suggested Brandon and his company would probably fit in there very nicely.

"You thinking about going over to The Spot tonight?" Louie asked. He was in the process of turning off his computer, which suggested to me that he was ready to head over now.

"I want to give Heidi a call just to see how she's doing. You going over there now?"

"Yeah, why don't you make your call and then join me? I'll tell Mike you're picking up the first round."

"Sounds good to me. Let me check in with her, and then Morton and I will be over."

I phoned Heidi as Louie made his way down the stairs. I was just about to hang up when she answered. "Mmm-mmm, Dev?" she asked with what sounded like a mouth full of food.

"Yeah, Heidi, how you doing? You sound a lot better than earlier today."

She took another bite of whatever she was eating and said. "Mmm-mmm, coming around. God, I wish you didn't eat that cookie. I could really go for that about now."

"Sorry about that. It's all I had for lunch. I ended up working all afternoon."

"Working? You've actually got a client?"

"Yeah, she called me this morning. Wants me to get pictures of her misbehaving husband while she's out of town, so she can file for divorce."

"That doesn't sound like fun," she said then continued to chew.

"No, it never is. First glance, they both seem like nice people, but who knows. Hey, I'm just checking in. You're sounding like you're heading back to normal. How's the head?"

"Much better. Nothing that twenty-four hours won't cure. I napped this afternoon. Kind of a raw throat, but that's probably due to last night's stupidity. Thanks again for dinner and for putting up with me after the Benedetti thingy. Oh, and thanks for this corned beef on Russian rye sandwich, too," she said then apparently took another bite.

"You figure out what you're going to do about Benedetti?"

"I'm not even going to begin to think about him until tomorrow. I'm still not at a hundred percent yet, but I'm getting there."

"Anything you need?"

"Oh, you're so sweet, Dev. But no, you've done more than enough. Thank you. I'm going to look for a series to watch, then turn in early tonight. And don't worry. I know I owe you, so just be patient."

"I will be as long as you are," I said. "Hey, I'll check in with you tomorrow. Have a quiet night and no alcohol."

"Oh, believe me, you don't even have to say that. I'll chat tomorrow. Thanks for checking up on me and thanks for the food. The chicken soup made all the difference."

"Talk tomorrow," I said, but she'd already hung up.

I got the coffee ready for the morning, turned off the lights, and stuffed the manila envelope with Tracy's information under my arm. Morton and I headed over to The Spot. On the way, I tossed the envelope in the front seat of my car.

As we drew closer to The Spot, Morton started wagging his tail and picking up speed. By the time I opened the door, he was straining at his leash. Louie was seated on his usual stool at the far end of the bar, and Morton nearly pulled my arm out of the socket as he strained on his leash to get to Louie.

Louie took a sip from his drink, laughed, and reached into the bag of deep-fat-fried pork rinds. I had to pick up speed for the next half-dozen steps or risk being dragged across the barroom floor.

"Morton, you were finally able to drag his worthless ass over here. Good job, Morton. Way to go," Louie said and reached down with a handful of pork rinds. "Everything okay with Heidi?"

"Yeah, just got off the phone with her. She sounded a hundred percent better. As we talked, she couldn't stop eating the sandwich I brought her, which is a good sign."

"She give you any indication about what she plans to do with this Benedetti character?"

"No, in fact, she said she wasn't even going to think about it until tomorrow, which is probably a good thing. I just don't know what she's going to do."

"She's a smart person. Didn't get where she is by being intimidated by people. I'd guess she might have an in with one or two powerful people who could make life hell for Benedetti," Louie said and took another sip.

Mike was suddenly there. He was wearing latex gloves and a face mask and drumming his fingers on the bar. "You thinking of ordering, or are you just going to take up a portion of the limited space we have to offer our customers in these trying times."

Including Louie, Mike, and me, there were eight people in the place. Three guys spread out along the bar and a guy and his wife in a booth. "Just a beer for me, Mike. How's business been?"

He shook his head and said, "You're looking at it. The new normal, I'm afraid."

"You think it'll ever get back to what it was?" I asked Louie.

"I honestly can't see it happening," Louie said, "at least not until we get an inoculation, a vaccine, or something. Even then, the economy is such a disaster. Talk about trickle down. It was supposed to be money, not debt and hard times that trickled down."

Louie had a second drink over the course of thirty minutes. I took a pass and paid the tab with one of the hundred-dollar bills Tracy sent me. Mike gave me the change, and I handed him a five for a tip. "Thanks, Dev, a tip is a pretty rare thing nowadays. Much appreciated."

"Thanks for taking care of us, Mike. You stay sane. Louie, I've got the coffee set for tomorrow morning. All you have to do is turn on the pot."

Louie drained his glass and slid off his bar stool. "What time you think you two will be in tomorrow."

"Not sure, I'm going to see if I can catch this Brandon Lovelace coming out of his office right now and check him out. I don't want to spend too much time on it tonight. I'll begin in earnest tomorrow. We shouldn't be any later than about nine. You in court tomorrow?"

"Yeah, but not until eleven, and that's just for a sentencing hearing, so unless things are really backed up, it shouldn't take more than fifteen or twenty minutes. I'll be in the office first thing. See you tomorrow, Dev. Morton, you take care, hang in there, and don't let Dev get you down."

Eight

I put Morton in the back seat and drove downtown to the Northwestern Building, hoping I might catch a glimpse of Brandon Lovelace leaving for the day. It was just a little before five. Traffic was heavy enough given the hour, but nothing compared to what rush hour had been just a few months ago.

I found a parking place right in front of the Northwestern Building. I pulled Brandon's photos from the envelope, studied them for a moment, and set them on the passenger seat. Maybe an hour later, he stepped out of the building and headed up the street. I didn't even have to guess; it was definitely him, and he was even better looking in person than in the photos. Walking with him was an attractive looking dark-haired woman. I thought she might be in her early thirties. They appeared to be engaged in a fairly animated conversation. At one point, he made a comment, and she hit him on the arm, and they both laughed. They headed into a parking ramp, maybe a block away. I kicked myself for not having my camera with me. But there was no point in taking a photo from behind, and if I needed to take a picture, I'd just have to use my cellphone.

I pulled ahead to the no parking zone just before the ramp and waited. Brandon appeared about four minutes later, driving the white SUV Tracy had mentioned in her description. The license plate matched the information she had provided. He was alone in the car. He inserted a white card into the ticket machine, which suggested he paid a monthly fee for a reserved spot. He made a right turn out of the ramp and headed up Fourth Street. I followed him, thinking the woman may have been an employee or a casual friend he just happened to run into as he left the building. He drove through downtown, turned onto Kellogg Boulevard, and took the exit to Shepard Road, a four-lane road that ran along the Mississippi River. He headed upriver, and I was pretty sure he was going home.

A little more than ten minutes later, Shepard Road turned into the River Boulevard, residential on one side and a scenic view overlooking the Mississippi River Valley on the other side. Two blocks after that he turned into a long asphalt driveway leading up to a one-story brick home with white trim and a stone front. An attached double garage with a large white door was set back slightly from the front of the house.

I slowed as I drove past. The address matched the one Tracy had provided. It was a home in a lovely, upscale part of the city. Brandon hopped out of his car and headed toward the front door.

I took a right on Cleveland Avenue and headed home. I got Morton settled in, made myself a ham sandwich, and filled a thermos with water. I tossed in a half-eaten package of mint fudge covered Oreo cookies. I'd had a three-week relationship with a woman named Christine who loved the things. Unfortunately, she turned out not to be that wild about me. I kept the cookies after she told

me to never, ever call her again.

I headed back to see what Brandon might be up to this evening. There was no parking allowed on either side of the River Boulevard where Brandon lived, but he was two lots from the corner, so I parked there. Since the River Boulevard has an asphalt pedestrian walkway and bike path with occasional benches overlooking the river, no one would think it strange if I sat facing the river, eating a sandwich for dinner. Thankfully, there was a bench almost directly across from Brandon and Tracy's home. I wore a surgical mask more to prevent Brandon from recognizing me than from any fear of infection. I settled in on the bench facing the river and waited.

I'd finished the sandwich and had gone through almost half of the fudge covered Oreos when I saw him maybe a quarter mile away heading toward me. He was dressed in tight black running shorts and what looked like a self-wicking dark gray running shirt. As he drew closer, I recognized the Under Armour logo on the shirt. He ran past me without glancing over, focused on some distant object. He slowed to a walk maybe thirty yards

beyond and then walked another thirty yards further before crossing the street and heading back toward his
house. He cut across a portion of his neighbors' front
lawn, walked up the driveway, and into his house. A
light went on toward the back of the house in what I presumed was the kitchen.

Obviously, he'd set off running before I had returned. I checked the time on my phone, twenty minutes
before eight. Given the pace he was moving, he'd probably done four or five miles. I made a mental note.

After another hour, it was dusk, and I stretched out
on the bench. I reminded myself to pack a pillow the next
time I did this. I remained on the bench until close to ten.
Brandon never left the house, and no one came to visit. I
walked back and forth for a block or two, keeping an eye
on his car in the driveway, but he never stepped out of
the house.

Sometime after eleven, I climbed in my car parked
around the corner. I had just settled in behind the wheel
when a police car drove past along the River Boulevard.
I wondered if it was a coincidence or if someone had
called the police and reported me loitering on the bench
for the past four hours.

I started the car, turned onto the River Boulevard,
and headed in the opposite direction from the police.
Morton was asleep somewhere upstairs when I arrived
home. I set the coffee pot for the morning, checked my
emails, and headed up to bed. Fortunately, Morton was
stretched out on his bed for a change. I climbed into bed

and drifted off to sleep as I planned my activity for tomorrow.

Nine

I was up before my alarm went off. Sometime during the middle of the night, Morton had climbed onto my bed and stretched out. He was taking up a good two-thirds of the bed. As I crawled out, he seemed to levitate and shift slightly, so that now he took up the entire bed. I headed into the bathroom and grabbed a shower.

I was downstairs on my third cup of coffee, reading through a series of online posts regarding Tommy Benedetti. I heard Morton jump off the bed, and a couple of minutes later, he wandered into the kitchen. I let him out the kitchen door after giving him the mandatory head scratch, filled his food and water dish, and went back to reading up on Benedetti.

He was not what one might refer to as the perfect neighbor. There was the case of a property line dispute three years ago; Benedetti lost. A charge of property damage two years ago; Benedetti settled out of court. He was a gambler, as in cards and betting, although he was banned from a number of Las Vegas casinos. That made me wonder exactly where he was gambling nowadays. I supposed he could be doing it online, although that didn't strike me as too much fun. Over the years, he had been charged at least a half-dozen different times with everything from possession to intent to distribute, assault, sexual exploitation of a minor, not to mention attempted rape. He must have an awfully good lawyer on staff because he was never found guilty.

At half-past-seven, dressed in gray sweat pants and a gray sweatshirt, I drove back over to Brandon Lovelace's home, parked around the corner, and pretended to stretch before running, all the while waiting to see when he left for the office. He finally left about an hour later. I hopped in the car and followed him down to the same parking ramp as yesterday, which pretty much convinced me he had a reserved spot in there that he paid for monthly.

After I watched him head into the Northwestern Building, I drove home and changed into jeans and a retro 70s Rolling Stones t-shirt. Morton and I drove down to the office. Louie was already in, seated in his desk chair with his feet up on the desk. He was just finishing up on the phone.

"Alright then, I'll present that to him and see what he wants to do. Thank you for the call. Have a nice day," he said and hung up. Once he had disconnected, he mumbled, "Bitch. Oh, not you, Dev. Just finishing up a call. Someone willing to drop the charges against my client provided he agrees to pick up her car payment."

"Is that a good deal?"

"It might be if he had the money. But he's a bartender at the Hilton. He hasn't worked since March, and it's going to be another month at least before he's called back. Just like everybody, he's got his own debts to be dealing with."

"Assault charges?" I asked.

"More like self-defense. The girlfriend came at him with a pair of scissors then drove off after driving into the fence along his driveway. Anyway, how was your evening?"

"I'd forgotten how absolutely boring my line of work can be." After I poured myself a cup of coffee, I topped up Louie's cup. I went on to give him a brief description of my evening on the park bench.

"Anything on Benedetti?" Louie asked.

"Only the history I read online. None of it good. The guy is a real loser. He's been charged at least a half-dozen times for some pretty serious stuff, but he's never been convicted. Being chauffeured around town in a stretch limo, he's gotta have money coming from somewhere. Listen to this. How bad do you have to be to get banned from Las Vegas casinos?"

"He was banned?" Louie asked.

"Yeah, MGM, Caesars, and Stations."

"Was he winning so much they wouldn't let him play anymore?"

"Benedetti? No way, in fact, just the opposite. He was in some poker tournament. It wasn't clear in the article I read if he was dealt bad hands or simply played them so poorly that he lost. Either way, he lost a ton of money, which isn't unusual for Vegas. But then he goes and moons the table he's at and takes off his shoes and throws them at the dealer. Security gets involved. He decides to fight them off, which didn't end well. He was arrested, charged with a number of crimes. He makes a plea deal, promises to never darken the casino doors again, and pays a fine. Let's just say the state of Nevada and the Vegas gaming industry weren't very impressed with Mr. Benedetti. I don't know this, but if you found out they'd stop him at the airport and send him packing if he ever flew back there, it wouldn't surprise me."

"And this is the guy who threatened Heidi the other night?"

"Yeah."

Louie shook his head and said, "You know, I might have someone you could contact on this guy. She's more than a little crazy, but if she could help get this guy to back off…"

"Who? God, at this stage, anything would help."

"Her name is Candi Mangle. I think she's originally from Tennessee or Arkansas or someplace. Works for the Fed's, the FBI. She was involved in a lot of undercover work. I think currently she's dealing with identity theft cases. She might have some ideas for you, might even be interested with Benedetti trying to pressure Heidi to let him invest in the fund."

"I'd love to talk to her. You got a phone number?" I asked as Louie began rifling through his Rolodex.

"Yeah, here we go. Her office, that's the FBI office over in Minneapolis, is…" He gave me the number, and I wrote it on the back cover of a Swank magazine I'd been looking at. "Then surprise, surprise, here's her home number, well, as of two years ago. But try it." He gave me that number, and I wrote it next to the Minneapolis number.

"Thanks, man. Let me call Heidi first, and then I'll give her a call." I speed-dialed Heidi's number and, after four rings, got dumped into her voicemail. "Heidi, it's Dev, just checking in. Give me a call when you have time. I've done a little research on your friend, Benedetti. Just for starters, he's banned from casinos in Vegas. It goes downhill from there. Talk to you later," I said and hung up.

I decided not to call the FBI office over in Minneapolis and instead called Candi Mangle's home number. After two rings, I was dumped into her voicemail. "Hi, sorry, but I can't take your call right now. Leave a message, and I'll get back to you as soon as possible. Thanks." Beep.

"Hi, Candi. My name is Dev Haskell. I'm a private investigator in St. Paul. Please give me a call. I may have some information for you. Thank you." I added my phone number and hung up. I fired up my laptop and went back to researching Tommy Benedetti. From what I read over the next ninety minutes, nothing changed my opinion. The guy was a thug, a self-absorbed jerk, and too stupid to realize it.

I called an acquaintance in the Department of Motor Vehicles. "This is Gerry," was how he answered.

"Hi Gerry, Dev Haskell."

There was a brief pause and then, in a voice a lot softer than the one he'd used to answer the phone, he said, "Don't tell me, let me guess. You're looking for someone's address. Right? What? Is she blonde, a red-head, or brunette?"

"You're only half-right, Gerry. I am looking for someone's address, but I'm serving a court summons on a guy, and it's looking like he either closed his office in the last thirty days, or he lied about his address. Hoping you might be able to help."

"God, Dev, when did you start serving summons?"

"You been watching the news over the past few months? Just about everything has tanked. You're lucky you're working for the state."

"Yeah, and you're not the only person to tell me that. Okay, give me her name."

"It's actually a guy, Gerry."

"A guy? You playing both sides of the field now, Dev?"

"Very funny, not. Here, the guy's name is Thomas Benedetti." I spelled out the last name for him and heard him tapping keys.

"Yeah, here he is, Thomas Benedetti, age fifty-two," he said a moment later. "You got a pen there?"

"Yeah, go ahead." I wrote the address on the back cover of Swank, just below Candi Mangle's phone number.

"Anything else you need?" Gerry asked.

"No, this is great. Many thanks. I owe you one."

"You owe me a lot more than just one. I'll add this to the list, and if things ever clear up to the point where we can go out at night again, you're buying."

"You got it, Gerry. Thanks."

"You stay sane and stay in touch," he said and hung up.

Benedetti apparently lived in Mahtomedi, a northern suburb of St. Paul. The city had newer homes, farms, a vineyard, and sat along the shore of White Bear Lake. Benedetti's home was on Park Ave. Looking at Google maps, White Bear Lake was apparently his backyard. Google brought up an image of a large, two-story home with a large paved brick area behind what looked like a wrought iron fence. What appeared to be a three-car garage sat next to the fence and some distance from the house. In the Google image, there were two cars parked in the circular drive. One was a black SUV, impossible to determine the make. The other vehicle was a white Lexus SUV. I wondered if the Lexus suggested Benedetti had a wife and possibly children?

I entered the address into the GPS on my phone, grabbed Morton's leash off the windowsill and said, "Louie, I'm going to go check out some stuff. I should be back in an hour or so. You in this afternoon?"

"Yeah, I think so. I'm about to head over to the courthouse now. If all goes according to plan, I'll be here this afternoon. Everything okay on your end?"

"Yeah, I'm in a holding pattern with Heidi and your FBI pal, Candi. I'm guessing Tracy's husband is in his office until the end of the workday. You know how it goes, about the time he heads out the door both women will call, and I'll suddenly be juggling three things at once."

"It never fails," Louie said.

I attached the leash to Morton's collar. I thought about calling Heidi again, decided against it, and we headed out the door. I hopped onto 35E heading north, merged onto 694, and turned off onto Hilton Trail a few miles later. The trip took less than twenty minutes. Once again, the traffic was heavier than last month, but nothing like it had been at one time. God, how long was this pandemic going to last?

Hilton Trail took me into the town of Mahtomedi. The average home looked to be maybe twenty-five to thirty years old. I took a left off Hilton Trail and headed toward Park Avenue. My guess at house prices seemed to climb by fifty grand every couple of blocks, but then, I was basing those numbers on an economy that didn't exist anymore, so who knew? Along the way, I passed maybe a half-dozen people walking, all retirement age, wearing face masks, and keeping their distance.

I turned right, pulled onto Park Avenue, and wove my way through the high scale neighborhood. I caught a view of White Bear Lake in between the gorgeous homes on the left-hand side. I slowed down three houses before Tommy Benedetti's and actually stopped for a brief moment in front of his place and studied his home.

The entire area, from the street up to the house and in front of the three-car garage, was paved in buff-colored brick. A white Lexus, newer than the one I'd seen in the online image, was parked in front of the house. No other vehicles were around.

I didn't see anything that suggested a stretch limo was a regular attendee. There was no way the stretch limo would be able to fit in the garage. That made me wonder if maybe the limo the other night was just a prop to suggest Tommy Benedetti was a bigger player than he actually was. But then, there were the three thugs, and they had clearly been armed. I drove down the road, turned around in a driveway, and went back to take another look. Evergreen bushes were planted in front of the wrought iron fence. In front of the bushes, and all the way out to the curb, the area was covered with wood chips.

It would be interesting to see the place from the lake side, and I drove along the street looking for a home that wasn't fenced in. I passed three over the course of almost a mile. None of them close enough to warrant cutting through.

I headed back to the interstate and drove into town. I parked across the street from the office. Morton and I

walked up to Rooster's BBQ, and I ordered a pork sandwich. On the way home, rather than strain at the leash,
Morton walked next to me, like the well-trained dog he
wasn't. He kept an eye on the bag with the BBQ pork
sandwich all the way up to the office.

Once in the office, I tossed him a biscuit. He gob-
bled it up in two or three bites then seemed to shrug and
settled onto his pillow.

Ten

While I ate my pork sandwich, I thought some more about Tommy Benedetti. I phoned my pal Aaron LaZelle down at the police department and left a message. I phoned Heidi and left another message. I thought about phoning Candi Mangle again, but based on the fact no one seemed to be answering my phone calls, I decided against it.

Louie strolled in about a half-hour later. He was red-faced from climbing the stairs. He gave me a little wave as he tried to catch his breath, tossed his briefcase on the picnic table, and settled into his desk chair. I got up, filled his almost empty coffee mug with what was left in the pot, turned off the burner, and set the mug on his desk. He nodded thanks, took a sip, grimaced, and shook his head.

After a couple of sips, he cleared his throat and said, "You learn anything on this Benedetti character?"

"Yeah, he's a scumbag. Not that it should be news to anyone who knows the guy. He's been tried on a number of different charges and never convicted." I listed the laundry list of charges to Louie and said, "I drove past his home this morning. It's in Mahtomedi and backs up onto White Bear Lake. Nice looking place. I'm guessing it would go for a million bucks, maybe more, at least in last year's market. It had a three-car garage, but there was no way anyone would be able to park a stretch limo in there. A white Lexus SUV was parked in the drive. I'm guessing it might belong to a wife. Maybe he's got kids. I don't know."

Louie nodded and set his coffee off to the side. "I asked a couple of folks I know down at the courthouse about him. They were aware of the guy, knew about the various charges against him, and the fact that nothing ever stuck. One guy suggested you might want to check on the house. He thought Benedetti was in arrears on the mortgage and owed some back taxes on the property."

"In arrears? How does someone in arrears manage to force a metal briefcase with two hundred grand on a woman like Heidi? A woman he's never met."

"You told me earlier this morning he's a gambler. Apparently, he took a chance."

"Yeah, he's a gambler, or at least used to be, and apparently not a very good one."

"Well then, maybe it fits. Maybe the whole thing was an act. You know, I'm thinking she just might want to get those bills tested. They could be counterfeit," Louie said.

"Counterfeit? God, I never even thought of that. You know, it makes sense in a crazy way. His act the other night with the stretch limo. What if he rented or borrowed the thing for an hour, and the thugs were just pals or something? Although, they didn't seem to be fooling around, and the one jerk had no problem knocking me to the ground."

Louie shook his head. "Well, Benedetti clearly has a history, and it seems to be wrought with failure. Given the times, being in arrears on a mortgage and/or property taxes right now wouldn't be all that unusual."

I pulled my laptop in front of me, lifted the screen, and turned it on. "We can find out about the property taxes in just a moment."

I clicked on the Google link and got into the Washington County site. I entered Benedetti's address, and a moment later, the tax record was displayed. The property taxes on the home for the first six months had not been paid. They're usually due on the fifteenth of May, but that had been extended this year to July fifteenth, due to the virus.

"You learn anything? Are the property taxes paid?" Louie asked.

"No, but with the date extended to the fifteenth of July, he's just a little more than two weeks late. I don't know."

"Yeah, maybe," Louie said. "Unless as part of his mortgage payment, an additional amount for property taxes is included. That isn't mandatory, but it is pretty standard. If he was up to date with his mortgage, the taxes would have been paid in May regardless of the July extension. I wonder if that means he's months behind on the mortgage."

I thought back to the safety deposit box with Heidi. The crisp, fresh bills in bundles with a rubber band wrapped around them. Not the standard paper wrap that would have been labeled $10,000. Instead, these had a rubber band, and $10,000 was written with a black Sharpie on a piece of lined paper that had been torn from some pocket notebook.

Louie slurped some coffee and said, "You thinking or daydreaming?"

"I'm thinking of that two hundred grand Benedetti gave Heidi. The stuff looked fresh, brand new. Now I'm wondering if it might be fake, counterfeit. Maybe this is all a big scam to get into the fund, and what? Loot it somehow? Be paid to leave? Could it be his latest crime?"

"You called Candi Mangle at the FBI, didn't you?"

"Yeah, I called her earlier this morning, ended up leaving a message."

"She'll get back to you. Mention this cash to her. If she uncovers a counterfeit scheme no one else is aware of, it could be a hell of a career boost. Might give you a little more bargaining power."

"Let me call Heidi again," I said, picking up my cellphone. I hit the button for Heidi, and amazingly, after three rings, she picked up. The first thing she did was cough into the phone before she managed to squeak out my name. "Dev?" Cough, cough, cough.

"What the hell? Heidi, you sound like a mad dog barking. You okay?"

Cough. "God, I don't know where I got this from. I just woke up with it about four this morning. It seems to be getting worse."

"You get exposed to someone?"

"Yeah, you. You feeling anything like this?"

"No, I'm doing fine." More coughing in the background. "Heidi?"

"Relax, I'll be okay. I took my temperature about an hour ago. It's fine. Relax, will you?"

"You come up with a plan on Benedetti?" I asked.

"To be honest, I really haven't thought about him. I'm trying to get rid of this stupid cough. I've got a vaporizer going, and I've been taking Robitussin. Hopefully, it will kick in soon." Cough, cough, cough.

"Can I get you anything?"

"Thanks, but I'm fine, and please, relax. My temperature is just fine. Believe me, I'm keeping an eye on it. Probably stress related with everything going on right now. Thanks for checking in, Dev. I'm staying in bed so I can beat this thing. Hopefully, we'll talk tomorrow." Cough, cough, cough. Click

"God, could you hear her coughing, Louie? She sounded like shit."

"You think she might have contracted the virus?"

"Heidi? I really doubt it. She's a fanatic on health. It was one of the reasons we had dinner at Chez Charles the other night. They're all into the social distancing and stuff. I mean, with the bottle of wine, it was close to two hundred bucks for the two of us, and all the staff were wearing face masks and latex gloves. No groups larger than four allowed. Let me tell you, for a moment, I thought I'd reserved a table at the city morgue."

"They're just playing by the rules, Dev. Trying to keep staff and customers safe."

"Oh, yeah, I get that, not a complaint, actually. But other than that night, I mean, it's not like she's been going out. She's been working from home since the middle of last March. She scrubs everything down with an alcohol wipe. I was afraid she was going to do that to me if we went to bed. Not that I had anything to worry about once Benedetti ruined the night."

"You think maybe she might have picked up the virus in his stretch limo?"

I shook my head. "I don't think that happened. I'm thinking it's maybe more a result of her pounding down all that vodka until she was absolutely ossified. Along with killing a bunch of brain cells, she probably did some temporary damage to her throat. Hopefully she'll learn a lesson."

"Talk about the pot calling the kettle black," Louie chuckled.

"What are you talking about? I haven't learned any lessons, but she's smarter than me, a lot smarter."

"You won't hear any argument from me."

I went back to delving into the online information on Benedetti. In between worrying about Heidi's health, the national response to the damn virus, and Benedetti, I didn't really accomplish much. Louie left the office, and

I watched him hurry across the street to The Spot. When I grabbed Morton's leash, he hopped off his pillow and met me at the door. We went for a walk. Morton took his time investigating every other gate and tree, plus every fire hydrant along the way.

We were a block away when my cellphone rang. The number came across as unknown, so I answered, "Haskell Investigations."

"Yes, I'd like to speak to Devlin Haskell, please."

"Speaking."

"Mr. Haskell, my name is Candi Mangle. I'm returning a call you left for me earlier this morning."

Eleven

I was a little surprised and very grateful that she called. "Thanks for returning my call, Ms. Mangle."

"You can stop with the formalities and call me Candi. Let me ask you something. How did you get my home number? It's unlisted."

"I'm a private investigator and—"

"You told me that in your message."

"And I deal with a number of folks at the courthouse and in the St. Paul police department. Your name came up more than once."

"You still haven't told me how you got my number."

Definitely with the FBI. "Some of the people I spoke with knew you or knew of you. All positive referrals, by the way. Someone gave me your number, but I can't remember who it was."

"I understand that along with conducting investigations, you also paint."

Obviously, she checked me out. "Paint? I'm not an artist if that's what you're thinking. I don't—"

"An artist? Hardly. From what I hear, Haskell, you've got a bit of a reputation. By the way, I meant painting with a roller. I've got a living room that needs a fresh coat."

"I've got a reputation as a painter?"

"Among other things. Interested in doing my living room?"

"I don't think I'd be able to fit that in right now," I lied.

"Mmm-mmm, we'll see about that. So why did you contact me?"

"I've come across something that might be of interest to you."

"Ahh, you're going to have to be just a little more specific," she said, sounding like she might be losing what little patience she had.

"Someone I know was forced to meet a guy. The guy is a thug, has a pretty extensive record, although I don't believe he's served any time. He's been charged with a number of crimes over the years, never found guilty. He's banned from some Las Vegas casinos. He forced my friend into a stretch limo and gave my friend two hundred grand in cash. All crisp, fresh, hundred-dollar bills. Someone suggested they might be counterfeit."

"How do you know they're counterfeit? Did you check the serial numbers? Look for fibers in the paper? Did you—"

"There wasn't time for that, and to be honest, it didn't even occur to us."

"So, what would you like from me?"

"I'd like to meet with you. Tell you what I know about this guy who gave my friend the money. See what you might suggest."

She seemed to think about that for a long moment. "Hello?"

"Yeah, still here, Haskell. Thinking where we might meet. Tell you what. You know where Davanni's is on Cleveland Avenue?"

"I do. You name the time, and I'll be happy to meet you."

"You free tonight?"

"I can be."

"I have a couple of items I need to take care of. Why don't we meet at Davanni's at seven-thirty? Will that work for you?"

"I'll see you there," I said, and she disconnected. So much for keeping an eye on Brandon Lovelace tonight. Maybe if I kept the meeting short, I could swing past Brandon's and see what he was up to after I met with Candi Mangle.

We headed into The Spot. Louie was at the end of the bar on his usual stool. Mike was bartending, wearing latex gloves and a face mask. Two other guys were seated at the bar, five stools apart, and both were wearing masks. One guy's mask looked like a clown face, white, with big red lips and a red nose. Morton began straining at his leash as Louie waved. Mike looked at me and held up an empty beer glass.

"Yeah, thanks, Mike. One's my limit. I gotta meet with someone later tonight. Better give Louie another of whatever he's drinking."

"He's having his usual. I'll bring them down to you," he said.

Louie dumped a half-dozen pork rinds into his hand and bent down as Morton rounded the corner of the bar. "Oh, good to see you, Morton. Here, a little reward for helping Dev find his way over here. Yeah, that's right, eat them up. You earned it."

Mike delivered my beer and Louie's drink as I took a twenty out of my wallet and tossed it on the bar. He took the bill and headed to the cash register. Morton sat at attention, staring at Louie. I picked up my beer glass and raised it toward Louie. He clinked glasses with me, drained the glass he'd been drinking, and picked up the fresh drink.

"Perfect timing on your part, Dev."

"Yeah, as always. Hey, I just got off the phone with that FBI woman you mentioned, Candi Mangle. I'm thinking of calling her The Mangler."

Louie smiled and took a sip. "Just don't let her know that. She any help?"

"We'll see. I'm meeting her down at Davanni's at seven-thirty. Hopefully, she'll have some ideas. I suppose it's too much to ask that she just lock up Benedetti and throw away the key."

"Did you mention his name to her?

"No, I didn't, and she didn't ask. But she agreed to meet, so that suggests to me she's at least a little interested. She did say she heard I did some painting from time to time and asked if I wanted to paint her living room."

"You going to do that?"

"Are you kidding? Why would I do that?"

"Because, up until the other day, you haven't had a client or a case for almost two months and you need the money? I don't know, just a wild guess. Or, maybe because it would be nice to have the FBI watching your back when you have to deal with this Benedetti, and you will have to deal with him at some point."

I took a sip of beer and considered what Louie had just said. "Yeah, maybe."

"Well, think about it," Louie said.

"She asked if I did anything to check to see if the bills were counterfeit."

"Like what?"

"Look for some kind of fibers in the paper or check the serial numbers. Hell, Heidi and I were both so surprised, it never even occurred to us the stuff might be fake. Heidi just wanted to get it all in a safety deposit box, so it was safe while she tries to figure out what the hell to do."

"And she can't just give it back to this guy?"

"I'm pretty sure that's not an option with Benedetti. He made that pretty clear when one of his thugs knocked me on my ass and encouraged her to get in the limo.

She's usually not the kind of woman you direct and tell what to do. The fact that she ended up with this mess actually speaks volumes on what a jerk Benedetti is."

"Yeah, and now she's sick," Louie said and took another drink.

"Hopefully, she just caught some cough she can beat."

"You better keep an eye on her, Dev. If she somehow got this virus shit, she's going to need all the help she can get."

"I'd probably be the last person to know what to do."

"Then you might just want to study up on it now, while you got the chance."

"You really thinking she's caught this shit?" I asked and drained my beer glass.

"I'm thinking right now, based on how fast that cough seems to have kicked in, there's about an eighty percent chance. You'll know for sure in the next forty-eight hours. She's just independent enough to think she can beat it, and then all of a sudden, she's too sick to move, and there's nothing she can do. If I were you, Dev, I'd keep your fingers crossed and hope to God I'm wrong."

Twelve

fter my uplifting conversation with Louie, Morton and I headed home. I let him out into the backyard, then hurried upstairs, grabbed a quick shower, shaved, and pulled on a reasonably clean, blue polo shirt. I headed over to Davanni's. It was normally about a fifteen-minute drive. I made it in about eight minutes and parked on a side street.

Davanni's was a pizza and sandwich place that currently offered only take-out although there were tables that seated four arranged outside on the sidewalk. There was a line of a half-dozen guys, waiting to order. Three guys wore masks. Everyone except me wore gloves. It appeared I had arrived before Candi Mangle.

Menus were taped on the windows, and as I read one, my stomach began to growl. I decided on the BBQ chicken pizza and stepped to the curb rather than wait in line.

My stomach continued to growl as seven-thirty came and went. At ten minutes before eight, I decided to go ahead and order. I stepped to the back of the line, now eight guys long. A few minutes later, a dark-haired woman strolled around the corner.

I pegged her at maybe late thirties, early forties. She was wearing tight blue jeans and a strappy black tank top with buttons down the front. Half the buttons were undone, revealing a deep, tanned cleavage. All the guys in line turned their heads and stared, including me.

She stepped next to the guy behind me. He had a shaved head, a gray goatee, and a beer belly. He smiled as she nodded and asked, "Are you, Dev Haskell?"

"No, but I'm buying," he said and laughed.

I raised my hand and said, "Hi, Candi. Over here."

"Sorry about that," she said to the guy with the goatee and stepped up next to me. "Nice to meet you," she said, sticking her right foot toward me, more as a joke.

I lifted my foot to touch hers and said, "Thanks for coming, Candi. I'm ordering the BBQ chicken pizza. Get whatever you want. I'm buying," I said loud enough, so the guy behind me heard.

He glanced up from his phone and laughed.

"You can check that menu on the window. I'm not sharing my pizza."

She smiled and said, "I'll have the chicken, bacon, honey mustard hot hoagie."

She must be a regular if she didn't even have to look at the menu. "You want to stake out a table? I'll place our order. It should only take a few minutes."

"Actually, I was thinking we might eat at my place. I'm just a couple of blocks away, and I've got beer and wine on ice. That is, if you don't mind."

"Works just fine for me," I said, thinking I was glad I'd grabbed a shower.

Once I ordered, we stood out at the curb, chatting about things in general, basically just the status of life at the moment and what changes we thought might be coming down the pike. She seemed fairly nice and, based on guys' reactions arriving or leaving, a head-turner.

About twenty minutes later, a kid stepped out of Davanni's carrying a brown paper bag with handles and called, "Haskell?"

"Yeah, over here," I said and met him halfway.

"Thank you, sir, enjoy your evening and come back soon."

"We will," I said and stepped back to Candi. "You sure you don't want to eat here?"

"I'd prefer my place if you don't mind."

"Sounds good. You want me to follow you?"

"You could, but it would be a slow drive. I walked over. How 'bout you drive, and I give you directions."

"Sounds good." She followed me around the corner to my Ford Taurus. The car was gray. It looked okay, actually, except for the hood I had replaced, which was primed flat black. Oh, and the vertical crease in the middle of the front passenger door. I was going to open the door for her, but she opened it herself, didn't say anything about the loud squeak it made, and climbed in.

I hurried around to the driver's side, set the food bag in the back seat, and started the car on the second try.

"Take a right at the corner," she said as she buckled up. I took a right and drove for three blocks.

"Take this next right. I'm on the right-hand side, down on the next block."

I made the turn and headed down the block, past the cross street, and began to slow. "It's that cream-colored house two doors down with the white trim," she said.

There were two parking spaces in front of her house, and I pulled in. She lived in a Cape Cod style place with a narrow porch that ran along the front and a driveway along the right side. A small hexagonal blue sign with white letters in the front garden announced that the home was secured by ADT. I noticed there were cameras on both corners of the house as well as one above the front door.

"Thanks for the lift," she said as she opened the passenger door. I grabbed the bag from the back seat and followed her across the sidewalk and up three steps leading to the front porch. Her front door was oak with three panels of beveled glass toward the top of the door. There was a peephole below the glass panels and an ornate brass doorknob that looked original to the house.

She unlocked the door, and the moment she opened it, an alarm sounded from inside. She stepped in, input a code on the keypad, and the alarm stopped. "Come on back to the kitchen, Dev. Would you like a beer or wine? I've got red or white."

"A beer would be great," I said, following her through the dining room and into the kitchen. On the way, I glanced at the living room behind me. The woodwork was all dark oak, and the walls had been painted a fire engine red, stylish maybe ten or fifteen years ago. There was a fireplace centered on the far wall. The fireplace was red brick with an oak mantel and built-in bookcases on either side of the fireplace. A stained glass window with a floral pattern was above each bookcase.

She pushed through a swinging door and entered the kitchen. "Do you want to warm that pizza in the oven for a few minutes?"

"No, it'll be great just the way it is," I said, and my stomach growled.

"Oh, good lord, let's get you fed. Are you up for eating outside?"

"That sounds fine to me," I said.

She opened the refrigerator and handed me a can of beer. She pulled out a bottle of white wine, filled a glass already sitting on the counter, and headed toward a back entryway. I followed her outside to a glass-topped table sitting on a small brick patio. An apple tree was at the end of the yard, and flowers and plants lined a wooden garden fence the length of the backyard.

"Pull up a seat and dig in. I don't know about you, but I'm starving," she said.

Thirteen

Neither one of us talked for the next few minutes. I was busy stuffing the fourth slice of pizza in my mouth. Candi was on the second half of her hoagie. She took a bite, chewed, swallowed, and said, "So tell me about this money you think might be counterfeit."

"Yeah, sure. My friend is on the board of an investment fund. She's been doing this for a number of years. She's very successful and has a great reputation. She's coming out of a restaurant the other night, a high-class place over on University Ave. The valet runs off to get her car, and while she's waiting, a stretch limo pulls out of the lot, stops next to her, and the door opens. Some thug gets out of the limo, and a guy calls her by name from the back seat and invites her into the limo."

"So, she knew the guy."

"No, she didn't, but he obviously knew who she was. She hesitates, and a couple of thugs climb out of the limo and encourage her to get in the back seat. She—"

"She's alone?"

"No. There was a guy with her. Nice guy, really nice, as a matter of fact. He tries to stop it, but there's, umm, three thugs, and they eventually fight the guy off. They're armed, and he isn't. They more or less force her into the limo and then take off."

"Did this guy call the cops?"

"No. They said they'd drop her off at her home in a half-hour, and he was afraid, if he alerted the police, these guys might hurt her."

"So did they bring her home?"

"Yeah, actually they did, and he was there waiting for her. She got out of the limo with a metal briefcase. It held two hundred grand, and the guy in the limo wanted her to invest it in the fund."

Candi shook her head and took another bite of her hoagie. "Mmm-mmm, strange, very strange. I have a couple of questions."

"Yeah, okay," I said. Without thinking, I held up a slice of pizza, tilted my head back, and then bit off half the piece.

Candi sat and stared for a moment.

"Oh, sorry, umm, you said you had some questions."

She shook her head, mumbled something I couldn't understand, and said, "So, she has two hundred grand in cash. All hundreds?"

"Yeah."

"What does she do? It's nighttime. No banks are open."

I half-chuckled. "She gets totally drunk on Grey Goose vodka."

"Grey Goose. Well, at least she has good taste. And the two hundred grand?"

"The guy hides it in the house then stays up all night looking out the window in case someone shows up and tries to rob her."

"Mmm, sounds like a nice guy. So, you said you actually saw the money."

"Oh, yeah. The next morning I went back, I mean, I went over first thing. She showed me the money, and I convinced her to put it somewhere safe. Then I drove her down to the First National Bank. She had a contact there. She rented a safety deposit box, put all the money in there, and as far as I know, that's where it remains today."

"How long ago was this?" Candi asked and stuffed the last of the hoagie into her mouth.

"Just a couple days ago. I'm pretty sure she hasn't returned to the bank since."

"Tell me about the currency. What did it feel like?"

"Feel like? It felt like cash. I fanned through two of the bundles. They were all hundreds."

"How'd the paper feel? Did you think it might have been a little thick?"

"Thick? No, I didn't get that sense, but I was picking up bundles, not individual bills."

"Was any of it sticky?"

"No, at least not that I could tell, but I didn't touch all the bundles."

"And you didn't look at the serial numbers on the bills, right?"

"I didn't, but I think I would have noticed if they were all the same."

"Pretty safe bet they wouldn't be. But, if you hold the bill up to the light, a thread next to the image of Ben Franklin reads 'USA' and '100.' The ink just to the left of the serial number changes from copper to green when you move the bill around. The serial number should correspond to the series. There are probably a half-dozen things you can do to check, depending on when the bill was printed. It would be interesting to take a look at these. What got you thinking they might be counterfeit?"

"Actually, none of the things you just said. But you know how bundles of cash from a bank usually have that paper wrap around them with the amount printed on it? A thousand, five thousand, or ten thousand dollars? These bundles didn't have that. They had a rubber band and a piece of paper torn from a little pocket notebook. $10,000 was written on the paper with a black sharpie. So she's got what looks like two hundred grand in hundred-dollar bills, and they aren't even wrapped properly. That doesn't seem right."

"I'd have to agree, Dev. I'm presuming you know who gave this briefcase to your friend."

"I know his name, Tommy Benedetti. I've never met him. All I know about him I've learned in the last two days just reading online or talking to people. Can you tell me anything about him?"

"What can I tell you? Well, I can give you some general information, off the top of my head. You want another beer? I'm going to grab another glass of wine."

"Yeah, I'd take another beer."

"I'll get it. You finished?" she asked, looking at my empty pizza box.

"Yeah, good choice. It's been a while since I've been to Davanni's, but I really like it."

"God, I'm there once a week when I'm in town. I'll be right back," she said, picking up my pizza box and the wrapper from her hoagie. I enjoyed the view as Candi strutted up the back steps and into her house. She was back out with my beer and another glass of white wine about ten minutes later. As she sat down, the slightest hint of a nice perfume wafted over.

"So," she said, "Tommy Benedetti. Tell me what you know."

"What I know, well…" I started in with him being banned from the Las Vegas casinos, mentioned the crimes I could recall him being charged with. I was quick to add that he had never been convicted. I described his house in Mahtomedi, told her I'd driven past it just that morning. I purposely left out my meeting with Tubby Gustafson the other day. "… and that's pretty much the extent of what I know."

"All in all, it sounds pretty accurate. I can maybe give you an update. The white Lexus at the Mahtomedi property does indeed belong to his wife, Gina. They have two teenage boys, Thomas, age sixteen, named after his father, and Michael, age fourteen. Both boys attend Mahtomedi High School. They're 'B' students and play in the school band."

"Does the wife work?"

Candi gave me a look suggesting I didn't know what I was talking about. "No, she does not. She's an exercise fanatic, and when not exercising, she's at home. Gina and Tommy Benedetti have been separated for maybe the past nine or ten months. She has the two boys in the home on the lake. The last I heard, he was shacking up with a girlfriend in some condo in Lowertown."

"Does she know he's in arrears on the property taxes and most likely the mortgage?"

She shook her head and said, "I have no idea. The only reason I'm even remotely aware of him is I was involved in tracking a major identity theft scheme. His name was mentioned as a key player. At this point, we could say he remains under consideration. Say I'm thinking of another glass of wine. How about another beer?"

"Yeah that would be great. Can I help with anything? Dishes or something?"

She gave a little laugh as she grabbed my empty beer can and her wine glass. "Dev, honey, we didn't have any dishes. Well, other than my wine glass. You ate your pizza out of the box, and I ate my hoagie out of the wrapper. Thanks for picking up that tab, by the way. That was really sweet of you. Back in a moment."

She was back about fifteen minutes later, attired in a loose-fitting t-shirt cut off above her navel and red and black stretch shorts that left nothing to the imagination. The black pattern on the shorts was designed to look like a garter belt. She set the beer can on the table, turned around, and took her time pushing her chair back a foot or two. All the while giving me a view of her perfect rear and the chance to glance up inside the loose fitting t-shirt.

"Hope you don't mind, but it's already been a long day. I just need to relax and, you know, get rid of some of the day's tension."

"You won't hear a complaint from me."

"Good. I'll maybe try to help you with this Benedetti situation, but I'm not sure what, exactly, I can do. I think the first thing is we should see if this two hundred-grand is counterfeit."

"Okay," I said.

"I'd like to examine it. If it's counterfeit, that opens up a number of options. From what I know of Benedetti, having that amount of cash and passing it off to someone as an incentive to invest in a fund doesn't sound like the best idea for the fund. But then, I'm not sure he's ever had a good idea." She took a long sip of her wine and said, "Let's maybe step inside. I want to show you the living room. Just to get an idea and see what you think."

"Ladies first," I said as Candi strutted up the steps and inside. She knew I was watching and seemed more than willing to put on a show. If I wasn't holding the beer can I would have applauded.

She led me in the kitchen, through the swinging door, across the dining room, and into the living room. She gulped down her wine glass, set the empty on the fireplace mantel, and proceeded to stretch for a moment, bending down touching her toes, up, then back down. She did the routine a half-dozen times. Once again, I wasn't about to complain.

"So, as you can see, the room is way overdue for an update. I've already got the paint. A nice neutral color, Navajo White. You familiar with it?"

"As a matter of fact, I am. It's a soft, warm white, with a slight yellow tint to it. I've painted it in a couple of rooms." I remembered painting Patti's bedroom, thinking it was going to make my nights sleeping over even better. That was just before she dumped me and had her new boyfriend leave my ladder and paint trays on my front porch. Looking at Candi right now, I wondered if my luck with that color had maybe changed.

More wine and beer led to sitting on the couch in front of the fireplace. The fireplace was gas-fueled, so Candi could start the fire just by turning on a switch. She poured herself another glass of wine, and we headed toward the bedroom just after midnight.

The room was pink, with dimmed lighting. Two steps led to a round bed raised up on a platform. A large round mirror was attached to the ceiling over the bed. As we climbed into the bed, she pushed a button, and the bed began to vibrate softly. We drifted off to sleep a half-hour later.

She woke me a little after two, again at four, and once more at five-thirty. I got dressed after that, gave her a kiss, promised to call later, and let myself out. I only passed two cars on my way home at that hour. Both cars were traveling in the opposite direction. I made a pot of coffee, grabbed a shower, and climbed into bed. Fortunately, Morton had left enough room for me.

He barked me awake a little after eight-thirty. I pulled on a white robe that held a slight perfumed scent and let him out the kitchen door. I poured myself a cup of coffee and sat at the kitchen counter, trying to remember if I had promised to paint Candi Mangle's living room.

Fourteen

Morton and I made it down to the office just before ten. Louie was already in the office, typing away on his laptop. "How's it going?" he said without looking up.

"Good, Louie. How about you?"

He was in shirt sleeves with his tie loosened and the top button on his shirt undone. "Trying to get this finished. I'm pleading before Hoffman in an hour. I maybe stayed a little too late at The Spot last night. How'd things go with Candi Mangle?"

"Okay." I poured what was left from the coffee pot into my mug, barely filling it half-full. I debated starting a fresh pot, ended up turning off the burner and settling into my desk chair.

"She offer to take a look at the cash Heidi got from Benedetti?"

"Mmm, she certainly seemed interested. If she takes a look and it's counterfeit, that would open the door to all sorts of help and probably eliminate Benedetti as a problem for Heidi." I had a long yawn.

"She gave me a couple of things to look for that might determine if it's counterfeit. I might try that first and maybe be able to confirm things one way or the other. More than likely, she'll have to take a look at the stuff herself. The more she heard what happened with Benedetti, the more it sounded like a scam to her right from the get-go. In fact, let me call Heidi right now and give her an update."

I speed-dialed Heidi. Her phone rang twice and dumped me into voicemail. "Yeah, Heidi, it's Dev. Hey, I met with an FBI agent last night. I didn't mention your name. I've got an idea on a couple of things we can do to see if those funds from Benedetti might be counterfeit. I'd like to get on this sooner rather than later. If the stuff is counterfeit, it would seem to get you off the hook. Give me a call either way when you can. I'm around all day until about four-thirty, and then I have to work a case. Thanks. Oh, hope that cough is better." Click.

Louie turned his chair to face me. "You think she's okay?"

"Heidi? Yeah, why wouldn't she be?"

"Just that cough she had yesterday. You said it was pretty bad and unless I'm missing something, it seemed to come on pretty fast."

"If you're thinking the virus, I'd say the chance of that is pretty slim. God, she reaches for an alcohol wipe if I stand still for more than sixty seconds. Believe me, you could perform open-heart surgery on any flat surface in her house. The place is more germ-free than any op-erating theatre. She's been working from home for five or six weeks. She'll be fine. She's just paying the price after having a love affair with Grey Goose vodka the other night."

"If you say so." Louie said. "I'd just continue to check on her. This shit can hit hard and fast."

"I just checked in and left a message. Knowing her, she's probably already got a half-dozen attorneys lined up to go after Benedetti in court. Speaking of which, I'd better call Aaron LaZelle and bring him up to date."

I phoned Aaron, my pal on the police force and got dumped into his voicemail. "Hey, Aaron, left you a message yesterday. Give me a call. I've got something that may be of interest to you. Thanks." As I disconnected, Louie placed his laptop in his briefcase and slipped on his suit coat.

"Don't forget to button that shirt and straighten your tie," I said.

"Oh, yeah. Thanks, man. I would have been standing in front of Hoffman like this, and he'd like nothing better than to fillet me before I even got started. You gonna be out, or are you working from here today?"

"I've got a ton of work to do right here at my desk. I should be here when you get back. Good luck."

"Thanks, I'm going to need it. Catch you later," Louie said and headed out the door.

I heard the stairs creak as he made his way down to the main floor and out the door. He was parked just in front of my Taurus. I watched him waddle across the street and settle in behind the wheel. Once he started the car and drove off, I got comfortable in my chair and closed my eyes.

My phone ringing woke me two and a half hours later. I had to clear my throat a couple of times as I answered, "Haskell Investigations."

"Yeah, Dev. It's Aaron. Did I wake you?" he joked. If only he knew.

"Just slaving away in the office, Aaron. How are you doing?"

"The usual, jammed. Sorry I couldn't get back to you sooner. I was out at a crime scene on the Eastside. What's up?"

"A guy named Tommy Benedetti."

"Mmm, yeah, we know him. My advice, don't go anywhere near him. He's nothing but trouble, with a strong dose of bad luck thrown in."

"A little late for that advice," I said and went on to fill him in on some of the details.

"Two hundred grand, and you think it's counterfeit?"

"At this point, I don't know. I've been in touch with someone in the FBI." My mind suddenly jumped to Candi Mangle, waking me up around two, four, and again at five-thirty this morning. Talk about energy. I remember her sliding—

"You still there, Dev?"

"Yeah, I'm back. Sorry, I lost you there for a minute. What were you saying?"

"I said, it would be very helpful to be included in any aspect of an investigation of Benedetti. Believe me, the list is long of folks who would like to see his ass locked up for a number of years."

"More than willing to include the department. It's just that I don't have anything yet. I want to get back to that safety deposit box and take a good hard look at that cash. I think even if it seems okay, I'm going to want to call in this FBI agent and get a professional opinion. I can only hope it turns up counterfeit and Heidi can get Benedetti out of her life."

"So, you'll keep me posted?"

"You bet I will."

"Okay, much appreciated, Dev. I'll alert a couple of folks around here and let them know you'll be getting back to me. This could be very good, and God knows we could all use some good news for a change. Thanks for the call. Don't forget about us."

"As soon as I have something, I'll let you know, Aaron."

We disconnected, and I snuggled back into my chair. The stairs creaking sometime later got my attention. Just in case, I quickly opened my laptop and turned it on. It had just finished letting off its startup sound when I heard a groan on the other side of the door. A moment later, the door opened, and a red-faced Louie stumbled in. He set his computer bag on the picnic table and gave me a wave but didn't say anything. He gasped as he sat down behind the picnic table.

I pretended to be working on my laptop. After three or four minutes, I said, "How'd things go? I figured you'd be in court all afternoon."

"It went well. In fact, better than I could have hoped. I got her off with time served. If there's no violation over the course of the next twelve months, her record will be expunged."

"She going to be able to do that?"

"She'd better. She's an elementary teacher. The district will work with her on this one, but if it happens again, she's toast. Right now, the line is long of people who would kill to have her job. We had a little 'Come to Jesus' meeting before the proceeding. She seemed to get it. Now if she can just stay on task for the next twelve months, it'll be good. "How'd things go for you?"

"Good, I guess. Nothing from Heidi, yet. I did talk to Aaron LaZelle. They would love to be involved. I'm not exactly sure how the Feds will feel about that, but I can't worry about it now."

"Glad you're starting to make some progress. Anything from Candi Mangle?"

"I'll be calling her in a bit. She had something going on until about three." I didn't feel the need to mention it was sleeping off her hangover and resting her worn-out body after the number of wrestling matches we had last night.

At three on the dot, I placed a call to Candi's home phone and left a message. "Hi Candi, this is Dev Haskell. I just wanted to thank you for working with me last night.

It was great to get to know you. Please give me a call when you have a chance. Wishing you all the best, take care."

At four, Louie turned off his computer and said, "I'm heading over to The Spot if you'd care to join me."

"Oh, thanks, I'd love to, but I'm about to take Morton home and then spend the night keeping an eye on Brandon Lovelace. See if he goes anywhere or maybe has someone come in. Tracy's gone for two or three more days, so if he's going to misbehave, these next few days seem like the perfect time. I'll hopefully know soon enough."

"Just be careful. I'll see you in the morning," Louie said and headed out the door.

Fifteen

I took Morton home and let him out in the backyard. I ran upstairs and changed into running clothes. It was eighty-seven degrees out and humid. Shorts and a faded t-shirt were all I needed. I filled Morton's water dish, coaxed him in with the offer of a biscuit, and headed over to Brandon Lovelace's house. On the way, I stopped and got a fish fillet at McDonalds. Brandon's car was in the driveway when I drove past. I parked around the corner and then settled onto a bench about two hundred yards from his house, ate the fish fillet, and waited.

He came out maybe a half-hour later, walked across the street, and began doing stretching exercises. I didn't think he'd seen me sitting on the bench. His back was turned as he stretched and touched his toes, and I hurried off the bench. I walked down a small path leading over the river bluff and waited. He ran past maybe ten minutes later.

I walked back up the path and watched as he ran up the pedestrian walkway. When he was almost out of sight, I began to run slowly along the same route. I must have jogged a good two miles and never saw him again.

I figured he had probably headed up one of the side streets. So much for following him on his run.

Since I was ready to collapse, I stopped, turned around, and began to walk back in the direction of my car. After maybe thirty minutes, I gradually rounded a bend and could see his driveway maybe a quarter-mile away. That meant the side street where I had parked was maybe a hundred feet closer, and I had at least half a chance of making it to my car.

I heard fast-paced footsteps coming from behind. I stepped off the asphalt walk to let the runner pass. It turned out to be Brandon. Thankfully, he ran past without giving me a second look.

Just like the other day, he ran past his house. He slowed to a walk and continued walking for a couple of minutes. He checked for traffic, crossed the street, and headed back to his house. I made it to the bench I was seated on earlier and collapsed. Brandon disappeared into his house. I sat on the bench sweating and attempted to recover.

I was still on the bench forty-five minutes later, rubbing my aching thighs and calves when a shiny dark-blue car pulled into Brandon's driveway. A blonde guy in tan slacks, a t-shirt, and a blue sport coat slid out of the driver's seat carrying a bottle of wine and what looked like a laptop computer under his arm. He walked up to the front door and rang the doorbell.

Brandon opened the door, half-shouted a greeting I couldn't understand, and the guy walked in. I figured they'd probably have a glass of wine and then head out to dinner or eat at Brandon's and then maybe go out on the prowl for a couple of women. If they ran into agent Candi Mangle, it would take more than two of them.

I settled in on the bench and waited. The mosquitos biting eventually woke me. I could hear the things flying around looking for blood, my blood. I pulled out my phone and checked the time. It was after eleven. I groaned to my feet, swatted the mosquitos away, and limped over to my car. Amazingly, the car started on the first try.

I stopped at the corner, took a left, and drove past Brandon's house. The blue car turned out to be a BMW. I wrote the license number on the McDonalds bag and headed home. I parked in the driveway and groaned as I climbed the steps to the front porch and let myself in. So much for my watchdog. Morton was nowhere to be seen.

I turned off the first-floor lights and headed upstairs. Morton was out cold on the bed. What was left of a chewed rawhide bone rested on my pillow. I slipped off my running attire, left it on the floor, and headed into the shower. The long, hot shower seemed to ease some of the muscle pain in my legs, and I went to bed.

I don't think I moved until the alarm went off the following morning. I got dressed and left Morton asleep in the bed with his head under the pillow. My legs were stiff, and as I headed down the stairs, I had to hold onto the stair rail. I turned on the coffee and fired up my laptop. Morton joined me maybe forty-five minutes later.

Sixteen

We'd been in the office for the better part of an hour before Louie made his way up the stairs. I'd already done two sets of stretching exercises in an effort to keep my legs from seizing up. As Louie made his way into the office, I was bent over touching my toes.

"Mmm-mmm," Louie groaned by way of a greeting. He set his briefcase on the picnic table and collapsed in his desk chair. I finished stretching and filled both our coffee mugs. A few minutes later, he took another sip and said, "So, did you learn anything on your stakeout last night?"

"Yeah. It's been a long time since I ran any distance."

"What?"

I proceeded to fill him in on my attempt to follow Brandon Lovelace last night.

"And at the end of all that, he never left the house?"

"Yeah. I kept an eye on things until almost midnight and then went home. I don't know. Maybe they were watching a movie or talking business or something. I have no idea who the guy was yet. But I'll place a call to my pal Gerry over at the DMV and get a name and address."

"Careful you don't wear out your welcome with him. He could lose his job if word got out he was giving you private information. They might even come up with a way to fine you."

"Sound advice," I said, stood and began attempting to touch my toes again.

"So, you're taking up running?"

"I don't think so. I thought I'd follow him, but I lost him almost before I started. Next time, I think I'll just follow in my car." My phone rang, and I glanced at the number, Candi Mangle.

"Hi, Candi," was how I answered and gave Louie a nod when he glanced over at the sound of her name.

"Hi, Dev. Did you catch up on your sleep?"

"Oh, yeah. Thanks for asking and thanks again for a most enjoyable evening."

"Well, I aim to please."

"And you did a number of times."

Louie got a strange look on his face.

"Calling for two reasons. First, did you have an opportunity to examine the currency?"

I thought it best not to mention I slept for most of yesterday afternoon.

"No, unfortunately, I haven't been able to contact the woman with the safety deposit box. I'll give her a call as soon as we're off the line."

"Okay, and secondly, I'm leaving my alarm off and the key to the front door beneath the flowerpot on the back steps. What time do you think you'll be over this morning to begin painting?"

I suddenly had a vague memory of being in an awkward position in a pink bedroom in the middle of the night. At that particular moment, I would have agreed to just about anything Candi wanted. Paint her living room? I could ask myself, what was I thinking? But I already knew.

"Yeah, the living room. I was in early this morning just finishing up here at the office. It shouldn't be more than forty-five minutes, maybe an hour tops and I'll be over."

"Okay, I'll wait for a bit. I don't like leaving my home with the alarm off for more than a few minutes. Why don't you give me a call when you're ready to leave?"

"Be happy to. It shouldn't be too long. Talk to you shortly," I said and hung up.

"Everything, okay?" Louie asked without looking up from his laptop.

"Oh, yeah. That was Candi Mangle. She's got someone she'd like me to meet. She wants me to tell him about the Benedetti deal with Heidi. You gonna be around today?"

"I've got a proceeding at eleven and another at two so I'll be down at the courthouse for most of the day."

"Okay, I think I'll take Morton home and leave him in the backyard. Neither one of us needs to come back here and deal with a Morton mess."

At the sound of his name, Morton's head popped up. I grabbed the leash off the windowsill, clicked it onto his collar, and we headed out the door. Other than 'Goodbye,' Louie didn't say anything, but I had the distinct feeling he had figured out a lot more than he was letting on.

I brought Morton home, filled his water dish, gave him a biscuit, and let him out into the backyard. I went upstairs, pulled my painting jeans off the hook in the closet. I slipped into my painting shoes and pulled on an old t-shirt. I grabbed a roller, a paint tray, a couple of brushes, a step ladder, and tossed them all in the back of the Taurus. I phoned Candi as I pulled out of the driveway to let her know I was on the way.

The key to the front door was right where she said it would be. The paint and two drop cloths were in the corner of the now empty living room. The paintings were off the wall, all the woodwork was taped off with blue masking tape, and there was a note on top of one of the paint cans that said she had made me lunch, and it was in the refrigerator. Other than not wanting to paint, it wasn't that bad of a gig. I finished up a little after three, phoned her, and left a message.

"Hi Candi, this is Dev. I'll be finished for the day in maybe an hour. I'll lock the front door and leave the key beneath that flowerpot. Give me a call when you're able. You're going to need a second coat."

I had already cleaned my brushes and tray. I headed into the kitchen, opened the refrigerator, and there was a sandwich from Davanni's on the shelf with a note attached that said, *'Enjoy lunch, Dev.'*

I settled in at the kitchen counter and started in on the sandwich.

Seventeen

I was home a little after four. I called Heidi and ended up leaving another message. I phoned Gerry at the DMV. He answered on the fourth ring. "This is Gerry."

"Hi Gerry, Dev Haskell."

"Dev Haskell, gee, let me guess. You're calling to take me to dinner at the restaurant of my choice. After which, you just happen to have tickets to the Minnesota Twins game. Front seats along the first baseline. Right?"

"Well, that's maybe half-right. We can watch a softball game at the Highland Park city playground since there isn't a Twins game and the restaurant will be closed. If you'd like, we can get a couple of Big Mac's and take them to the softball game."

"No, thanks. What you got?"

"A shiny dark blue BMW. License number…" I went on to give him the number.

"Humph," he said a half-minute later "Guy's name is Dylan Finch." He spelled out the first name for me. "Doesn't look like any tickets or warnings in the last five years. Age twenty-nine. Date of birth, 19 August 1991. You want the home address?"

"Yeah, give it to me, and I won't have to bug you again."

"I'll put this on the list, Dev. I can't wait to be your guest at a place with the most expensive whiskey in town."

"Yeah, Gerry. If things ever open up again, we'll go."

"Counting on it. Gotta run. Take care."

A twenty-nine-year-old guy visiting Brandon Lovelace. It had to be a business deal.

I had some leftover pizza for dinner. Did more stretching exercises on my legs. At least they weren't feeling as bad as earlier in the day. Morton and I settled in to watch a movie I'd already seen. I dozed off, and when I woke, Morton had already headed upstairs. I got the coffee ready for the morning, turned off the lights, and went upstairs to bed. I was asleep about the time my head hit the pillow.

Morton's growling woke me a little before four in the morning. I tried to settle him down, but he wouldn't have it. He also wasn't going to get off the bed, which, if past experience was any indication, meant that something was going on just outside, and he was frightened. I hopped out of bed, pulled on a pair of jeans and a black t-shirt. I took out my Smith & Wesson 52 pistol from my nightstand. It's a .38 caliber and more than enough to deal with whatever was going on.

I left the lights off and groaned as I made my way down the stairs, holding onto the handrail. I couldn't see anything out the front windows and was heading into the kitchen when I heard what maybe sounded like a cough. Or, was it a bark? I peeked out the dining room windows, but all I saw was the neighbor's driveway. I headed into the kitchen and heard the noise again. It seemed to be coming from the back door.

I pressed my back against the kitchen wall, pointed the .38, and headed toward the door. I heard what sounded like someone hurrying down the steps. There was no way whoever was out there could have seen me. I peeked out the window next to the door just in time to catch a figure hurrying down the driveway. I unlocked the door, stepped outside, and listened for a moment before I went down the stairs.

I caught a glimpse of someone jogging across the sidewalk and into the street. He coughed a few times, sounding more like a bark than a cough, and started running down the street.

"Hey, stop now, or I'll shoot. I'm warning you. I'm going shoot," I shouted as he picked up speed. He headed toward a nondescript gray SUV parked halfway down the block. It was the only car on the street. He must have pressed his fob because the taillights suddenly flashed, and the horn gave off a quick beep.

"Stop, or I'll shoot," I shouted, having no intention of shooting. I was barefoot and not about to chase him.

He seemed to pick up speed and reached the driver's door in a half-dozen steps. As he opened the door, the interior light flashed on, and he glanced back in my direction. I recognized him almost immediately. I'd seen him just the other night as Heidi and I were leaving the Chez Charles restaurant. The muscular guy with the 'S' curved nose. The guy who held the limo door open. He was coughing that night, too. Now it sounded more like a mad dog barking.

I watched as his taillights disappeared around the corner. Somehow, Tommy Benedetti knew it was me with Heidi the other night. I thought for a half-second about giving her a call but quickly decided that wouldn't be the best move. Maybe Heidi had mentioned my name when she was in the stretch limo. Maybe she threatened Benedetti, although that didn't sound quite right.

I decided the best thing to do might be to hurry back into the house rather than get caught standing out on the street, holding a .38 at a little after four in the morning.

I went back in the kitchen door, locked it, and wedged a chair beneath the doorknob. I placed another chair up against the front door. I went through every room, double-checking to make sure all the first-floor windows were locked. I never really got back to sleep. At six, I headed into the shower. I pulled on a bathrobe and went downstairs for a coffee. I sent Louie an email letting him know I wouldn't be in until sometime after the noon hour. I was on the computer for about ninety minutes. I filled Morton's food and water dish and set them outside on the back porch.

I headed upstairs, put on my painting clothes, and gently woke Morton. He gave me a look that suggested something along the lines of 'What do you think you're doing?' Once it was apparent I wasn't going to leave, he groaned, hopped off the bed, stretched, and we headed downstairs. I gave him a good long scratch behind the ears and let him outside.

I called Candi. She picked up on the third ring. "Dev?"

"Hi Candi, hey, I'm wondering if I could come over and get that second coat on the living room?"

"This morning?"

"Yeah, if it wouldn't be too much trouble."

"Well, yeah, I suppose so. Umm, I guess that will work. Let's get it done."

Twenty minutes later, I was driving down Candi's street. A guy in a black Chevy Equinox with government plates was just pulling out of Candi's driveway. His hair was tangled, and he looked like he had just been rousted out of bed. As I pulled in front of the house he sped down the street in the opposite direction. I went to the front door and rang the doorbell. Candi answered a half-minute later. She was wearing a short, black silk robe with Asian lettering on the left side and drinking from a coffee mug. She gave me a peck on the cheek as I stepped in. "Coffee's in the kitchen, help yourself. I've got to get ready for work," she said. She headed into her bedroom and closed the door behind her.

I poured myself a mug of coffee and made note of the two wine glasses in the sink. Obviously, she was a busy lady. I walked into the living room, spread out the drop cloths, and went to work. Candi stepped out of her bedroom a half-hour later. She was dressed in a conservative, black business suit with a light blue blouse. Her shoes were black with maybe a two-inch heel.

"Let me know when you have something on that currency. The sooner, the better. Thanks for finishing this up so quickly. I owe you, big time," she said and raised her eyebrows. I glanced at her after that last comment, but she was busy rummaging through her purse.

"I'll leave the key on the kitchen table. The door locks automatically, but I would appreciate you using the key to do the second lock. Have a good day, thanks again, and call me when you're leaving. Bye, bye," she said and headed into the kitchen and out the back door. A minute later, I watched her as she backed out of the driveway and headed down the street.

I finished up before noon, cleaned my brushes, and opened the refrigerator to see what she'd left for lunch. There wasn't anything. I guess not surprising, given the fact she had been otherwise detained this morning. I loaded my ladder and equipment into the Taurus. I called Candi and let her know I was finished then drove home.

I showered, shaved, and was down at the office a little after one. Louie wasn't around. The coffee pot was empty and still on. I placed another call to Heidi and immediately ended up in her voicemail. "Heidi, it's Dev.

I'm getting worried. Call me, so I know you're okay. Thanks."

Eighteen

Heidi finally returned my call in the middle of the afternoon. Unfortunately, she did not sound good.

"Hi, Heidi," was how I answered.

She responded with a good thirty seconds of a non-stop barking cough. After which, she managed to get out a raspy, "Dev."

"Heidi, where are you? You sound like absolute shit. Have you been tested for the virus?"

"I can't get the test," cough, bark, bark, "for another four," bark cough, cough, "four days."

"It sounds to me like the test isn't going to matter. You've got the damn virus. I want you to get into bed. I'm coming over and—"

"No." Cough, bark, cough. "I think" cough, "Nora O'Rourke is," bark, bark, "is coming over to check on me. I can't remember."

Nora O'Rourke was Heidi's next-door neighbor and an ER nurse. I'd met her a half-dozen times. "Okay, I want you in bed and have Nora call me once she's taken a look at you. Don't worry. She'll know what to do."

Cough, cough, bark. "Dev," cough, cough. "I'm scared."

"Now listen to me. You get to bed now. Okay?"

Cough, bark, cough. "Okay," she said and hung up.

Not good. I planned to give Nora a call and see if she could get over there right away. I rummaged through my Rolodex three times, going through 'N,' 'O,' and 'R' knowing how I sometimes filed things. I couldn't find anything. She lived right next door to Heidi, and I knew her address within a number or two. I went online, Googled Nora's name, and then searched public records. It took maybe five minutes to get to her phone number, which, under the circumstances, seemed like five hours.

I phoned Nora, and she answered on the third ring. Before she could even say hello, I said, "Hi, Nora, this is Dev Haskell."

There was a pause before she said, "Oh, Dev, sorry it took me a minute. What can I do for you?"

"Have you spoken with Heidi today?"

"Heidi? Funny you should call. I got a text message from her this morning. But I'm working night shift in the ER. We've been working six days on, one day off, so I've been leaving my phone down in the kitchen when I come home and go to bed. I was going to stop over on my way to work later tonight. Is everything okay?"

"I don't think so." I went on to tell her about leaving three days' worth of phone messages and finally talking to Heidi fifteen minutes ago. "She had this raspy, barky, cough. Couldn't finish a sentence. She sounded confused. She's been a fanatic about staying isolated, rubbing everything that stays still with alcohol wipes, but I'm afraid she's contracted the virus somehow."

As I said that last part, I thought that damn Benedetti. That's where she probably got this thing.

"Oh, dear. That doesn't sound good. Let me suit up, and I'll run over there."

"Thanks, Nora. Please call me once you see her."

"Yeah, okay. Stay by the phone. I'll get back to you shortly. Thanks for the call, Dev." Nora called back ten minutes later.

I answered with, "Hi, Nora. What'd you find out?"

"Nothing. I couldn't get in. I rang the doorbell a bunch of times and phoned her twice. No answer. You wouldn't happen to have a key, would you?"

"I do," I said, heading out the office door and hurrying down the stairs. "I'm about ten minutes away."

"I'll be watching for you," she said. I disconnected, hurried across the street to my car, and sped toward Heidi's house. I screeched to a stop and was just getting out of the car when Nora hurried out of her house and across the front lawn. She was gowned up with a face mask, protective shield, gloves, and what looked like a one-piece polyester outfit. She handed me a pair of gloves and a face mask.

"I want you to put these on and don't touch anything. You got it? Do not touch anything. I want you to stay behind me at all times. If she's in her bedroom, you are not to go in. I will. You just wait in the hall. Understand?”

“Yeah, yeah, I got it. Come on. Let’s go,” I said and started to run toward the door.

“Dev, stop. Stop right there. Now calm down and put the gloves on.”

“Nora, I—”

“Put the damn gloves on, Dev. Okay, good. Now the mask. Okay, much better. Now, when you unlock the door, I want you to step aside and let me go in first.”

“Okay, okay, I got it.”

“All right, let’s go,” she said.

I didn’t run up to the front door, but I walked awfully damn fast. I inserted the key and heard the lock click. I turned the knob, opened the door, then stepped back and let Nora enter.

“You stay six feet behind me, and I’m not kidding. Six feet, Dev.”

I nodded and said, “Yeah, I got it,” as she hurried past me.

I followed her into Heidi’s living room and down the short hall. She called out Heidi’s name a couple of times as she made her way toward the master bedroom. “You wait out here,” she said before she opened the bedroom door.

“Heidi, can you hear me? It’s Nora. Heidi, I’m here with Dev. I want to check and see how you’re doing. I’m going to take your temperature, honey.”

Heidi barked a cough as Nora took a little white and blue thing that kind of looked like a gun and held it up to Heidi's forehead.

"Mmm-mmm, okay, you've got a bit of a fever." Nora glanced at the end table. An empty water glass and a bottle of Ibuprofen sat next to a Kindle. "I going to have Dev get you some fresh water. I want you to take two more Ibuprofen."

She handed me the water glass and said, "Put this one in the dishwasher and fill a clean water glass for her."

"Okay, now, Heidi. The best thing you can do is…" I hurried out to the kitchen and put the water glass in the sink on top of two plates and a bowl. Very unlike Heidi to leave dirty dishes in the sink. I filled a water glass and hurried back to the bedroom.

"Thanks, Dev. Give us a moment here. I'm going to help Heidi into the bathroom."

I went back into the kitchen, rinsed off the plates and bowl, and loaded them with the glass in the half-full dishwasher. The coffee pot was maybe a third full, and I poured the contents down the sink. I put soap in the dishwasher container and pressed the button to start it. I checked the refrigerator; nothing appeared to be spoiled. No food was left out in the kitchen, and I walked into the living room. I stared at the empty couch and suddenly got all choked up thinking about the wonderful nights we'd had on it, just chatting, laughing, and telling stories.

Heidi has a mailbox built into the wall. I opened it and pulled out the mail. Most of the envelopes were commercial offers, and I placed them in her recycling bin. There were three envelopes that appeared to be business, but they would just have to wait. I set them on the kitchen counter. I unplugged the cord to recharge the phone and took it into the bedroom. Nora was in the process of helping Heidi back into bed. Heidi glanced at me for a moment, but I'm not sure she really recognized me.

Nora tucked Heidi into bed and signaled me to make my way to the front door. Once outside, I locked the door behind us, and Nora said, "Well, I'm glad you phoned. She's definitely got the virus."

"Shit."

"Dev, she's not elderly. She doesn't have any preexisting conditions. She's in good shape. So she has a very good chance of coming through this. Let's stay in touch. I'll look in on her when I leave for work and again when I come home. I'm home a little after nine in the morning, and I have to be gowned up and on-site at nine in the evening. You should check on her around noon and maybe five or six in the evening. Let me see if I can get you some more protection gear. You can get those masks at Park Pharmacy along with a box of those gloves. Any questions?"

"What about medicine?"

"There really isn't any. The Ibuprofen is really for pain relief. Now, when you check on her, she will most likely be asleep. If she's awake, she may not be cognizant. That's more or less normal, so don't panic. Let's stay in touch."

"Thanks again, Nora. You really helped. I know you've had more than enough of this at work, so we really appreciate you helping."

"Sure thing. Okay, come on over to my place. I want you to dispose of that mask and those gloves properly and then wash your hands."

"Oh, you don't have to—"

"Dev, get with the program and cop on to what you just saw. Right now, that mask and those gloves are carrying the virus. So let's dispose of them. You should go home, shower, and then get your ass to the pharmacy and load up on masks and gloves. If you don't do that, you're just going to make things worse for Heidi."

"Okay, got it."

"Good, you have any questions?" she asked as we walked toward her back door.

"Just one. Heidi was in a car with four guys about five days ago. It was a stretch limo. They had a business meeting in the limo, and they dropped her off here at home once they were finished. I know for a fact one of the guys was coughing. I saw him last night, and his cough sounded more like a bark. As a matter of fact, he couldn't seem to stop coughing, and it sounded an awful lot like Heidi did when I spoke to her on the phone earlier today. Could she have caught the virus from that guy in the stretch limo?"

"I would say there's a pretty strong chance she did. You may want to contact those individuals and give them a warning if they aren't ill already."

"Oh, I'll be sure to contact them. I'll definitely give them a warning. Not to worry about that."

Nineteen

Ever the good student, I followed Nora's directions, went home, and took a long hot shower. I let Morton back in the house, gave him a biscuit, and then headed over to the Park Pharmacy. I purchased twenty masks, a box with a thousand gloves, and a packet of alcohol wipes. I stopped at the hardware store and had a spare key to Heidi's made for Nora. I decided to eat healthy and made myself a tomato and bacon sandwich for dinner. I sent Louie a text message telling him Morton and I would be in first thing in the morning, and then headed back to Heidi's.

I stopped along the way and picked up fresh fruit that she could eat if she felt like it. I put the gloves and the mask on while still in my car. I dropped the key into Nora's mailbox and let myself into Heidi's house. The sun was starting to think about setting, and I turned on a table lamp next to the front window after I entered. I placed the fruit in the refrigerator and quietly headed to Heidi's bedroom to check in on her. She was asleep, breathing heavily, and occasionally coughing. Though nothing like her coughing earlier in the day. I took her water glass out to the kitchen. I emptied the dishwasher, put the water glass in the dishwasher, and placed a fresh glass of water on her nightstand.

I wrote her a note on the back of an envelope from her recycling bin, telling her Nora was going to check on her before she left for work, and I would be by later in the morning. I ended the note with *'Fresh fruit in the fridge. Your favorite, strawberries.'*

I drove home wearing the gloves and mask. I wiped down the steering wheel on the Taurus as I climbed out of the car. Morton had been sitting on the couch looking out the front window, and he met me at the front door. I walked into the kitchen and tossed him a biscuit since he'd been so patient with me today. I washed my hands while singing three verses of Happy Birthday. I dished up a bowl of frozen yogurt and settled down in front of the TV. After the movie, I joined Morton already in bed and slept through the night until my alarm went off.

No sign of the coughing intruder from the night before, but then I'd threatened to shoot him, so he probably figured I'd be waiting up in case he returned. I was on the computer when Morton eventually wandered into the kitchen. He took two steps into the room, stopped, stretched, and then wandered over to have his head scratched. I let him out after that and filled his food and water dish.

We headed down to the office maybe a half-hour later. Louie wasn't in yet. Morton made a beeline for his pillow and snuggled down for an early morning nap. I made a fresh pot of coffee, pulled out my binoculars, and scanned the building across the street. Unfortunately, there was nothing to see. Just as the coffee finished perking, I saw Louie pull in behind my car. I put the binoculars away, filled our mugs, and set his on the picnic table.

He began to groan his way up the stairs as I settled in behind my desk. The door swung open, and he stood in the doorway for a moment, looking amazed he'd made it up the stairs. He gave me a little wave and set his briefcase on the picnic table as he headed toward his chair. Once he sat down, he noticed the steaming coffee mug and pulled it closer.

After three or four sips, his face wasn't quite so red, and he said, "How'd your day go?"

"Interesting," I said and gave him the lowdown on meeting with Nora and the two of us checking on Heidi. "So now I'm driving around with gloves, masks, and wipes in my car. I've got to check in on Heidi later this morning and in the early evening."

"But she's okay? What did she say?"

"Actually, she's not okay. She's out of it, Louie. Nora said she'll be having scary dreams, maybe hallucinating, dealing with back pain and muscle cramps for at least the next few days. The best thing would be if she just slept. We'll check on her breathing, make sure that's okay and just wait for her to improve."

Louie shook his head. "God, this whole mess is just incredible. What the hell is the new world going to be like? People working from home, no one going to bars. I can't imagine."

"Louie, just be glad neither one of us owns a restaurant or a store where people have to come in to buy stuff. There are going to be a hell of a lot of changes. Was there anyone in The Spot last night?"

Louie shook his head. "Four other people besides me. Nothing happening. No interesting conversations to listen in on. The television was playing a World Series game from 1991, Twins and Atlanta Braves. I was the last one to leave the place, and after watching that baseball game, I couldn't wait to get home. I was home before ten. I'm sure Mike locked the door to The Spot before I even made it to my car."

Twenty

Louie headed to the courthouse just before ten. I left Morton in charge of the office and drove out to Mahtomedi. I pulled in front of the Benedetti house. The white Lexus was parked over by the garage, and now a basketball net on wheels was set up close to the house. Two boys were shooting baskets. They looked similar, and I figured they were probably the Benedetti brothers. I got out of my car, opened the gate, and headed toward the house. The younger of the two, Michael, caught the ball as it bounced off the backboard and saw me approaching. He said something to his older brother, but I was too far away to hear what he said. He shot the ball, missed the basket, and his brother caught the rebound. They both turned and watched me as I approached.

"Hey, guys, how's it going?" I called.

"Fine," the older one said. The younger kid just nodded.

"Your mom, home? I wanted to talk to her about something."

"If this is about the mortgage, you're supposed to talk to our dad," Thomas, the older boy said.

"Yeah, and he's not here right now," Michael added.

"No, I don't know anything about the mortgage. Or taxes, or anything like that. Is she home?"

"Inside," Thomas said.

I pulled a business card out of my wallet and said, "Would you mind giving this to her and letting her know I have a question for her if she has a moment to talk?"

He glanced at the card, looked like he was about to say something, but then thought he better not. He bounced the basketball over to his brother, who dribbled twice, shot, and missed. The ball bounced to me. I grabbed it, took a shot, and the ball swished through the net.

"Do that again," Michael said and bounced the ball to me.

I repeated the shot, including the ball swishing through the net.

"Hmm-mmm, you're pretty good. Did you play for a team?"

"No, when I was a kid, there was a net on my neighbor's garage. I spent a lot of time out there in the alley, practicing."

"How do you aim?" he asked.

"Step over here, and I'll show you what I do. I miss once in a while, but I make the shot most of the time." I took the ball from him and explained how I lined it up with the rim and made sure I had enough of an arc. I took another shot, and mercifully, I made it. I grabbed the basketball and handed it to him.

"You go ahead. Line it up and shoot. It takes some practice, but you'll get it."

He lined up his shot, tossed it, and it bounced off the rim.

"Okay, you almost got it. You need to get it higher and just a little closer. But you got the right idea. Try it again."

He spent a little more time lining up the shot then tossed the ball. I thought he was going to make a basket, but the ball flipped back out of the hoop at the last moment.

"Oh, man, so close. Try it again," I said and bounced the ball to him.

He lined it up, and just as he shot a woman's voice said, "Mr. Haskell?"

The ball swirled inside the rim then dropped through the net. "Well, done, Michael," I said. Keep practicing that, move all around, and shoot. You've got it. You learned a lot quicker than it took me."

He flashed a wide grin and grabbed the ball.

I turned and faced the blonde woman standing in the doorway. "Hi, are you Gina Benedetti?" I asked, extending my hand as I headed toward her.

She folded her arms across her chest and nodded. She had that look of someone who had been a hot number for basically her entire life. Candi had described her as an exercise fanatic, and clearly, she was in shape. She wore a long sleeve blue stretch top and pants. The pants rose up to just above the navel on her flat stomach, and the top stopped just beneath her breasts, exposing maybe a five-inch wide view of perfectly tanned skin.

"Just what did you want to ask me? If it's anything financial, you'll have to talk to Tommy, or you can call my attorney." Interesting it was her attorney and not 'their' attorney. She'd obviously been dealing with creditors, collections, phone calls, and mail.

"Hey, Mom, watch this," Michael said and quickly shot the basketball. It bounced off the rim and off to the side.

"Remember to take your time, Mike. You got it," I said.

"Oh, thanks. He's always trying to beat his older brother at everything."

"Mmm, brothers. Yeah, it's only natural," I said. "I wonder if we might talk privately."

"You still haven't told me what this is about."

"I wanted to warn you about the virus."

"What?"

"I wanted to warn you, well, and by extension, your boys. A friend of mine had a brief meeting with your husband a few days ago. She's since come down with the Coronavirus."

"Why would you think she caught it from Tommy? Who, by the way, I've separated from."

"I heard you might have separated, but I don't know how to contact him. My friend was fanatic about working from home. She was leaving a restaurant, her first night out in a few months, and your husband pulled up in a stretch limo. A big guy stepped out with an 'S' curved nose."

"That sounds like Tony."

"Hmm, okay. Well, Tony was coughing, and they made my friend get into the limo. They drove around for maybe thirty or forty minutes. She's now got COVID 19. They were virtually the only people she'd physically interacted with over the last two months."

"And just what, exactly, do you mean by physically interacted with?"

"Nothing sexual if that's what you're asking. She's a financial person. Your husband wanted to invest in a certain hedge fund and he—"

"Are you shitting me? A hedge fund?" She screeched. I heard the basketball stop bouncing for a long moment before it started up again. "He hasn't paid the damn mortgage for months, and he didn't pay the property taxes this spring. The only reason the boys and I haven't been tossed out on the street is because the government put a temporary halt to evictions and foreclosures. But believe me, it's eventually going to happen. God, I go to sleep every night worried about being out on the street, and it's the first thing I think of every morning when I wake up. And that bastard Tommy wants to invest in a hedge fund? I'd say I can't believe it, but unfortunately, I can," she said and shook her head.

"Is there a way you know of that I could get in touch with him?"

"Well, he's shacked up with that skanky slut, Coco. You know her?"

"Coco? God, actually, I think I might. I mean, I don't exactly know her, but the name rings a bell." If it was the woman I was thinking of, Tommy Benedetti had his hands full. "Is she, umm, a dancer?"

"You mean, is she a stripper? Yeah, among a number of other things. I'm sure she probably does anything he or any other guy wants her to do. I've never met the bitch, and I don't intend to, ever. And just in case no one mentioned it, those aren't real, they're implants."

"All I heard was that he was with someone in Lowertown."

"Yeah, that would be Coco. She lives in The Market House down on Fifth Street. Coco Cummings. I think she's up on the fifth floor. Tommy took the boys down there on Easter. I told him never again. God, I had to burn their clothes when they got home. They reeked of cheap perfume. Mind if I ask you something?"

"No, not at all."

"Good, because I was gonna ask anyway. Exactly what did it cost him to get into this hedge fund bullshit?"

"Well, first of all, he's not in. Just the way he approached the matter set off all sorts of warning flags. That said, the woman who makes the decision of whether or not he does get in is so ill with the virus right now she can't even make a phone call let alone check out the viability of someone attempting to invest in the fund."

"Yeah, sure, but like they say, when money's talking nobody's walking. So, let me ask you again. Exactly what did it cost Tommy to get into this hedge fund bullshit?"

"He offered two hundred grand, but that—"

"Two hundred grand? Are you shitting me?" This time the basketball stopped bouncing and was now rolling onto the lawn as both wide-eyed boys stopped to watch us. Gina glanced over at them and said, "I'm talking with Mr. Hassle. If you're tired of shooting baskets, there's an hour of music practice that still has to be done today." Tommy quickly grabbed the ball and passed it to his younger brother. "Let's move out by your car. You can't be serious, two hundred grand?" she asked again. She opened the gate and stormed toward my car.

"Yes, but like I said, there are some questions about his offer."

"What kind of questions?" she asked, leaning against the side of my car and crossing her arms.

"Well, I'm not really at liberty to—"

"Hey, listen up here, Mr. Do Everything Right. Tommy Benedetti is a failed crook, a failed gambler, a failed husband, and it sounds like a soon to be failed financial investor. I've got two wonderful boys who are driving me crazy. Their stupid prick of a father rarely pays any attention to them, and when he does, they end up spending the afternoon with a stripper who has fake boobs. We're going to be evicted from this place about five minutes after the government lifts the ban on evictions. Who the hell in this town is going to hire me once they find out I was married to that putz, Tommy Benedetti? So, if he's dancing around town in a stretch limo with two hundred grand and begging some woman to take it, don't you think I just might have a right to know about that? Honest to God. How did I ever end up with this deadbeat?"

"Okay, listen, calm down, and I'll tell you what I suspect. I use that word cautiously because I don't really know." I went on to tell her about Tommy Benedetti pulling up in the stretch limo as Heidi came out of Chez Charles. I neglected to mention I was with her. I did tell her that I was with Heidi later as she polished off the better part of a bottle of Grey Goose. I told her I saw the cash myself, fanned a couple of bundles, and that they were wrapped with a rubber band and a note written with a Sharpie.

"Oh, God, that is vintage Tommy. He just never gets it right," she said, shaking her head. "Let me just ask you something here. What do you think a packet of those official $10,000 labels would cost? A buck? Two bucks? Certainly no more than five bucks. So instead of getting the proper wrapping around each bundle, he uses a rubber band and then pens a note with a damn color crayon."

"Actually, it was a Sharpie, a black Sharpie," I said, and she shot me a look. "Not that the Sharpie is important."

"Except that it is because right from the get-go, everyone knows somethings not adding up. Here's a question for you. You interested in picking up another client?"

"Another client?"

"I need to know the facts about all this and how it plays out. If this goes down the way I think it will, I don't give a damn what Tommy says, a simple separation will not give me or the boys enough distance. I'm going for a divorce. Capisce?"

"Well, umm, yeah. If I can help you in some way I will. No problem. I just don't know how you—"

"Okay, good. My attorney's name is Courtney Potter. I'm going to tell her to give you a call. God. I slept with the jerk for the better part of twenty years. I know a few things. Take for instance, that stretch limo. That thing isn't his. He's got an old high school pal who owns a limo service, Victor DeCulo. Usually, he rents that thing out for weddings or the occasional date when someone wants to get laid by a new girlfriend. Believe me, I know from personal experience. Oh, and just in case you had any questions, guess who was probably the driver?"

"The driver?"

"Of that limo. God, are you listening? It was more likely than not, Coco. She's got a class C commercial driver's license, drives a school bus when she's not shaking her implants on stage."

"Coco Cummings was the driver of the limo?"

"I'm almost certain of it. And that idiot you described with the nose that's been broken too many times to count. That's most likely Tommy's older brother, Tony. Hard to believe, but he's an even bigger loser than Tommy."

"And there were two other guys. One of them maybe knows Karate. He hit a guy in the chest and then chopped him on the back of the neck when he went down."

Gina nodded and said, "Most likely, Coco's brother, Melvin Cummings. He's another deadbeat whose only success in life has been getting jailed on a regular basis."

"Okay, so here's Tommy's main problem," I said. "The hedge fund folks think the money might be counterfeit. In fact, they're pretty sure it is, and they're in touch with the FBI to come in and examine it. Just in case that's not bad enough, I think the FBI contacted the St. Paul police and want them to be involved."

"Mother of God," Gina said, shaking her head. "It just doesn't end. Tommy's got an uncle named Arnold, same last name. He has a small printing shop downtown called Inkoholic. The authorities are aware of him. He scammed some pull tabs maybe ten years ago. True to the family way, he got caught and did three years. God, it would be just like him to print up bills and do a lousy job at it."

"How long were you married to Tommy?"

"Mmm, my oldest, the good Tommy, is sixteen now, so we were married for fourteen years. We've been separated for almost one. Believe me, I'm counting the days."

"Gina, I appreciate the updates, and I will keep you advised of what happens. I'll hopefully be in touch in the next few days."

"Let me give you my personal cellphone number. Tommy doesn't know I have this, so please don't give it to him." She gave me the number, and I punched it into my cellphone.

"Okay, thanks, Gina. Remember, I'm pretty sure at least one of these characters has the virus."

"Idiots," she said, shaking her head. "All absolute idiots." I watched as she closed the gate behind her and walked over to shoot a couple of baskets with her sons. I felt sorry for all of them. They had a tough road ahead and really nothing they could do except wait for it.

I got in my car and wrote down the names, Victor DeCulo, Tony Benedetti, Coco Cummings, Melvin Cummings, Arnold Benedetti, Inkoholic printing, and last but not least, Courtney Potter, all on the back of the McDonalds bag.

Twenty-one

On the way back home, I drove through downtown and cruised past The Market House, a refurbished warehouse where Tommy Benedetti was supposedly shacked up with Coco Cummings. I guessed the age of the building at maybe a hundred and twenty years. It looked great from the outside. Surprisingly, it was just two blocks from Brandon Lovelace's office. A car was pulling out of a parking place. I slowed, waited until he left, and pulled into the spot. I hurried across the street and into the lobby of The Market House.

The lobby was pretty typical, a room with security doors opposite the entrance. On either of the side walls were, and I counted them, seventy-five built-in mailboxes. Each box was locked and identified only by a unit number. If I had the time, I could have camped out in the lobby and waited for Coco or even Tommy Benedetti to wander in, but then what? Besides, I was feeling the urge to go check on Heidi and make sure she was okay. So I climbed back in my car and drove to Heidi's house.

I parked in front of Heidi's and pulled on my mask. I slipped my hands into the gloves, pulled a couple of alcohol wipes from the pack, and headed up to the front door. I unlocked the door and left it open. I called out Heidi's name a couple of times as I made my way to the bedroom. She was sound asleep and breathing heavily. She gave a slight cough twice during the four or five minutes I watched her.

I took her water glass out to the kitchen, rinsed it, and placed it in the dishwasher. I filled a fresh glass. I remembered she had a container of orange juice in the refrigerator and filled a second glass. I took both glasses into the bedroom and placed them on the end table. I watched Heidi for a couple more minutes, then locked up. I wiped the doorknobs down with the wipes and headed for my car. I placed my gloves, mask, and wipes in a plastic bag. I pulled out another wipe, cleaned my hands and the steering wheel, and headed down to the office.

Morton met me at the office door and headed down the stairs. I grabbed his leash and caught up to him on the first floor. We did a good twenty-minute walk through the neighborhood at Morton's pace, which meant a thorough investigation of every other tree, most of the front yard gates, and every fire hydrant.

When we headed up to the office, Louie was seated at his picnic table. He was red-faced which suggested he'd just arrived. "Hey, how's your day going?" I asked as I unclipped Morton's leash.

Louie nodded and flashed me the 'OK' sign using his thumb and forefinger. A couple of minutes later, he asked, "How about you?"

"Gee, thanks for asking. It went pretty well." I went on to tell him about checking on Heidi. Then I told him about talking with Gina Benedetti, although I was pretty light on the details and didn't mention any names.

He shook his head and said, "It sounds like a busy day. A lot of running around."

"Yeah, but all of it worthwhile, and I'm only half-done. I'm going to drop off Morton at home and then go over to Brandon Lovelace's and see what he's up to to-night. So far, he's been nothing if not boring. Tracy's back in forty-eight hours, and I don't have a thing to show her, except that Brandon has been in either a meeting or maybe watching a movie with this Dylan Finch guy."

"You think maybe she was mistaken? Could be since this Brandon is running his own business, maybe he's just been working long hours."

"Yeah, possibly. Anyway, we better get going here. Brandon seems to go for a run at the end of the day, and I want to be over there before he gets back from the run. You in tomorrow morning?"

"Yeah, and you don't have to tell me, I know. First one in makes the coffee," Louie said.

"Okay, Crabby. I'll see you in the morning. Have a good evening."

Louie gave me a wave and fired up his laptop.

I drove Morton home, let him out into the backyard then sent Nora O'Rourke a text message letting her know I'd checked on Heidi, and she was sound asleep. I let

Morton back in after a couple of minutes, tossed him a biscuit, then headed over to Brandon's.

His car was in the driveway as I drove past. I pulled around the corner and parked. I settled in on the bench across the street from his house and gazed at the river valley for the better part of an hour. I was beginning to wonder what was taking Brandon so long on his run when he strolled out of the house in jeans and a gray striped golf shirt.

Even from where I sat, he looked freshly showered, cleaned up, and dressed for a leisurely night out. He climbed in his car, backed out of the driveway, then turned at the corner and drove past my car.

I was immediately on my feet, heading to my car. It started on the second try and I followed him up Cleveland Avenue, maybe two blocks behind him. I kept a couple of cars between us as we drove through Highland Village, past Saint Catherine's, Davanni's, Saint Thomas, over I-94 and down to University Avenue. Brandon made a left-hand turn onto University and headed toward Minneapolis.

Just across the city line, Brandon turned into the parking lot next to a single-story pink stucco building. I knew where we were. The bar was called 'Going My Way.' I had been in there once before, only by mistake. Not that I was treated badly, in fact, just the opposite. Customers and staff could not have been nicer. But I decided I might be more comfortable somewhere else.

I pulled into the parking lot as Brandon was climbing out of his car and heading for the door. I parked, slipped on gloves and a mask, and hurried over to his car. His SUV was parked up next to the building. I took a couple of photos with my cellphone. The photos captured his car parked up against the pink building with the 'Going My Way' sign that was illuminated out in front of the building.

There were double doors leading into the place, and I stepped into the small lobby. Just like the last time I was here, there were probably twenty black and white framed photos of scenes from the 1944 Bing Crosby movie, Going My Way. A movie where Bing Crosby plays a priest. The only other time I'd been in here, it never dawned on me that Going My Way might just be one of the best names ever for a gay bar.

I walked into the bar, and it became immediately apparent I was probably the worst dressed person in there. I spotted two leather vests, one pair of leather trousers. A number of trendy shirts. A couple of sport coats, a few pairs of Italian loafers, and some trendy face masks, one of which had blue sequins. Yeah, I was obviously the worst dressed guy in the place in a faded t-shirt and jeans I'd been wearing for a couple of weeks. At least people seemed to be more or less keeping a six-foot distance. There was a band setting up on stage, actually just two guys, but it looked like there was going to be live music in a bit.

"What can I get you, sir?" a young bartender asked from behind his mask. He wore latex gloves on his hands.

I looked at the half-dozen beer taps and ordered a Summit IPA. I set a ten-dollar bill on the 'U' shaped bar then took a sip once my beer was placed in front of me. As I sipped, I glanced around the room for Brandon. I eventually saw him seated at a table with none other than Dylan Finch.

I thought for a long moment, gradually arriving at the realization that the affair Tracy suspected her husband was having had just become a bit more difficult to explain. I settled onto a barstool and watched the two guys set up onstage while at the same time keeping an eye on Brandon and Dylan.

I pretended to be sending a text message when I took three photos of them, leaning forward and talking to one another at the table. At one point, Brandon had his hand placed on Dylan's shoulder and seemed to be nodding in an understanding way. I took two more photos of them.

The guitar players were in the process of doing a final sound check when another guy suddenly arrived at the table. Brandon stood and hugged the guy, indicated a chair, and they all sat down. Some guy across the 'U' shaped bar raised his eyebrows at me. I tried not to respond and focused on the stage.

Maybe twenty minutes later, the guitar players broke into a song I didn't recognize. It sounded pretty good, and suddenly, there were four couples, all guys,

out on the floor dancing. They were all exceptional danc-
ers. Dylan and the guy who had just joined them stood
and headed to the dance floor at the start of the second
song. This one I recognized, Norah Jones, 'Come Away
With Me.' Of course, it helped that the guitar players announced the name of song before they started playing. I
stupidly glanced across the bar, and the guy who had
raised his eyebrows earlier now indicated the dance floor
with a nod of his head.

I shook my head, no.

Dylan and his dance partner were on the dance floor
for two songs and then sat down again with Brandon.
They all seemed to be involved in an intense discussion,
nothing that appeared negative, but they were laughing
back and forth and apparently interrupting and talking
over one another. Brandon signaled one of the waiters
and ordered another round for the table.

I signaled the bartender and ordered another IPA.
When the bartender delivered my beer, he leaned across
the bar toward me and said, "Excuse me, Cody said he
would like to buy you a drink." As he mentioned the
guy's name, he moved a little to the side, and the same
guy who had been raising his eyebrows, and indicating
the dance floor, nodded vigorously.

"Oh, thanks, but no. Tell Cody, thanks, but I'm,
umm, meeting someone in just a few minutes." I tossed
another ten-dollar bill on the bar, smiled, and said,
"Thanks and keep the change."

The bartender smiled, nodded, and shook his head 'no' to Cody across the way. I watched Brandon's table for five more minutes and finished my beer. I pulled my mask back over my nose and mouth and hurried out the door. Fortunately, no one followed me. I hurried to my car, and I headed home.

Twenty-two

The following morning, Louie was already work-ing at his desk when Morton and I arrived at the office. Amazingly, there was a fresh pot of cof-fee on. I filled both our mugs and settled in behind my desk. As I turned on my computer, Louie sat back in his chair and said, "So, did your pal Brandon Lovelace throw some wild, crazy party last night?"

I shook my head and said, "You won't believe it." I went on to give him all the details and finished up with, "So, on top of supposedly confirming he's having an af-fair, I'm going to have to tell Tracy that she's married to a gay guy."

"Dev, just because he was in that bar doesn't neces-sarily mean he's gay. And before you say anything," Louie said, holding up his hand to stop me from talking. "Just say for a moment one or both of these guys were potential clients or just someone he was doing business with, and that's where they wanted to meet."

"Louie, it didn't look like a business meeting. Were you listening? This Dylan and the other guy got up and danced two dances. One of them was a slow dance. You know with their arms around each other and—"

"And so what, Dev? I'll ask you again. What if he's trying to get them on board and do some project with them? You said this Dylan guy drives a pretty nice BMW. Seems to me that might mean he could be an investor or maybe a real estate developer. Let's be honest here. Both of us have done business with some very unsavory characters over the years. People involved in real crimes. These guys are just dancing together, big deal."

"Yeah, I get that. And I'm cool with that aspect." Louie shot me a questioning look. "What I'm not happy about is when I speak to Brandon's wife, Tracy. I'm going to have to tell her that her husband was hanging out in a gay pickup joint. You think she's going to want to hear that?"

"You think anyone who's hired you over the years to photograph a spouse really wants a confirmation of their suspicions?"

"Well, no, not really, but nine times out of ten, they actually know. That's why they hire me in the first place."

"So, tell her the truth. She probably knows it anyway. The guy might be having an affair, but you haven't proven anything yet. They didn't check into a hotel. No one spent the night at Brandon's, did they? He didn't kill someone. He hasn't kidnapped a child. He didn't rob a bank. You want to see some really awful people listen to the political news. Talk about a criminal class."

Twenty-three

It was noon, and I had just pulled in front of Heidi's house when my phone rang. The call came through as unknown. "Haskell Investigations."

"Devlin Haskell, private investigator, please." The woman sounded like she was reading my name from a phone book.

"Speaking," I said.

"Mr. Haskell, my name is Courtney Potter. I represent Gina Benedetti. I understand you met with her yesterday."

'Met with her' sounded way too formal. "I chatted with her out on the street as she leaned against my car. It was pretty casual. We just talked."

"Mmm-mmm. My understanding is you had information regarding her husband, Thomas, and a proposal he made to a financial consultant. If I understand correctly, he not only offered this individual two hundred thousand dollars, but he managed to pay her in advance."

"Thus far, you're correct that Tommy Benedetti is Gina's husband. Beyond that, you're not making much sense. I'll be happy to help you in any way I can. As a matter of fact, I told Gina as much. But saying that the person I know was paid in advance is completely false."

"Perhaps you might enlighten me."

"Be happy to," I said and then proceeded to fill her in on some of the details. I didn't mention Heidi's name. I didn't mention the assault on me or the fact that I was even present. I did tell her that I had the FBI and the police involved and maybe embellished that aspect a little. "As things develop, I would be more than happy to keep you and Gina informed. But I have to warn you, based on the introduction to Mr. Benedetti and his cohorts, I intend to be extremely cautious from here on in.

"I'm not attempting to prosecute or arrest anyone," I said. "But I do want my client to be safe, unharmed, and not get cheated. If the currency forced on my client proves to be counterfeit, the authorities will have that knowledge and act accordingly."

"And when do you think this might happen?"

"I can't say for sure, but I would hope within the next forty-eight to seventy-two hours."

"And you've been in touch with Federal authorities?"

"Yes, I've been in touch with local law enforcement as well as Federal authorities." I conjured up a memory of Candi Mangle in her pink bedroom but thought it best not to elaborate.

"Very well. I'll look forward to hearing from you."

"I look forward to getting this entire episode as far away from my client as possible. I'll let you know just as soon as my client is out of danger."

She seemed to think about that for a moment before she said, "Thank you for your time," and hung up. It couldn't have been more than a two-minute conversation, and already, I didn't like her.

I slipped on my gloves and a mask, grabbed a couple of wipes, and walked up the sidewalk to Heidi's front door. The table lamp next to the front window had been turned off, suggesting Nora had stopped in this morning. I headed toward Heidi's bedroom. She was in bed, and as I opened the door, her eyes blinked open. She had a mask pulled down around her neck.

It seemed to take a moment for her to recognize me. She gave me a nod and pulled the mask up over her mouth and nose.

"Are you doing okay, Heidi? Just nod if you can." She gave a slight nod.

"How is the head?" I asked.

She shook her head, and her eyes closed for a few seconds. I thought she might have drifted off to sleep, but they slowly opened again. Her water glass was empty, as was another glass on the end table. I thought it may have been the one I'd filled with orange juice.

"I'm going to get you some water and orange juice. I want you to take two of those Ibuprofen." I think she nodded, but I couldn't be sure. Her eyes closed and remained that way. I grabbed both glasses and headed into the kitchen. I put the glasses in the dishwasher, filled two clean glasses, and took them back to the bedroom.

Heidi's eyes opened for a moment as I entered. I took two Ibuprofen pills from the plastic bottle and gently shook her shoulder. Her eyes slowly opened. "Take these pills, Heidi. They'll help you get better."

She took the pills from my gloved hand and placed them in her mouth. I held the glass to her lips, and she swallowed three or four times. She didn't drink very much water, but at least she got some liquid and was able to swallow the pills. Her eyes closed, and I watched for a long moment, hoping she'd wake up again, but she didn't. I checked the bathroom to make sure she had enough toilet paper and toothpaste, although I wasn't sure she could even get out of bed on her own.

I went back to the kitchen and took some of the strawberries I'd gotten yesterday, cut them up and placed them in a bowl. I set the bowl on the nightstand next to her bed. I watched her for a minute or two then headed out the door. I placed my gloves and mask in the plastic bag. Wiped my hands, the door handle, and the steering wheel with two of the wipes, tossed those in the bag, and headed down to the office.

Morton was the only one in the office. He opened one eye as I entered, apparently recognized me, and went back to sleep. I didn't feel like lunch, so I poured the remnants of the coffee pot into my mug, turned off the burner, and fired up my computer.

Twenty-four

I'd been Googling people online, starting with Courtney Potter and moving on to Tommy Benedetti's
bunch of dunces. I thought I heard Louie slowly but
surely groaning his way up the stairs. I could hear the
stairs creaking, slower and with lots more creaking than
usual. I thought this might be the time to suggest to Louie
that he take Morton for a morning and afternoon walk.
Nothing crazy, just twenty minutes along the neighborhood streets so he could begin to let exercise enter his
daily regime and avoid the heart attack that had to be on
his horizon.

The creaking and groaning eventually stopped, and
I focused on the office door, waiting for Louie to stagger
in. The door opened, but it wasn't Louie. Instead, a massive individual dressed in PPE gear from head to toe
lumbered into the office. Behind him, an even larger ro-
tund figure similarly dressed waddled in. Along with the
mask and hood, the second figure wore a protective plastic face shield.

Morton raised his head for a brief moment and immediately lowered it. He somehow seemed to sink even
further into his pillow and placed his paws over his eyes.

The first guy in carried a packet of sanitary wipes and proceeded to rub one over my client chair. When finished, he dropped the wipe on the floor. He pulled a fresh wipe from the packet, which he then used to wipe down the front and top of my desk.

I wondered if someone had seen me enter Heidi's home wearing just a mask and gloves and had reported me. "Is this about checking in on Heidi Bauer and only wearing a pair of—"

"Silencio! You dunderhead!" the individual waiting to sit down shouted.

At the word 'Silencio', I suddenly recognized both of them. "Tub— err, I mean, Mister Gustafson?"

"Yes, Haskell. It would appear I now have to risk my life just to obtain basic information from you." I could tell he was shouting, but with the face mask and the protective plastic shield, it sounded like he was shouting from inside a walk-in cooler. I had to focus to hear him.

Not only was he attired in a massive blue outfit, size double-triple extra-large, including a hood covering his head, but he had little blue booties covering the shoes on his feet. Of course, his hands were covered in latex gloves, probably two pairs. He wore a mask over his nose and mouth with the hood pulled tight. Literally, all I was able to see were his eyes. Quite the change from the naked guy on the massage table I watched on the computer screen while locked in the small room beneath his staircase.

Once I recognized Tubby, it was obvious Fat Freddy Zimmerman was the one duly wiping down the chairs and the front of my desk. When he finished wiping down the chair, Tubby directed him to pull the chair back four or five feet— no doubt, social distancing.

"Mr. Gustafson, this is indeed an honor, and I want to thank you for taking the trouble to drop by and—"

"Did you hear what I said, you one-watt idiot? You were supposed to provide me with information on that mistake of a human being, Tommy Benedetti. Instead, I'm literally forced to risk my life and come to this hell-hole of yours on the second floor. Tell me what you've found out and quickly so we can get back to an uncontaminated area," he said as he sat down. "Oh. My. God. I can literally feel the virus beginning to close in as I sit here. Hurry up, what have you learned?"

"Can I offer either of you a cup of coffee or a pastry? I think we might have a doughnut left over from—"

"You and your ilk are the very reason this nation has become infected. No, Haskell. Stay seated and do not even think about coming near me. Benedetti, what in the hell have you learned?"

"I've learned he appears to be broke. He's behind in his mortgage payments. He owes back taxes. The limo he was traveling in was owned by a friend." I pulled the McDonalds bag in front of me with Dylan Finch's license plate number and the names of Tommy Benedetti's crew that Gina had given me. Tubby shook his hooded head as I read the note on the bag. "That limo is actually owned by some guy named Victor DeCulo."

"And you got this information from someone at McDonalds?" Tubby asked. He didn't seem to be kidding.

"No, sir, I've been talking to a number of people. I can tell you that there is a very strong suspicion that the funds Mr. Benedetti offered are actually counterfeit. I'm in the process of having the FBI and the St. Paul police check them out."

"When do you expect to have confirmation?"

"Very soon, sir."

Tubby shook his head and said, "I want to know within the next twenty-four hours. Next, I want you to set up a meeting for me with the woman Benedetti approached to gain access to this fund. I'll offer her an investment with terms she can't refuse, and I'll expect—"

"I'm afraid at this stage that can't happen, sir. You see I was just—"

"Haskell, big mistake. Very big mistake. Don't you ever tell me something can't happen. Never ever, do you hear me? Never!" he shouted.

"Sir, if I might be allowed to finish what I was—"

"Silencio. One more word, Frederick, and I want you to throw this malcontent out the window. Do I make myself clear, Haskell?"

"Yes, sir, very clear. The only problem is that..." With a wave of his hand, Tubby signaled Fat Freddy to grab me. "...the problem is she's come down with the virus, sir. She'll be out of commission for at least a few weeks, probably longer. I was just there checking in on her an hour or so ago. The last thing I want you to do is risk your life. I think—"

"Checking in on her? You mean you actually saw her? You went to the hospital?"

"No, sir. She's at home, in bed. But she definitely has the virus. I gave her a couple of pills and poured her a fresh glass of water." Tubby was suddenly on his feet, heading for the door. "I cut up some strawberries and left them next to the bed. Hopefully, she'll eat a couple, you know just to increase her vitamin C level," I yelled as Tubby and Fat Freddy hurried out the door and down the stairs.

I watched as the two of them waddled across the street. Tubby waited for Freddy to open the car door and then slid into the back seat. Freddy didn't bother to look up and give me the finger. He just slid behind the wheel and fired up the Escalade. The car rolled forward about two feet and jerked to a stop. The driver's door suddenly opened, Freddy hopped out, rubbed the door handles with an alcohol wipe. He dropped the wipe in the street, looked up, and then gave me the finger as he climbed back in and took off. Mission accomplished.

Twenty-five

I had just tossed Fat Freddy's sanitary wipes in the trash and was about to move the chair back when Louie opened the door. Morton barked excitedly and hurried over to Louie with his tail wagging. Louie almost tripped over the chair Tubby had been sitting in. "Oh, God," he wheezed, red-faced. "You," gasp, "thinking of rearranging," gasp, "the office?"

"Sorry, Louie. You just missed my visitors. Excellent timing on your part."

"Who?" he asked and collapsed into his desk chair.

"None other than Tubby Gustafson and Fat Freddy Zimmerman. You just missed them, although they couldn't have been here for more than a couple of minutes. They fled the scene as soon as I mentioned seeing Heidi."

"What the hell did those two want? Whatever it is, it can't be good."

I pushed the chair back in front of my desk, gave a quick glance around to see if they'd left any more debris, and sat down. "They wanted information on Benedetti."

"I suppose he's a friend of Tubby Gustafson's."

"Surprisingly, no. At least not from what I'm picking up. But knowing Tubby, there has to be some self-serving motive in the not too distant future. I told them about thinking Benedetti's two hundred grand might be counterfeit. I told him I had the cops and the FBI looking into it."

"And they bought that?"

"Maybe. Tubby wants answers in the next twenty-four hours."

"So what are you supposed to do? Tell the Feds that Tubby Gustafson is giving them twenty-four hours to perform or else? You should have him call the Feds. That would be interesting."

"I was going to call Candi Mangle today anyway. The problem is the money is in the safety deposit box that only Heidi is authorized to have access to. So I can't get in there to check it out."

"Dev, Candi is with the FBI. Have her get a search warrant. She could probably get the thing in under sixty seconds. You said she had all sorts of ways to tell if the currency is real or not. Get her involved, get Heidi's key, and do it."

"But Heidi will want to—"

"Earth to Dev. Heidi is ill, extremely ill. She doesn't want to deal with these funds, correct? She's less than impressed with Tommy Benedetti. She would like the problem to just disappear, so she doesn't have to take on Benedetti as an investor. Correct?"

"Well, yeah."

"Okay, so wouldn't it be nice to eliminate the Benedetti problem for Heidi and make you look like Superman at the same time? All you have to do is have Candi look at the currency. I'll give her thirty seconds before she declares it counterfeit. Suddenly, you're the hero. You've saved Heidi's fund. You've got Benedetti on counterfeit charges. You've got the feds and the St. Paul cops owing you a big favor. Think about it, man. You should be on the phone with Candi now. Tell her about Heidi being ill, get the damn search warrant, and get your ass over there. Plus, you'll get Tubby and that fatty guy off your back. Simple as that," Louie said.

I nodded, pulled out my phone, and called Candi. At no surprise, I ended up leaving a message. "Hi, Candi, Dev Haskell here. Hey, I'm calling to see if you can get a search warrant so we can get into that safety deposit box and check out the currency from Tommy Benedetti. I've also been investigating, and I have a list of names of people involved with Benedetti for you. Among the names is an uncle of Benedetti's who just happens to own a small printing company. Please give me a call as soon as possible," I said and hung up.

"Nicely done," Louie said. "Now, what about Aaron LaZelle? It might be wise to give him a heads-up call."

I thought about that for a half-second, phoned Aaron, and left a similar message. When I hung up, I felt like I'd actually accomplished something.

"See, well done. Problem solved," Louie said. "You can pay for the drinks tonight at The Spot to show your appreciation."

"Yeah, well, let's just see if either one actually picks up the phone and calls me back. The way my luck has been running lately, I probably won't hear—" My phone ringing cut me off, and I picked up.

"Haskell Investigations."

"Hi, Dev," Candi said, "I got your phone message. Interesting. You can get into the safety deposit box?"

"I can get the key, and if you can get the search warrant, we can get in there and take a look."

"Perfect timing, I just picked out a new color for the dining room last night."

"A new color? Candi, I'm talking about you getting a search warrant and checking out this two hundred grand. I thought—"

"And I'm talking about a new color for my dining room and, umm, a painting project with benefits. Multiple benefits," she said, "one of which would be the search warrant, and the other just might be another sleepless night."

"Did you already get the paint, or do you want me to pick it up?"

twenty-six

It was a little after one, and I nicely suggested to Louie he might want to get on an exercise program as an additional way of protection from the virus, mentioning that maybe taking Morton for a walk would be a good way to start. Louie decided that walking up to Roosters and getting two BBQ pork sandwiches that I was going to pay for might be a better way. He took the twenty I gave him and left.

I fired up my computer and did a search on Tommy Benedetti's brother, Tony. Maybe not surprising, when I Googled Tony Benedetti, the first thing that came up was his full name, Antonio Luca Benedetti, followed by three mugshots. Tony looking straight ahead, followed by a right and left side image. The date on the photos was October 18, 1990.

I pegged Tony at maybe fifty-four, two years older than his slime ball brother, Tommy, which made him maybe twenty-four in the mugshot. He already had the 'S' curved nose suggesting he was probably a pain in the ass from his earliest days. He'd been in and out of the Red Wing Juvenile Detention Center, the Ramsey County Jail, the workhouse, the Minneapolis jail, and two state institutions on a variety of charges. By 1990, he'd been incarcerated in one or another institution for the past ten years, and he was only twenty-four in the mugshot.

No doubt he was one of those guys that the cops knew on a first name basis, although I'm sure the name they used wasn't Tony. Apparently, he was always involved in some criminal undertaking, and based on what I read and Gina's comments the other day, rarely, if ever, successful. It seemed obvious he always seemed to get caught, and I wondered, when would he ever catch on? The answer, of course, was never.

I placed a call to Gina Benedetti. She answered after a couple of rings, "Hi, Dev." Her friendly tone actually caught me off-guard. "Hello?"

"Hi, Gina, sorry I was just finishing something. Quick question for you. Would you happen to have an address for Tommy's brother, Tony?"

It sounded like she half-snorted into the phone. "An address. You mean when he's not residing at taxpayer expense?"

"Yeah, just want to check out a couple of things."

"Give me a minute to look him up. I just have to go upstairs and check the address book. Of course, he seems to move every six or eight months. So there's no telling if the address I'll give you is correct or not. Michael, shouldn't you still be practicing your violin? I didn't hear the timer go off."

"Aw, Mom, do I have to. I—"

"I'm paying for lessons that you wanted to take. Now get back on it. Ten more minutes, honey, and then you can go outside. Okay?"

"Yeah, I guess," Michael said, not sounding all that thrilled about it.

"Sorry about that," Gina said. "I'm in the office. Let me just find that address book."

"How's Michael doing with the basketball shooting?"

"Well, I have to give you credit. You landed on something he apparently likes to do. He was out there last night until dark. Out after breakfast and just now wanted to cut his music practice short and sneak outside."

I had to laugh and for a half-second remembered doing the same thing, well, except I never took music lessons. "Is he making any baskets?"

"Oh, yeah, marked improvement. Okay, here we go. The most recent address for Tony is 458 Thomas Avenue, in Saint Paul. I've never been there. Do you know where that is?"

"I do," I said, typing the address into Google and bringing it up on my laptop. The property came up as a three-story, tan-colored house with white trim. Given the image and the location, I figured the structure was probably built as a single-family home back in the 1880s and converted to apartments in the 40s or 50s. Not the best neighborhood in town but not the worst either.

As I looked at the images, Gina said, "I told Tommy I wasn't going to go to Tony's apartment ever again, and that was at least ten years ago. There had been a shooting next door to Tony. The police suspected him, but he was never charged. His landlord evicted him thirty days later."

I changed the subject and said, "I spoke with Courtney Potter yesterday."

"I know. She told me she was going to talk to you. Everything go okay?" she said. I suspected Gina had called Potter and told her to call me.

"Oh, yeah. We only spoke for a couple of minutes, and I told her when I had something definite, I'd get back to her."

"Okay. Anything else I can help you with?" she asked, bringing our conversation to a close.

"No, I appreciate the help, Gina. Tell Mike to keep practicing the basketball, oh, of course, once he's finished his music lesson."

"I'll be sure to do that," she laughed, suggesting I was leaving on a fairly good note.

Once she hung up, I went through the online photos of Tony Benedetti's last known address. There were three interior shots of an apartment. The place had a small kitchen, a living room with gray carpet, and two small bedrooms. There was no romance to the apartment. But then, given the fact the unit was rented to the likes of Tony Benedetti, a landlord would be crazy to put any money into the place.

Louie returned with a bag from Roosters holding two BBQ pork sandwiches. We sat and chatted at our desks while eating the sandwiches. Morton looked back and forth at us, pasting a mournful look on his face. I opened my bottom desk drawer, pulled a biscuit from the box, and tossed it to him. He hurried back to his pillow and settled into it.

Once I finished my sandwich, I grabbed Morton's leash, took him for a quick walk, and then put him in the car. We drove up the hill to Lexington Avenue, took a right, drove to Thomas Avenue, and took another right. 458 Thomas sat on the south side of the street close to, but not on, the corner. It looked just like the photo I'd seen online only a little more rundown.

The asphalt shingled roof looked like it should have been torn off and replaced at least five years ago. The screen door on the front had apparently been torn off, although the steel hinges were still attached to the door frame. There were five black mailboxes attached to the exterior next to the front door. A small pad with five buttons was screwed onto the trim around the front door. Unit number 4 had the name T. Benedetti. I pressed the buzzer and waited. Nothing happened. I pressed it two more times and got the same result.

I opened the mailbox labeled four. There were a number of envelopes and pamphlets stuffed in the mailbox. I pulled them out and quickly fanned through them. With the exception of one envelope, they were all addressed to resident or occupant. The one exception was an envelope addressed to A. Benedetti from the Ramsey County Attorney's office. I returned everything to the mailbox, rang the doorbell one more time, and then headed back to my car.

Twenty-seven

Louie was busy typing away when we returned to the office. Morton immediately settled onto his pillow, and before I turned on my computer, his eyes were closed.

Louie finished up typing a few minutes later and turned off his laptop. "You find out anything?"

"Maybe," I said. "It's a five-plex. The place looks pretty much like a dump. Tony Benedetti's name is still on the mailbox. A bunch of junk mail in there and a letter from the Ramsey County Attorney's office. I rang his doorbell four separate times, but he never answered. Maybe he was out. Maybe he saw it was me and decided not to answer. I don't know. Not that I really wanted to see him, anyway. The way he was coughing the other night, I'm sure he's got this damn virus. With any luck, he'll just become another statistic."

Louie shook his head and mumbled, "You're heartless, man."

"I've got to meet with Candi Mangle later today. I want to give her the info on Heidi's safety deposit box so she can get that search warrant and determine if that currency is counterfeit or not."

"Sounds good," Louie said, but he said it in a way that suggested he knew there was more to my meeting Candi than simply giving her information. Fortunately, he didn't pursue that particular line of questioning. "I'm guessing you're not going to make it over to The Spot."

"I'd love to, but I better take a pass. Like I said, I have to meet with Candi. Then I've got to head over to Brandon Lovelace's and see what he's up to. God, his wife is back in town sometime tomorrow, and I don't really have anything to tell her."

"Maybe that's a good thing. I'll see you two tomorrow morning," Louie said. He placed his laptop in his briefcase and headed over to The Spot.

I got a pot of coffee ready for the morning, and we headed out. I drove to Heidi's, slipped the gloves on, pulled a mask over my nose and mouth, and walked up to the front door. I stepped inside, turned on the table lamp for Nora when she checked on Heidi later tonight, and emptied Heidi's mailbox. It was the same as Tony Benedetti's, all junk mail. At least Heidi didn't have a letter from the Ramsey County Attorney's office. I tossed the mail in the recycling bin and peeked in on Heidi. She was sound asleep. Her water glass was only half-empty. She had raspy sounding breathing that seemed worse than yesterday or even earlier today.

I brought her water glass out and put it in the dishwasher. I filled a fresh glass of water for her and carried it back to the bedroom. I took two Ibuprofen from the bottle and placed them on the bedside table next to the water glass.

I walked into her office. There, sitting right on the top of her desk was an envelope from the First National Bank. I opened the envelope and pulled out the form letter, listing the number on her safety deposit box, 744, and stating the annual fee of two hundred and seventy-five dollars that would be debited from her account. The letter was signed by Dennis Constantine, the bank officer we'd met with the other day. The key to the safety deposit box was in the envelope. I placed the form letter back in the envelope with the key and headed back to my car.

Once in the car, I sent Nora a text message, stating I was just leaving and mentioning my thoughts on Heidi's breathing. I put the envelope in my glove compartment and headed home.

I let Morton out the back and phoned Candi. I was prepared to get dropped into her voicemail. "Hello, Dev, mmm-mmm, what's on your mind?" she said, sounding like some sex kitten in a movie.

"I was hoping to get your dining room painted tonight. Were you able to get the paint?"

"No, not yet, but I was about to leave. I'll pick it up on the way home and make some dinner. See you in forty-five minutes?"

"Works for me," I said. I hung up, shaved, grabbed a quick shower, and changed into my painting clothes. I loaded my ladder, paint trays, brushes, and drop cloths into the car and let Morton in. I turned on a couple of lights for Morton then headed over to Candi's place. Once again, the traffic wasn't as heavy as what I considered a normal rush hour, but there definitely were more cars than a week or two before.

Candi's car was parked in front of her garage, and I pulled in behind it. I made three trips carrying my equipment to the back door before I knocked. Candi answered a moment later.

"Oh, perfect timing. I've got lasagna for dinner, and it's in the oven. Can I help carry something?"

"No, don't bother. I got it," I said. I carried the ladder into the dining room, expecting to have to move the table, chairs, sideboard, and a china cabinet, but they were all arranged in the living room. The dining room was empty, and once again, all the woodwork was expertly taped off with masking tape.

"Oh, wow, this will save all sorts of time. That's a lot of work moving everything out of the dining room. Who'd you find to do it?"

"Oh, I moved it myself, umm, took hours, and I had to go lay down afterward."

I didn't really believe her, but then I was just glad I didn't have to move everything. "I'll bring the rest of my equipment in here."

"Perfect, and I'll dish up the lasagna. Would you like a glass of wine?"

"Yes, I would, but I'd better not have any until after I've finished painting."

"How long do you think it will take you?"

"Maybe three or four hours. At least a good hour to edge around your crown molding and the baseboard. Two plus hours to roll the walls. What color did you choose?"

She grinned and said, "It's a light gray called spare white. Have you used it before?"

"No, I don't think so." I pretended for a moment to be thinking about all sorts of places I painted. "Let me get that stuff in here and get set up."

"I'll dish up dinner," Candi said.

I laid the drop cloths down and got the ladder set up. Then I went out to the car and got Heidi's letter from First National. Candi copied the information - safety deposit box number, Dennis Constantine's name, address, phone number - and handed the envelope back to me.

"Shouldn't take more than a day, two at the most to obtain the search warrant. Then once we actually get hold of the currency, it will just take a couple of minutes to run a few of the tests. I'm guessing you'd like to be there?"

"Yeah, and I'd like the St. Paul Police involved, too."

She seemed to think about that for a moment. "This is going to be our case, mine in particular, at least initially. Ultimately, it will be turned over to the Secret Service. But police involvement is fine with me. I'll be able to take the initial credit and not have to do any of the work." She raised her wine glass, and I clinked it with my can of Coke.

"Sounds like a good plan," I said as we sat down at the kitchen counter. The lasagna was delicious. There were six slices of garlic bread as well, and I ate four of them. Not that I really cared, but I was more than a little suspicious when Candi told me she'd made everything. I was guessing it was takeout from somewhere.

She more or less shoved me out of the kitchen so I'd get going on painting her dining room. She popped her head in about an hour later. I'd just finished edging and was filling my paint tray.

"How's it going?" she asked, looking around the room.

"Very well, covering nicely. Give me about a half-hour and pop back in. I should have one of the walls done by then."

She stuck her head back in maybe an hour later. I had three walls finished and was starting on the final one. "Oh, Dev, it looks absolutely wonderful. Oh, my. It just brightens up the room so wonderfully."

"So, you like it?"

"I do, very much, thank you. Oh, I'm just thrilled. I was a little worried about the color, but it really works."

I heard the bathroom door close about ten minutes later. A couple minutes after that, it sounded like the shower was running. I finished rolling the walls. I did some touch-up in the corners then cleaned up my brushes and paint tray down in the basement laundry tubs. As I came up the basement stairs, Candi met me at the top of the stairs. She wore her black silk robe with the Asian lettering on the left-hand side and a smile.

She handed me a glass of wine and said, "I think you should take a shower and get cleaned up. I'll be in the bedroom waiting."

"You sure I need a shower? I—"

"Trust me, Dev," she said and then leaned over and nibbled on my ear.

"Okay, yeah, a shower might be just the thing. I'll only be a couple of minutes."

I took a quick shower. Candi left a fluffy towel and a white bathrobe with a monogram that said 'Jewel Hotel' over the left breast. I figured she probably stole the bathrobe. I took a big gulp of wine, looked at myself in the mirror, and headed into the bedroom.

Candi was lying in bed with the sheet pulled up to her chin and a smile on her face. The bedroom lights were dimmed, which was great because it disguised the nuclear pink walls. Soft, romantic music came out of the speakers hanging in the corners and drifted throughout the room. I climbed the two steps to her bed, and as I drew closer, I heard a buzzing sound and must have given her a look.

"Oh, sorry, Dev. I couldn't wait, so I started without you."

Twenty-eight

J ust like the last time I'd spent the night, she woke me a number of times. After the five o'clock wake up, I whispered, "I'm going to head home. Let me know what happens with the search warrant."

That seemed to infuse her with enough energy for another twenty minutes. Once she drifted off to sleep, I climbed out of bed, dressed, and let myself out the back door. I debated checking in on Heidi, but Nora would be checking on her just after 9:00, so I decided to wait until noon. I drove home and figured I would climb in bed for thirty minutes. Morton woke me just before 9:00. I quickly pulled on some jeans, let him outside, filled his food and water dish, and hurried upstairs to shower.

We walked into the office forty-five minutes later. Louie was typing away on his laptop. "Morning. Working late last night?"

"Yeah, and didn't sleep very well," I said, not mentioning Candi's name.

Louie nodded and kept typing. I filled my mug with coffee and settled in at my desk. I'd barely taken a sip of coffee when my phone rang, Nora O'Rourke.

"Hi Nora, everything all right?"

"Mmm, she's definitely getting worse. I was afraid of this."

"You think we should get her to the hospital?"

"Unfortunately, it doesn't work like that right now. If these were normal times, yes, absolutely. But right now, with beds at a premium, you just about have to be at death's door before you'll get admitted. We just need to keep a close eye on her. She's getting fluid in her lungs. Are you able to stop by around noon?"

"Yeah, I was planning to check on her. I've been going over there twice a day."

"Good. Me too, so let's keep it up. Before you go over, stop at my house. Go to the back door. I've got some more PPE for you, a surgical gown, and more gloves and masks. I'll leave them in a box at my back door. From now on, Dev, I want you to gown up before you see Heidi. Do not remove any of the PPE until you are safely outside. You'll have to reuse the surgical gown. They're in short supply so I could only get one. But dispose of the mask and gloves after every visit. Okay?"

"Yeah, got you. Thanks for that. I've read a couple of things, and I'm wondering if they might help."

"Like what? If you're thinking of giving her hydroxychloroquine, don't."

"No, I wasn't thinking of that. But I read that back rubs can sometimes help, and the other thing was a sleep apnea mask that might help her breathe."

"Yes, to the back rubs if she can deal with them. She may start to experience chest pain if her case gets much worse, and a back rub would actually be added torture, so use your head and see how she does. With the sleep apnea mask, it won't do any harm and might do some good, so try it. Even if you tell her what you're going to do, she's at the stage now where everything will be getting hazy, and she simply won't remember. It's going to be touch and go for the next three or four days, and either she'll start to improve or we'll have to get her into the hospital. Just keep your fingers crossed."

"Okay, Nora. Thanks for the call. I'll be over there in a couple of hours. Get some sleep."

"Thanks, Dev, send me a text message after you've seen her."

"Will do," I said and hung up.

"Everything okay?" Louie said as he turned to face me.

I gave him the update then said, "I'm going to order one of those sleep apnea devices for Heidi." I clicked onto the Amazon site and looked up Sleep Apnea. There were pages and pages of masks, straps, ventilators, and hoses. It went on and on.

After twenty minutes of looking at everything, I was no further ahead. "Hey, Louie, come over here and look at this stuff for a minute. I need to get something that will help Heidi breathe. Nora said the next few days are going to be the worst."

"Yeah, I know. You already told me," he said, rising out of his chair and walking over. "Let's see what you got."

He leaned down to look on the screen as I slowly moved through the hundreds of different options. "This is bullshit," he said, pulling the laptop toward him. He typed in something at the top, and the screen flashed to ventilator kits, masks, and the complete setup.

"Here's the deal, Dev. There's a chance some of that other stuff will work. But if it doesn't, you're not going to know until her condition worsens, and at that point, you'd do anything to get this heavy-duty stuff. You'll need it immediately, and if you order it, it might not be here for a few days, maybe. I know it's a big chunk of change, but wouldn't it be nice to know you have more than enough backup?"

I must have given him a look.

"Think of it this way, Dev. There's a guy getting ready to shoot at you, and you have to make a choice. You can ask him not to. You can use the BB gun you've got. Or, you've got a grenade launcher. What's your choice?"

"Thanks for putting it in terms I'd understand."

"That's why I make the big bucks," Louie said and walked back to his desk.

I placed an order for the ventilator, the mask, tubing, the works, and then paid an additional twenty-five bucks to have it shipped overnight. Amazingly, my credit card

was accepted, and a moment later, I had a copy of my
order and the shipping information.

Twenty-nine

I drove over to Heidi's at noon. I walked along the side of Nora's house, opened her backyard gate, and saw the box of personal protective equipment sitting on the back steps. I grabbed the box, unlocked Heidi's front door, and went inside.

The surgical gown was blue with a hood. Very similar to the ones Tubby and Fat Freddy had been wearing. I stepped out of my shoes and slipped into the gown. The gown had elastic at the wrists, ankles, and waist and a zipper to pull it closed from the waist up to my chin. I pulled the face mask on, slipped the hood over my head, and pulled on the gloves. I walked into Heidi's bedroom.

As I entered, she opened her eyes. Not surprisingly, she gave no indication of recognizing me and instead barked three or four times with a vicious cough. She couldn't possibly talk.

"Heidi, it's me, Dev. How about a back rub? Would you like that?"

I think she nodded, but I couldn't be sure. But then she attempted to roll over, so I helped her get comfortable on her stomach and proceeded to massage her shoulders and back. Her eyes gradually closed, and I kept up the massage for another thirty minutes. Working the shoulders, her neck, going up and down her spine. I worked the middle of her back, hoping it would, in some way, loosen up the congestion and the fluid building up in her lungs. She remained asleep once I finished. I got her a fresh glass of water, emptied her mailbox, then slipped out of the isolation gown and left.

I went to the McDonalds drive-through and ordered a Quarter Pounder with bacon and cheese, onion rings, and a strawberry shake. I took the meal back to the office. Louie wasn't there, and Morton gave me his undivided attention until I tossed him a dog biscuit and told him to get back on his pillow. Not that he listened, but he got the message, and I more or less ate in peace.

I sent Nora O'Rourke an update on Heidi. I told her I gave Heidi a back rub, it seemed to relax her a bit, and that she was asleep when I left. I mentioned that I'd ordered a ventilator and a sleep apnea mask that would be delivered tomorrow and that I would be back to check on Heidi around six tonight. Just as I was thinking about heading over to Tony Benedetti's place on Thomas Avenue, my phone rang.

"Haskell Investigations."

"Hi, Dev, this is Tracy Kelly."

Shit. Tracy Kelly and I didn't have a thing to tell her.

"Tracy, great to hear from you. Are you still in Chicago?"

"I'm actually about to head to the airport. I'll be back in the twin cities around six this evening."

"How's Chicago?"

"Oh, fine, under the circumstances. Most people are playing by the rules, and then there are certain folks who won't wear gloves, or masks, or social distance. You know, it only takes one to infect all the rest of us."

"Yeah, believe me. I know what you're talking about, Tracy. Of course, life being what it is, you and I will get infected, and they'll just continue on in their own little world, and nothing will ever happen to them."

"I was wondering if there was a time we might meet tomorrow. I'd be happy to come to your office."

"I can meet tomorrow," I said, hoping she wouldn't want to. "I've got an appointment at noon and another around six in the evening tomorrow. A friend of mine has contracted the virus. She's attempting to recover at home, and I'm checking in on her. I've been doing that every day and will continue to do so, but I wanted to let you know in case you would prefer not to meet for a while," I said, hoping I could buy some more time.

She seemed to think about that for a long moment then said, "You're wearing protection when you check on this person?"

"Yes, gloves and a mask every day, and as of today, I'm also wearing a surgical gown. But if you have some concerns, I completely understand, and if you'd feel more comfortable once my friend is on the road to recovery, I would be happy to wait until then. At no additional charge, of course," I said, hoping I'd given her a good reason not to meet with me.

"How about this," she said, "if the weather is nice, we could meet outside or in a park someplace. We'll be able to social distance, and you can bring me up to date on what you've discovered. I don't want to hear the news over the phone because, if it's bad, I might just try to jump out of the airplane."

Perfect, that didn't add any pressure. She thinks her husband is having an affair, and I get to tell her he's not seeing a woman… because he's gay. "Sure, a park sounds perfect. You pick the place, and I'll meet you there," I said, thinking she would probably pick the Minnesota zoo, and then she could throw herself in with the lions once she listened to what I have to say.

"Oh, taxi's here. I've got to hurry. I'll phone you tomorrow. Looking forward to being able to meet you in person, Dev. Bye, bye, bye."

So much for putting the meeting off until I actually had something. I was not looking forward to meeting Tracy tomorrow. I left Louie a note and headed over to Tony Benedetti's again, on the odd chance he might be home and actually answer the door.

I pulled in front of the dive Tony lived in, slipped on a mask and gloves, and walked up to the front door. I checked the mailbox. It was still full of mail. I rang his doorbell twice and didn't get an answer. There were five units in the building. If the fifth unit was in what used to be the attic, that probably meant Tony's unit four and unit three were on the same floor. I pushed the doorbell for unit three and waited. I was about to push the doorbell again when the door suddenly opened.

"Yeah?" the heavyset woman said. It was more a snarl than a question. She wore jeans, a gray t-shirt, and red flip-flops. She looked at me with the mask and gloves and shook her head.

"Oh, sorry. I must have pushed the wrong button. I was hoping to get Mr. Benedetti."

She seemed to examine me for a moment and said, "I hope you're here to arrest that piece of shit."

"Actually, no. At least, not exactly. But I'd like to talk to him about an incident, and depending on how he answers, I may or may not get the police involved."

"Anything I can do to help?" she said, suddenly sounding a lot nicer.

"Would you happen to know where he is?"

"Unfortunately, I don't. I try and stay as far away from that deadbeat as I can. But I do know how to get into his apartment if you wanted to take a look in the place."

"Thank you, but I don't think I—"

"You might just find what you're looking for. Be a shame to waste the opportunity. He hasn't been around for a few days. Might be out planning another crime; at least, that's what I'm thinking."

"How, umm, do you plan to get into his apartment?"

"With the key."

"The key? Are you the landlord?"

"Of this hell-hole. No way, dude. That idiot Tony left the key in the door one night. I'm going to work the following morning, and there it was, the key to his place. Just waiting to be pulled out of the lock, so I did it. Took the damn key. The Dude still ain't caught on yet."

"I suppose it wouldn't hurt to just take a look around."

"Follow me. By the way, my name's Joyce," she said and headed for the staircase. I stepped inside and followed.

The stairs had the remnants of what at one time had been an ornate, oak Victorian banister. The newel post was carved in a floral pattern. I followed her up the stairs. Halfway up, someone had spray-painted ALB in that almost indecipherable script popular with graffiti aficionados. It suddenly dawned on me that ALB might stand for Antonio Luca Benedetti.

"Gee, that's a lousy thing to do. Who spray painted the wall?" I asked.

"Mmm, funny, it happened about a week after Tony moved in. Now, when stuff like that happens, the owner just leaves it. I can't say that I really blame him. How are you ever going to catch someone unless you're standing right here?"

We walked down a hall on the second floor, walking past three places where doors had been removed and a sheetrock wall installed. The doors to apartments three and four were almost directly opposite one another.

"Let me just get that key and I'll be right back," Joyce said as she opened the door labeled three and closed it behind her. I detected the automatic lock snapping into place when she closed the door. She was back out thirty seconds later.

"Like I told you, I come out on my way to work one morning, and this here key was still hanging in the lock. Probably came home drunk again, and then when I took it he just figured he lost it. The owner charges you fifteen dollars for a new one. He ain't left one in there ever since."

She was about to insert the key in the lock when I said, "Hold on. Just in case." I knocked on the door, then knocked on it again, even harder. No sound came from inside.

Joyce looked at me and said, "Happy?" She inserted the key, opened the door, and stepped inside. "Just one big pig pen."

The place was somewhat familiar to the images I'd seen online. The gray carpet looked a lot dirtier, with a definite path heading from a bedroom to the kitchen. There was a black, faux-leather couch with a slit cut in one of the cushions and two bricks holding up an end where the leg was missing. A small flat screen rested on top of a half-barrel, presumably empty. Two piles of dirty clothes were on the floor just outside the bedroom door.

Peeking into the kitchen, I saw a sink filled with dirty dishes. A stack of paper plates sat on a small Formica counter, and a four-burner stove had a dirty pan sitting on each burner. Alongside the stove was a small window. A mousetrap on the floor next to the stove held a dead mouse. It looked like it had been there for quite a while.

"Not sure I'd want to eat anything coming from this kitchen," I said.

"Oh, gross. Check this out," she said and led me into the bedroom. There was a definite locker room odor, and I held my breath. The mattress on the floor had only one sheet; it was grayed and beyond repair. Joyce bent down and lifted the sweat-stained pillow using just her thumb and forefinger. What looked like a Colt .45 Defender with a stainless steel finish and a three-inch barrel rested beneath the pillow. Based on Tony's criminal record, he'd be back behind bars if the cops ever found it.

I opened the closet door, clothes on the floor and a Minnesota Vikings jersey on a hanger.

"God, this place is awful. What's in the other room?" I said.

"Pretty empty. Come on, and I'll show you."

The second bedroom was smaller than the first and empty except for a cardboard box containing what looked like an old carburetor. "Does he own a car?"

Joyce shook her head. "Not that I know of. Every once in a while, he's driving something, but I think he just borrows 'em from family or maybe a friend if he has one." There was a closet door, and I walked over and opened it. A half-dozen metal hangers hung from the hanging rod. There was a shelf with the remnants of a dead plant in a pot wrapped in red foil. On the floor was a black plastic trash bag. I glanced inside and quickly closed the bag.

"What's in there," Joyce asked.

"Just garbage from the kitchen," I lied. "Let's get out of here before he shows up."

"I already told you. That asshole ain't been around for a couple of days. I'm thinking maybe he went and skipped out on the rent."

"Maybe. It certainly wouldn't be surprising, but just in case."

She seemed to think about that for a moment.

"Besides, Joyce, if we're in here for much longer, we'll probably catch a bunch of diseases that'll be even worse than the virus."

That seemed to get her moving toward the hallway. She locked the door once we were out of the unit. "Hey, Joyce, you mind if I get your phone number? If I hear of something happening with Tony I can give you a call and keep you up to date."

She nodded and reeled off her phone number.

I pulled out my cell and said, "Give me that number again." When she finished, I watched her step into her apartment and thanked my lucky stars it wasn't me living across the hall from Tony Benedetti. I headed down the stairs, shook my head as I passed the ALB spray-painted on the wall, and stepped outside. Once in the car, I pulled off the mask and gloves and placed them in the plastic bag.

As I pulled away and headed down the street, a gray SUV passed me, traveling in the opposite direction. Two guys sat in the front. They looked somewhat familiar, and I thought they might have been two of guys with Tommy Benedetti the night they forced Heidi into the car, but I couldn't be sure. I watched in the rearview mirror as their brake lights came on in front of Tony Benedetti's place. Just in case they recognized me, I turned right, headed down an alley, turned onto the street at the end of the alley, and pulled to the curb. I sat there waiting for ten minutes. Fortunately nothing happened and I drove back to the office.

Thirty

Once I was back in the office, I took Morton for a walk through the neighborhood. I left Louie a note telling him I was going to check on Heidi, and I'd meet him at The Spot. We drove over to Heidi's, and I was just about to get out of the car when my phone rang.

"Hi, Candi. I was just going to call you," I lied.

"Hi, Dev, glad I got you. I just wanted to let you know that I've obtained the warrant. I've been in touch with George Turner. He's the Secret Service Agent I mentioned. We're meeting at the First National Bank tomorrow morning at 11:00. I would love to have you join us. I plan on calling Dennis Constantine at First National tomorrow morning once we meet in front of the bank. If you would like to get in touch with your contact in the St. Paul Police Department, that would be fine. But please, do not contact them until tomorrow morning."

"Okay, I can do that. Let me ask you a question."

"By all means," she said.

"If I have a thought there may be more of this currency around, would it make sense to get a search warrant for other locations before tomorrow?"

She didn't even pause to think about an answer. "Let's wait. Make sure we know what we're dealing with. At this point, I'm ninety-eight percent sure we'll be able to confirm the currency is counterfeit. But let's make sure that's the case and then quietly obtain warrants to search homes and businesses of all individuals involved."

"Okay, so I'll call the police tomorrow, and we'll meet you at 11:00 at the bank."

"Yes, and Dev?"

"Yeah."

"Don't forget the key to the Safety Deposit Box."

"Oh, yeah, thanks for reminding me," I said.

We disconnected, and I pulled on the gloves and the mask. I let myself in Heidi's front door, stepped into the surgical gown I'd left hanging on the closet doorknob, and headed toward the bedroom. I heard Heidi coughing before I made it to her room.

"Hey, how you doing, lady?" I asked.

Heidi attempted to focus on me for a moment, but she was clearly out of it. She coughed again and closed her eyes. I brought her water glass out to the kitchen and placed it in the dishwasher. I filled a fresh glass and brought it back to her. I more or less stuffed two Ibuprofen into her mouth then placed the water glass to her lips. She swallowed the first three sips, then flew into a coughing jag, spitting out the last bit of water. When she finally stopped coughing, her eyes were closed, and I stared at her just to make sure she was still breathing. She was, but they were shallow breaths.

I went back into the kitchen, turned on the dishwasher, then made my way toward the front door. I turned on the table lamp in the living room, then took a wipe from the packet and cleaned off the doorknob before I stepped out of my surgical gown and hung it up. Out in the car, I took a wipe from the packet on the front seat, wiped the steering wheel, then took off my gloves and mask and placed them in the bag.

I pulled out my cellphone and sent Nora an update on Heidi's condition. I drove back to the office, grabbed Morton and we headed over to The Spot. There were only three customers in the place tonight. A couple wearing gloves were sitting in a booth and Louie was sitting on his regular stool. Mike was behind the bar wearing gloves and a mask.

Bob Seger was singing 'Old Time Rock and Roll' on the jukebox. It may sound crazy, but it brought a lump in my throat for a moment. We, in fact the world, were on a new track to God only knew where.

"A beer for me and whatever Louie's drinking," I said to Mike as I strolled down to Louie. I let go of the leash, and Morton took off along the bar. He ran toward Louie who was in the process of opening a bag of pork rinds.

"Hello, Morton," Louie said as he leaned down and rubbed him behind the ears. "Oh, so good to see you. You've been so patient, taking Dev for his walk. Trying to get him to move along instead of staring at every woman who happens to drive down the street. Here, Morton, Dev told me not to, but I saved a bag of pork rinds just for you. It's a health food."

"Careful, Louie, or you'll spoil him."

"Ahh, he needs it. Were you checking in on Heidi? How's she doing?"

"Not so great. Nora says she's still not bad enough to be admitted to the hospital. But she was coughing an awful lot. She looked at me, but I don't think she recognized me, and it wasn't because I had a mask on. She's just out of it. Asleep most of the time, and if she is awake, it's only for a moment."

"Maybe sleeping like that or drifting out of consciousness, whatever it is, would be a good thing. It suggests her body is directing all its resources to fighting the virus."

"Yeah, I suppose," I said as Mike set our glasses on the bar. I tossed a twenty-dollar bill across the bar to him then raised a glass with Louie and took a large drink.

"Heidi didn't have any preexisting condition, did she?" Louie asked.

"You kidding? Except for some goofy diet she's on from time to time, she takes very good care of herself. I can attest to the fact she's in excellent shape."

Louie nodded and said, "Your description of her current condition pretty much matches what I've heard from a friend who had this virus. He had five or six days where he was really out of it and then gradually began to recover. I'd say it was close to another month before he was back at a hundred percent."

"This week will determine if she can recover at home or if she needs to go into the hospital. Oh, hey, I almost forgot to tell you. Just as I pulled in front of Heidi's, I got a call from Candi Mangle."

"And?"

"And, she's got the warrant. We're going to meet tomorrow. She's got some guy from the Secret Service involved. They're going to run tests on Benedetti's currency. Hopefully, it will test counterfeit, and that will get him out of the picture."

"Good news," Louie said. "You tell his wife?"

"No. In fact, I probably shouldn't have even told you. I'll get back to her when I have some solid information. If the stuff comes up as counterfeit, that's just the first step in the process. I don't want to be sending that guy a warning."

"Well, it sounds like things are starting to go your way." Louie raised his glass, emptied it, and signaled Mike for another round.

"Yeah, they're going my way for the moment. But, I spoke with Tracy Kelly this afternoon and—"

"Were you able to tell her anything?"

"No. You might even say I dodged the question, not that she asked one. I just don't have anything conclusive yet. And the little I do have suggests that her husband is in a relationship with another guy. Not good."

"Yeah," Louie said. "It's not going to be good, Dev. You've done these cases before. A spouse suspects their partner is involved with someone else, and your job is to confirm that. It's been a big part of your business. So what's the problem?"

"The problem, Louie, is that I don't have real confirmation. I don't have the money shot of him in bed with some guy. I don't have a shot of the two of them having sex in the back of a car. All I've got are a few images of Brandon Lovelace basically doing nothing out of line."

"So, you stay on the case until you get the images, and you tell Tracy you're going to need more time. It's not your fault. My God, Dev. The guy hasn't been misbehaving. Would it be such a bad deal if you had to tell her that, while she was gone and he had the perfect opportunity to misbehave, he didn't? You've had enough experience delivering bad information, confirming a spouse's suspicions. Maybe take a deep breath and enjoy the fact you tried and came up empty-handed. It would seem to me that would be information Tracy would love to hear.

I finished my beer. Morton got another handful of pork rinds, and we headed out the door. We were home just after eight. I found a bowl of chili and rice in the back of the refrigerator that looked okay, so I heated it up in the microwave. I settled in front of the tv and wasted two hours of my life watching a worthless movie I'd seen before. I went upstairs to bed at 11:00, pushed Morton over, and fell asleep.

Thirty-one

Morton's barking a little after four woke me. Once again, he was acting in a way that suggested he'd heard something and was frightened. This time I was out of bed, armed, and moving downstairs in about thirty seconds. I saw nothing out the front or side windows of the house. I entered the kitchen and looked out the window next to the kitchen door.

There were two figures standing at the bottom of the back door steps. One was whispering to the other. When he finished, he looked up at the back porch. I recognized him as the guy who'd given me the Karate chop to the back of my neck when they forced Heidi into the stretch limo. Melvin Cummings. Coco's brother. I thought the other guy maybe looked like the Google image I saw of Victor DeCulo but couldn't be sure.

I was tempted to open the door, invite them in, and shoot both of them. After all, a man's home is his castle and all that stuff. I waited and watched. The guy I thought was DeCulo kept shaking his head. After a long minute, Melvin threw his hands up, shook his head, and stormed off down my driveway. DeCulo watched him for a long moment then hurried after him.

I watched out the front window as they headed toward a gray SUV, just like the one I'd seen yesterday as I left Tony Benedetti's. In fact, no doubt the same car. I thought about shooting out the tires for maybe a half-second. The odds were right around a hundred percent that both of them would be armed, so bad idea. They climbed into the SUV, apparently carrying on a rather animated conversation. A moment later, the vehicle started, and they took off down the street. I prayed they'd run into a police car or hit a phone pole but no such luck. They disappeared into the darkness a few seconds later.

I went back upstairs to bed. I set the pistol on top of the nightstand, just in case and drifted back to sleep. My alarm woke me a few hours later.

Thirty-two

I was up, showered, and dressed in a reasonably clean dark-gray golf shirt and black jeans. The shirt was missing the top button, but I wasn't going to button it anyway, so it didn't matter. I was on my computer for a good hour before Morton made his way downstairs. I gave him a rub behind his ears and let him out the kitchen door. After I filled his food and water dish, I stepped outside, looked up and down the driveway to see if Melvin Cummins or Victor DeCulo had left any clue as to what they'd planned on doing. I didn't find anything.

Morton was sitting in the corner of the yard with his head raised and his eyes closed, enjoying the morning sun. After I called him three or four times, he followed me inside for breakfast. We headed down to the office thirty minutes later.

Louie was at his picnic table reading a file. The coffee was on. As I stepped into the office, I said, "You're in bright and early."

"Yeah, I've got a 10:00 appearance. First timer, I've advised a guilty plea. Don't say anything. We'll pay the fine and leave. Should be short and simple, as long as my client shuts the hell up."

"Is it some pain in the ass guy who wants to give his point of view?"

"Half-right," Louie said. "A nice woman, actually. But she has this habit of just explaining something one more time so you'll finally see the wisdom of her viewpoint."

"Let me guess, a DUI. She blew over the limit, and she was arrested. What else is there to consider?"

"Yeah, that's been my point. She, on the other hand, would like to remind everyone that she was returning from a family funeral. Her grandfather, who was a Vietnam veteran and a police officer. Therefore, everyone should apparently look the other way."

"And that's not happening?"

"Correct," Louie said.

"What was the guy's name?"

"Emmett Casey. Did you know him?" Louie asked.

I shook my head. "No, can't say that I did."

"I'd guess, if he were around she'd be getting a piece of his mind. Anyway, that's my morning. And you're down to the bank this morning?"

"We're meeting out front at 11:00. As a matter of fact, let me give Aaron a call, bring him up to date." I phoned Aaron and was about to leave a message when he answered.

"Yeah, Dev."

"Hi, Aaron. I'm meeting this morning with the FBI agent, Candi Mangle, and some Secret Service guy who'll actually be doing the tests on Tommy Benedetti's currency. I expect them to test counterfeit. Do you have someone who wants to be there?"

"Yeah, I spoke with Delton Lange. He's in fraud and forgery. He'll be our man on the scene. What time and where?"

"We're meeting at the First National Bank at 11:00. I could be down at the station at 10:00, and we could go over together. That would help to introduce him to the team rather than be treated as a tag along. Before we get started, I've got a couple of items I want to run past him, see what he thinks."

"Okay, I'll call him now. He's a, how can I say it, a rather meticulous guy. That's one of the reasons he's so good at what he does. If you say you're going to be here at 10:00, Dev, he'll be expecting you, at 10:00, not five after."

"Sounds like a welcome change from what I'm used to down there."

"Yeah, Dev. God forbid anyone here would have something else going on when you wash up on shore and want the phone number of some woman you saw in the liquor store."

"I don't call you guys for people's phone numbers."

"Yeah, I know, you call Gerry Sanchez over at the DMV." I was tempted to ask how he knew that but didn't say anything. "I'll call Lange now and let him know you'll be down here at exactly 10:00. Later," Aaron said and hung up.

I was at the police station ten minutes early. I dodged most of the potholes in the gravel visitor's parking lot and found a parking space in the back of the lot. I got the bank envelope with the safety deposit box number and the key from my glove compartment. I grabbed a pair of gloves and a mask and made it inside with plenty of time to spare. I didn't recognize the sergeant working reception.

"Hi, I'm here to see Delton Lange in fraud and forgery. He's expecting me. My name is Dev Haskell," I said and handed him my business card. He didn't seem all that impressed with the fact my business card said 'Private Investigator.'

"Might as well take a seat, and I'll give him a call."

I sat down in a black plastic chair. Some older guy in need of a shave and a shower was snoring in a chair across from me and down three seats. A tear-stained woman sat two seats away to the right, dabbing her eyes. A bored looking couple sat directly across from her. I guess it was the rare person who was here on a positive note. I was lucky. I was about to get Tommy Benedetti out of Heidi's life.

Maybe four minutes later, someone called "Devlin Haskell?"

I stood, gave a wave so he saw me and hurried over to the security door. "Hi, I'm Dev Haskell. Are you Delton Lange?"

He nodded, and we shook hands. He wore a gray suit, with a light blue shirt and a dark blue tie. His black shoes were shined, and his hair, black with a touch of gray, was neatly trimmed. He smiled and said, "Nice to meet you. Let's go to my section, and you can bring me up to date. Care for a coffee before we get started?"

I knew better than to drink a coffee from one of the machines here. "No, thank you."

I was used to taking the elevator up to Aaron's homicide office, so I was a little surprised when we walked past the elevator and headed down the hall. Lange led me into a conference room with a black case and a laptop computer sitting on the table. He closed the door behind me as we stepped in.

"Take a seat, Mr. Haskell."

"Feel free to call me Dev."

"All right, Dev. So, bring me up to date."

We sat at the table, and I started at the beginning, telling him about Heidi and me leaving Chez Charles and Tommy Benedetti pulling up in the stretch limo. I told him about the guys with Tommy, including his brother, Tony. I mentioned Coco Cummings as the probable driver and her brother Melvin as the guy who assaulted me. I told him we were suspicious of the funds from Tommy Benedetti right off the bat. The rubber bands and the $10,000 written with a Sharpie did nothing to change our impression. He laughed at that part and shook his head. I went on to tell him about Candi Mangle with the FBI and George Turner with the Secret Service.

"I know Turner. He's good," Lange said. "And I've heard of Agent Mangle," he said but didn't comment any further.

I didn't tell him about the black plastic trash bag in the closet at Tony Benedetti's apartment. I did mention the uncle, Arnold Benedetti, the owner of the printshop, Inkoholic.

At the mention of Inkoholic, he fired up his computer and did a quick search. He clicked the keys on the keyboard then nodded and looked up at me. "Oh yeah, the pull tabs," he said.

"That's what I heard." I remembered what Gina had told me, but I wanted to keep her out of it, so I didn't mention her name.

"A bad job right from the get-go. Arnold Benedetti got thirty-six months," Lange said and shook his head.

"I guess apples don't fall far from the tree. Doing a lousy job and getting caught seems to be a family trait."

"Interesting, so how, exactly, do you see this working?" he asked.

I gave a little shrug and said, "To tell you the truth, I'm not really sure. It would seem that at least initially, George Turner with the secret service will be making the calls. Hopefully, he'll determine the funds are counterfeit. I'm guessing they'll take possession of them at that time. Get an arrest warrant for Benedetti. Maybe arrest the others, Cummings, DeCulo, and Tony Benedetti."

"So let's cut to the chase. If the Feds are in on this, why are you here talking to me?"

"I have a lot of interaction with the St. Paul Police department. On a rare occasion, it hasn't always been on the most positive note. I just want to stay on everyone's good side."

"Okay, fair enough. And the Feds know I'll be there?"

"They know I was going to contact the department and hopefully bring someone with me. To my knowledge, they do not know that someone is you. But maybe your reputation proceeds you, and you're the logical choice."

He flashed a quick smile at that and looked at his watch. "We're just a couple of minutes away but no harm in being the first ones. Let's go. I'll drive," he said.

He grabbed the black case off the table, and we headed out the door. We went out the back of the building and into an enclosed parking area with two guard stations. Lange headed into the back lane of the parking area and clicked on a key fob.

A set of headlights flashed about three cars down. A white Ford Taurus, theoretically an unmarked car except, when you looked at the black tires without any semblance of a whitewall and the spotlight mounted next to the sideview mirror on the driver's side, anyone with an ounce of brains would be pretty sure it was an unmarked vehicle.

"Hop in," Lange said as he set his case in the backseat and climbed behind the wheel.

Thirty-three

It was a six-minute drive over to the First National Bank, and that included waiting for a stoplight to change. Lange pulled into a parking place just across the street from the entrance to the bank. The parking spaces were numbered, and he ran a credit card through the parking meter pay station and set the receipt on the dashboard. He pulled his case out of the back seat, and we walked across the street to the front entrance of the First National Bank building.

"I'll just give them a call and let them know we're here," I said. We were ten minutes early. I called Candi Mangle. She answered on the first ring.

"Good morning, Dev. I hope you're still able to join us."

"Oh, yes. In fact, I'm out in front of the main entrance with Officer Delton Lange. He's with the fraud and forgery division of the police department. We're all set."

"Perfect, we're ten or fifteen minutes away. I'll phone Dennis Constantine when we get there. Did you remember to bring the key?"

"Amazingly, yes. See you when you get here."

"See you shortly," she said and hung up.

"They'll be here in about ten minutes," I said to Lange.

He quickly checked his watch. I figured he was probably setting an internal alarm. God help Candi if it took them longer than ten minutes. "Say, I noticed while you were on the phone that you're missing the top button on your shirt," Lange said.

"Oh, really?" I said, pretending I didn't know. Just to prove the point, I reached up and felt the area where the button would have been. "Hmm, I wonder how that happened? Thank you for telling me. I'll get it taken care of."

Lange nodded as if that made sense.

Candi and George Turner arrived fifteen minutes later. They were in a black Chevy Equinox LT with government plates. Turner was driving. They pulled up in front of us and climbed out. Turner pulled a black case that looked just like Lange's from the back seat. He opened the driver's door, turned on the flashing lights, and locked the car. As he walked around the front of the car, Candi slid out of the passenger seat, smiled, and gave me a nod. Turner stepped onto the sidewalk, kept the proper distance, smiled at Lange, and said, "Hello, Delton, wonderful to see you again. Let me introduce Agent Candi Mangle. Candi, Delton Lange, the officer I mentioned earlier."

Candi and Delton flashed a smile at one another and nodded.

"Has it already been a year, Delton?" Turner said.

"Almost. It will be a year next month on the twelfth. Time flies," Lange said.

"Faster and faster. And pardon me, you must be Devlin Haskell. Agent Mangle has told me if it wasn't for you working a case, we wouldn't even be here. Thank you for your diligence."

"My pleasure. Hopefully, this will work out to everyone's advantage," I said. I had to wipe the smile off my face. I recognized Turner and his car from the morning I arrived at Candi's to paint her living room. It was him pulling out of her driveway and heading in the opposite direction.

"Let me place this call to Mr. Constantine, now," Candi said, pulling out her phone. "Yes, Dennis Constantine, please," she said into her phone a moment later. "Mmm-mmm, I think it would be best if you called him out of the meeting. This is Agent Mangle. I'm with the Federal Bureau of Investigation. The FBI. No, I will not leave a message. Please put him on the line now. Yes, I'll hold." She flashed a look that suggested something like, *'Do you believe this?'*

It was close to five minutes before she said, "Yes, Mr. Constantine. Thank you for finally taking my call." She spoke in a tone that was anything but polite. "We have a warrant to open a client's safety deposit box, and we are on our way. If you would please make yourself available. We're under a bit of a time constraint."

Hearing 'time constraint', I looked at Candi and then Turner. He simply smiled and raised his eyebrows.

Candi suddenly nodded and pointed toward the door. "We should be there shortly, maybe two or three minutes. Thank you," she said and disconnected. "If you would be so kind as to lead the way, Dev."

We walked into the building and headed for the elevator. Using my elbow, I pushed the up button on the elevator. At this point, everyone but me had latex gloves on and was wearing a mask. I quickly donned my mask just as the doors opened on the elevator. I pushed the button for the second floor, and we stepped off fifteen seconds later.

Four people approaching the receptionist's desk in the bank lobby, two of them carrying black cases, caused a few heads to turn. Candi led the pack and seemed to be picking up speed with every step. She looked like she was about to give the receptionist a piece of her mind when a voice said, "Agent Mangle?"

Dennis Constantine appeared around the corner. Candi took a deep breath and made very brief introductions. Given her tone and the look on her face, if I thought there might have been some earlier history between Candi and Constantine, I was even more convinced now. Her tone seemed to suggest that, if Constantine didn't comply, he might find himself in Federal prison by early afternoon.

Thirty-four

Constantine quickly led us into a conference room. Once we were all seated, Candi stood and thrust the warrant at him as if it were a dagger. "We need immediate access to safety deposit box number seven-forty-four."

He examined the warrant for a long moment, reading it word for word. "I'm afraid I'll have to run this past our legal team before I can grant—"

"You know it doesn't work like that, Dennis. We need access immediately, or I'll have you placed under arrest by Officer Lange."

Lange didn't even blink, he simply flashed a slight smile, pulled his suit coat to the side revealing the badge on his belt, and nodded.

Secret Service Agent Turner said, "You'll be found in violation of a number of federal laws. I'd say it's certainly liable to end your career here at First National, and most likely close the door to just about anywhere in the financial industry. Your choice, of course, but I'd caution you to choose carefully."

The woman wore a name tag that read Gretchen. She was blonde, maybe forty-five, and very attractive with sparkling blue eyes. I couldn't help but focus on her as she led us into the vault.

"Seven-forty-four?" she asked, inserting her key and turning it.

"Yep, this is the one," I said, placing Heidi's key in the lock and opening the box. Gretchen pulled the safety deposit box out maybe six inches, flashed a smile at me, and said, "Would you mind?"

I pulled the box out the rest of the way, and we followed Gretchen from the vault into a small room just next door. "I'll be waiting outside. Just let me know when you're finished in here." She flashed another smile and quickly left the room.

I set the metal box on the table, lifted the lid, pulled out the metal briefcase and opened it. The funds appeared just as we'd left them, bundled with rubber bands and the $10,000 notes scribbled with a black Sharpie.

Turner took four photographs of the bundles sitting in the safety deposit box then said, "Delton, if you would pull them out and line them up on the table, please."

Lange began to take the bundles out one by one and arrange them along the edge of the table.

Turner took a number of photos, adjusting the lens on the camera three or four different times as he photographed. "Initial comments?" he asked once he'd finished taking the photos.

Lange looked at Candi and I. We both seemed to be caught off-guard for a moment. He nodded and said, "Of course, the first impression is the rubber band and the hand-written note. It's so basic that I'm wondering if this wasn't some spur of the moment idea with virtually no thought put into it. The next thing I notice is that some of the bundles appear to be a slightly different size, just a bit thicker than the other bundles. Here, here, these two, and that one down at the end," he said, pointing to the far end. "Either they didn't count the bills properly, or there may have been a paper change, using a thicker stock."

Turner nodded and said, "I'm thinking we may be dealing with some first-timers here." He opened his case and pulled out a rectangular magnifying glass on a stand. A cord ran along one side, and he plugged it into an outlet on the wall. He grabbed the bundle closest to him and pulled off the top bill.

He felt the bill between his thumb and forefinger. "Hmm, it feels normal." He held the bill in both hands and moved it back and forth. "Color shifting ink gold to green."

I looked at Candi, but she was focused on Turner. Apparently, I was the only one who didn't know what he was talking about.

He turned the switch on the magnifying glass and held the bill against the light, glancing back and forth. "The watermark matches," he said as he adjusted the magnifying glass and studied the boarders. "Borders aren't blurred," he said, looking up and flashing a questioning look at Candi. He moved the bill and seemed to be studying the portrait of Benjamin Franklin. "Damn, security thread is there. Just the way it should be."

"Delton, do you have an ultraviolet light?"

Lange was already in his case, rummaging around. He pulled out a small light with a glass screen and plugged it in. He set the light on the table next to the magnifying glass. Turner pulled the light closer, turned it on, and placed the bill against the glass.

Turner looked up at Lange and said, "The security thread is red." He set the bill on the table, pulled his glasses off, looked at Candi, and said, "I don't know. If this bill is counterfeit, it may just be the best I've ever seen."

Lange reached over and examined the bill then looked at Turner. "Serial number is L, and the series is 2009 alpha. That's a match."

"They can't be real," I said. "Don't you guys have one of those pens they use in the grocery stores?"

They looked at one another and shook their heads. "They're highly inaccurate, Dev," Lange said. He pulled a bill from the top of another pile, and they went through the process again, only in about half the time.

"Jesus Christ, I don't believe it," Turner said more than once. He stood, walked down the line, and pulled another bill from the top of a random pile. Unfortunately, he came up with the same result.

"I'm sorry, but these are not counterfeit. We've tested these three. I suggest we take them back to the lab and conduct a more thorough examination," Turner said. He looked down the length of the table and shook his head. "This just can't be."

"Mind if I suggest something?" I said.

"Haskell, the pens don't work. Honest, believe me. Right about now, I wish they did. The sooner we can get these back to the lab, the sooner we can begin our testing."

"Just humor me, take the next bill from that first bundle."

Turner looked at me, and I could suddenly see the wheels starting to turn. He grabbed the bundle, pulled a bill out from the middle of the bundle, and took off his glove. He rubbed the bill between his thumb and forefinger, and a smile suddenly spread across his face. "Bingo," he said and handed the bill to Lange.

Turner pulled a bill from the middle of another pile. He smiled as he rubbed the bill between his thumb and forefinger, then held the bill up to the light behind the magnifying glass and began to chuckle. "No watermark, Delton," he said to Lange. "Way to go, Haskell. We would have caught it, but this saves us hours, even days. We'll test all of these, but no doubt they're counterfeit with an actual hundred-dollar bill at the top of every bundle. Absolute bush league. And what was the name of the printer you mentioned?"

"Inkoholic," I said. "Owned by a guy named Arnold Benedetti, an uncle of the guy that passed these bills on."

"You got him, Candi. Joint arrest, we both get credit?"

"I wouldn't have it any other way," she said, pushing her chair back and standing. "Let me just inform Dennis we'll be taking all this as evidence." She smiled and hurried out of the room to give Dennis the news. We could hear her voice on the other side of the door asking Gretchen to get Dennis.

"I'd say she's enjoying this," I said.

Turner smiled and said. "Believe me, one of the many ways she can pleasure herself. I moved the furniture out of her living room and then out of her dining room so she could have some guy in to paint the rooms. After I moved the furniture, she had me tape off all the woodwork."

"Sounds like an awful lot of work," Lange said.

"Yeah, my back was killing me for two days afterward," Turner said.

Lange began placing the bundles of cash back into the metal briefcase. "I hoped you got paid, Agent Turner."

"Oh, yeah, in a manner of speaking."

Thirty-five

It was another hour before Candi had the proper documents emailed to Dennis Constantine. I'd given her Heidi's email address, and she sent the documents to Heidi as well. We said our goodbyes out on the street. Lange and I waited for a couple of cars to pass then hurried across the street to the unmarked white Taurus. Turner and Candi pulled away from the curb and disappeared around the corner.

On the drive back to the station, I said to Lange, "So, I gave Candi a list of the guys that were with Benedetti the night he forced Heidi into the stretch limo and told her she had to take that money. I'm guessing they're going to be arresting these clowns in short order. Are you going to be able to participate in the arrests?"

He looked at me and shook his head. "Thanks, Dev, but that's not the way it works. We all got along great back there, and don't get me wrong. I was happy, no, make that delighted to participate, but from here on in, they'll steal all the thunder, and it's going to be their show. That's just the way it is."

"Would you want to participate?" I asked.

He shot me a look and said, "I suddenly have the feeling there's maybe something you've been keeping to yourself."

"Here's what I want. You tell me if this works. I want this Tommy Benedetti to get sentenced for a number of years. They can fine him, but my sense is he'll present a pretty strong case of being bankrupt. So hopefully, instead of a fine, they add some years to his sentence. I'd like his wife and two sons protected from a team of federal agents or St. Paul Police arriving at six in the morning to arrest Benedetti and conduct a search of the home."

"I really can't do anything to stop that. I would guess they're probably on the phone to get those warrants now, and with almost two hundred grand in counterfeit cash, they won't have any problem getting them."

"Yeah, I know that. Here's what the Feds don't know. Tommy Benedetti isn't living at his home. In fact, he hasn't been for the better part of the year."

"Okay…"

"And, I think these guys printed up a lot more dough than what we saw today. I might be able to find out where it is, and if you could make the arrests or searches of these places, they would have to acknowledge you, and you might get more than just a passing thank you."

He seemed to think about that as he drove the next three blocks then turned into the police parking lot. He showed his ID to the guard at the gate then parked in the exact same spot where the car had been originally. He turned off the engine then looked at me. "Okay, I'm game. What do you have?"

"Benedetti isn't at his home in Mahtomedi. Tommy Benedetti is currently living with a woman named Coco Cummings. I think, but can't prove, that she was the driver of that stretch limo when they forced the funds on my friend. Coco lives in The Market House over on Fifth Street. I don't know the unit number, but I believe she is up on the fifth floor. Tommy Benedetti and possibly his brother Tony may be there. Tony lives at 458 Thomas Avenue in St. Paul. He's in unit four. It's a house about a hundred and twenty years old that was converted into five units. Not the nicest place, and he hasn't been seen there in five or six days. I think, if you search the place, you might find more counterfeit funds there."

"And what are you getting out of all of this?"

"I pretty much already have it. My friend, the woman who had this counterfeit currency forced on her, gets Tommy Benedetti and, by extension, his thug friends off her back. And his wife, who is struggling with two teenage boys and is going to lose just about everything, can file for divorce and hopefully limit some of the liabilities she'll be facing."

"Okay, try this on for size. We get warrants for the woman's unit in The Market House and for this place over on Thomas Avenue. We arrest whoever is on the scene and sort it out later. Let me find out the time they expect to raid Benedetti's home, and you can give the wife a thirty-minute warning so she can get herself and those kids out of there."

"Thirty minutes?"

"When the Feds go there, it will be at an early hour. When they find the place empty, they're going to suspect the family was warned. They're going to think Benedetti was there and somehow got a warning."

"So, what do we do?"

"Trust me, and we're liable to make you look like a real nice guy," he said.

"Well, there you go. You can fool some of the people some of the time."

Thirty-six

I left Lange and hurried out to my car. I drove over to Heidi's, slipped on my gloves and mask, and hurried into the house. It was almost 1:00, and I should have been there an hour ago. My surgical gown was hanging on the closet door. I stepped into it, zipped it up, and walked back to Heidi's room.

She was asleep. I took two more Ibuprofen from the bottle and set them on the nightstand then brought her water glass out to the kitchen. I set it in the dishwasher, filled the soap compartment, and turned on the dishwasher. I pulled a clean glass from the cabinet, filled it, and brought it back into Heidi's room. Her breathing seemed somewhat regular but coming in short breaths. I watched her for five minutes then quietly left. Once in the car, I sent a text message to Nora, giving her an update.

I was about to pull away from the curb when my phone rang, Tracy. God, I had completely forgotten about her. "Hey, Tracy, how's it going? Did you make it back from Chicago yesterday?"

"Yes, no problem. Thankfully, the plane was only about half-full. Everyone was required to wear masks, and everyone kept their distance."

"Thank goodness. What about Chicago's O'Hare?"

"The usual, most people are wearing masks, but there's always a few idiots, no matter what the rules are. They're always above the law and don't have to follow the rules like the rest of us."

"Yeah, I've got a pal who says, if you're placing your safety in God's hands, why bother wearing a seatbelt?"

She laughed at that then said, "Are we still on for meeting at Como Park at two?"

I looked at the clock on my dash. That was just forty minutes away. "I can if you'd like. I think, as I mentioned, I don't have much confirming information at this point." I waited, holding my breath, hoping she'd decide to meet another day.

"When do you think you might get it?"

"Actually, Tracy, it's not like that. I mean, I know how really stressful it is to wait, but consider this. I don't have anything that would convince you Brandon is having an affair. I watched him. I've followed him running. I've seen him coming in and out of his office building. You've been gone for the better part of a week. If he were going to carry on, this past week would have been the perfect time. I did not see any indication he was doing anything out of line," I said, deciding I wasn't going to mention Brandon's evening at 'Going My Way' just yet.

"So, where do we stand?" she said.

"Give me a couple more days. If nothing happens, you can decide to cancel me, or we can discuss what other options may exist. Oh, and I won't charge you for the next couple of days. I think that's the least I can do because you've been so patient."

She seemed to think about that for a moment then said, "Okay. But only a couple days and then let's look at what you have. I'm starting to pull my hair out just thinking about this."

"Fair enough. Thanks for your patience, Tracy."

"Okay, talk to you in a few days," she said and hung up.

I breathed a big sigh of relief and headed to the office. Louie was at his desk, going over a file. As I stepped into the office, he looked up and said, "So?"

I grinned. "It's counterfeit and not a very good job of counterfeiting." I went on to tell him about the meeting at the First National Bank, Dennis Constantine, and the real hundred-dollar bills on the top of every bundle of cash.

"Perfect," Louie said and clapped his hands. "With any luck, the Feds will be rounding up Benedetti and his gang in the next twenty-four hours."

"Yeah, I'm sure they will. Good riddance is all I can say. The longer they lock these guys up, the better it will be for Heidi."

"Oh, hey, glad you mentioned her. I signed for a delivery. It's at your desk."

I glanced over at my desk. A small cardboard box sat on the desk. "What the hell is this thing?" I said, walking over, and then saw the box on the floor behind the desk and the two other boxes stacked on my chair.

"Oh, great, the sleep apnea ventilator I ordered for Heidi. This is perfect and not a moment too soon. Wonderful." I pulled out my phone and sent a text to Nora, telling her the ventilator had arrived.

I got a reply five minutes later. *'Can you get it over there now? Sooner the better.'*

'On my way.' I replied. "Hey, Louie, you going to be here for a while?"

"Yeah, rest of the afternoon. Everything okay?"

"Yeah, Nora just sent a text telling me to hook Heidi up to this thing as soon as possible. I'm going to run over there now if that's okay. If you want, I can take Morton home."

"No, leave him here. If we're not here when you get back, it's because Morton made me go over to The Spot."

"Thanks, see you in a bit," I said. I stacked up the boxes, hurried down the stairs, and dumped them in the back seat. I hopped behind the wheel and headed up the street toward Heidi's. I'd maybe gone three blocks when I glanced in my rearview mirror and recognized the nondescript gray SUV following me. There were two guys seated in the front. I couldn't tell if anyone was in the back or if Tommy Benedetti was even in the car.

I was coming up to PJ Murphy's bakery, a two-story white structure on the corner. Two cops were just getting out of their squad car and heading toward the bakery. I quickly pulled ahead of their vehicle, parked in a bus stop, and hopped out, waving at the cops.

The gray SUV sped up as it passed me, and I recognized the two guys as part of Tommy Benedetti's bunch of idiots. The same two idiots who'd been in my driveway the other night, Melvin Cummings and Victor DeCulo. I checked the license plate as they sped past, repeating the number, EMA 268, in my head.

One of the cops gave me a funny look and said, "Excuse me sir, you're parked in a bus stop. It would be best to move, or we'll have to ticket you."

EMA 268, EMA 268. "Okay, officers, if you could just direct me. I'm a bit lost. Can you direct me to Fairview Avenue?" EMA 268, EMA 268

The cop nodded. "Little more than a mile down this road, the third stoplight is Fairview Avenue."

"Thank you so much. I'm moving my car right now. Thank you." EMA 268

I climbed back behind the wheel, waited for two cars to pass, then put on my blinker and pulled into the traffic lane. I gave a little toot on the horn as the cops stepped into the bakery.

At the first stoplight, I took a left, not usually where I'd turn, but I didn't want to run into Benedetti's crew. It was plain old luck of the draw that I noticed them following and was able to pull over to the cops. I drove down the road another mile then turned right and took a round-about route to Heidi's house.

Heidi has a double garage behind her house facing the alley. I pulled in front of her garage then hurried into her backyard and unlocked the garage door. I opened the second garage door, got back in my car, and pulled in alongside her red Mercedes. I got the boxes out of my back seat, lowered the garage door, and hurried around to the front of the house.

Before I went inside, I phoned Candi Mangle. She answered on the second ring.

"Everything all right, Dev?"

"Yeah, but I think I dodged a bullet." I went on to explain the gray SUV following me and then gave her the license plate number.

"And you're sure these two individuals were involved?"

"Absolutely, I recognized Melvin Cummings and Victor DeCulo, who was driving."

"All right, look, as long as you're okay, this is another step forward. I'll get this to our folks right away." Interestingly, she didn't mention the Saint Paul Police. We said our good-byes, disconnected, and I phoned Delton Lange and gave him the information.

"Thank you, Dev. I'll put a BOLO out on this plate number. With any luck, we'll get them."

"Thanks, Delton. Anything else happens on this end, I'll let you know."

I slipped on my surgical gown, the gloves, and the mask, and checked in on Heidi. She was either unconscious or sound asleep. I couldn't tell which and didn't want to wake her. The important thing was she was breathing.

I brought the half-empty water glass into the kitchen. Then lined up the boxes in the living room, opened them, and pulled out the contents. It actually looked a lot simpler than I feared. There was a ventilator, air-tube, full face mask, six feet of air hose, a hose holder, and a wedge pillow. I read through the directions twice.

I carried everything into Heidi's room and proceeded to set things up. It only took about ten minutes. She seemed to struggle slightly as I slipped the wedge pillow beneath her shoulders. She shook her head back and forth as I pulled the full-face mask over her head, but then she settled back down. I brought the fresh glass of water in from the kitchen then set the direction booklet for the ventilator on the chest of drawers next to her bed and left the bedroom. I cleaned up all the packing material in the living room and placed it in the recycling bin.

I checked on Heidi again, and was it just my imagination, or was she actually breathing better? I sat at the kitchen counter, in my surgical gown, gloves, and mask for the next hour, checking on Heidi every ten minutes.

She seemed to be doing well, thank God, and she really did seem to be breathing better.

I sent Nora a text message giving her an update and then waited for fifteen minutes. When I didn't hear from her, I checked on Heidi once more then hung up my surgical gown and headed out the door.

Thirty-seven

It was mid-afternoon once I climbed behind the wheel, I debated going back to the office. I made a command decision and headed out to Mahtomedi. Along the way, I checked in my rearview mirror for the gray SUV every other minute, but fortunately, I never saw it. I was heading down Park Avenue toward the Benedetti home twenty minutes later. As I parked in front of the entrance, I noticed the white Lexus parked up near the house. The basketball net was in the exact same spot as the other day. No one was out shooting baskets right now.

I climbed out of my car and gave a careful look up and down the street. I couldn't see a gray SUV anywhere. I opened the gate, walked across the brick-paved area, and rang the doorbell. Gina opened the door a few moments later.

"Dev? Everything okay?" As she asked, she looked over her shoulder, checking for the boys, and then stepped outside, closing the door behind her. "What's happened?"

I told her about the currency being identified as counterfeit. "So here is what's going to happen. They're getting warrants for your husband, his brother Tony, Melvin and Coco Cummings, his uncle Arnold Benedetti, Victor DeCulo, and anyone else they can link to this. I don't know for sure, but my sense is they'll try to roust everyone early tomorrow morning, probably between four and six in the morning."

"Good, that's great news. I want to call my lawyer right now and have her file my divorce—"

"You need to wait until tomorrow morning, Gina. You need to wait until they've made the raids."

"But why? If they're going to arrest him. Wouldn't it make sense to—"

"Actually, no. If you alert your attorney before the raids and they can't find Tommy, or don't arrest everyone, say if Tommy isn't at Coco's, or Tony hasn't returned to his apartment, then automatically you will be under suspicion as having alerted them and therefore an accessory to the crime."

"But, I haven't done anything. Why the hell do I—"

"Gina, listen to me. They are going to kick in that door behind you early tomorrow morning, and they aren't going to find Tommy here, are they?"

"Of course they won't. That's the whole point. That limp bastard hasn't slept here for over ten months."

"Exactly. But as far as they know, this is where he lives. They expect him to be here. So when they come here, they are not going to ring the doorbell or politely knock. They're going to kick it in."

"They can't do that."

"Please, just listen to me. When they come, you're going to tell them you knew they were coming and that Tommy's not here. And then they're going to arrest you as an accessory, take you away, and place your two boys with child protection. Because you're not listening."

"They can't do that."

"They can, and they will."

"Then I'll call the police right now and tell them that Tommy isn't here."

"Good idea. That will be proof positive that you knew about the planned raid and alerted Tommy."

"But I, I won't do that."

"And, then, when you do file for divorce, even if they release you, Tommy will have a bargaining chip, thanks to you. He'll tell the police that you warned him, and that's why he got away, at least for a while. Unless you do whatever he wants in the divorce, and then he just might, maybe, not tell that lie to the police. But you go ahead and do it your way, Gina. You don't have to listen to me. Just remember, for the rest of their lives, those two young boys in the house will think you were somehow in on Tommy's scam. In case they have any doubts, they were sound asleep, right here in the house when the cops kicked in the door and handcuffed you and the boys until they searched the place. At which point, the boys will have been taken to the police station and eventually placed with child protection until everything gets sorted out."

"But you're not listening, Dev. I'm not going to tell Tommy."

"Unfortunately, I was listening, Gina. And when you call the police and tell them not to come here, they're going to know that you have inside information. They're going to think you told Tommy. They are not going to believe anything you tell them because, at the end of the day, to them, you are Mrs. Tommy Benedetti."

Finally, that seemed to get to her, and a light suddenly flashed on. "I can call my sister Mona, and she'll let us spend the night there."

"Good, call her, spend the night there, maybe two nights. If anyone asks you later, tell them you and the boys were having a sleepover at your sister's house. Bring some ice cream or cookies or something, so it seems like a party. Don't mention anything to your sister because the police will ultimately question her, and if she doesn't know anything, she'll be safe. But please, go there tonight. Be safe. Please, just do it and don't call the police."

"Okay, I will, and Dev, thanks for listening to me. I know you're right. It's just one more damn thing Tommy has brought down on the boys and me."

"Hey, Gina, you go to your sisters, and you've just beat him at his own game, and he doesn't even know you're playing."

She nodded, rose up on her toes, and gave me a kiss on the cheek. "Thanks, Dev. I'll call you tomorrow."

"Let me call you. In case they check your phone, and they probably will, I don't want to have the police finding any more phone calls between us. Okay? You're good to go?"

She nodded and hurried back into the house, calling, "Tommy, Michael, turn off the game. We're going to Aunt Mona's now. Come on, let's go…"

Thirty-eight

I drove back to the office. Morton was asleep. As I stepped into the office, he opened one eye, recognized me, and went back to sleep. Louie was at his picnic table desk. He looked up and asked, "You get that ventilator working?"

"Seems to be working fine. Heidi didn't seem too pleased initially, but she settled down and appeared to be breathing much better. I stayed there for at least an hour and checked on her every ten minutes. Her breathing appeared to be a little more regular and deeper. I just hope we're past the worst of it and slowly but surely, she'll begin to recover."

"You feeling okay?"

"Yeah, no problems. I drove out to Gina Benedetti's."

"You tell her the money was counterfeit?"

"Yeah, and I told her, most likely, there was going to be a raid on the house early tomorrow morning."

"She's going to get out of there, right?"

"I hope so. I explained the facts to her in no uncertain terms more than once. She seemed to get it finally. It never ceases to amaze me, when you tell someone what's going to happen, and they decide to come up with an alternate plan. She figured, if she just called the police and told them Tommy wasn't at the house, it would save them the trouble of coming over. I explained to her how that would most likely lead to her arrest and possible charges as an accomplice."

"Did she start getting the message when she heard that?"

"Not at first. Actually, not until I said her sons would be placed in child protection. Once she heard that, things began to click. They'll all be spending tonight at her sister's place, and I said I'd call her with an update tomorrow. Benedetti has been pretty much out of the picture for the last ten months where the family is concerned. My fear is that, with this latest scam collapsing, he's liable to try anything. It would just be better if they kept a low profile until he's behind bars."

Louie nodded and said, "Kind of a busy day for a change."

"You know, I'd just like things to quiet down. If nothing else happened today, it would be all right with me. I—"

"Haskell? Haskell, are you up there. Haskell?" a nasally sounding voice seemed to be shouting from outside. "Dev Haskell, you dumb shit, get down here."

"What the hell is that?" I said, stepping over to the window.

"Haskell! Haskell? Time to wake up. Nap time is over."

"Is that who I think it is?" Louie asked, getting out of his chair and hurrying to the window. Morton was right behind him.

We looked across the street to the black Cadillac Escalade parked in front of Louie's car. There was Tubby Gustafson in a powder blue surgical gown, blue booties, latex gloves, a face mask, and a face shield. He was shouting into a megaphone. Fat Freddy Zimmerman, dressed in similar attire, stood next to Tubby holding the megaphone.

Tubby pointed up at me as I stepped to the window. He shouted, "Haskell, you sorry excuse for a thinking human being. I see you. Now get your worthless ass down here."

"God, I can't believe it. Damn it. That moron, he'll have the entire neighborhood looking out their windows. That fat bastard," I said and headed for the door.

"You might want to take a mask and some gloves," Louie said.

"Yeah, God only knows what I could catch from Tubby." I pulled a mask and two gloves from my wastebasket and hurried out the door. On the way down the stairs, I blew into the gloves so I'd be able to slip them on.

"Haskell, I saw you up there a moment ago. Where are you? Haskell do you hear— Well, finally. Hope I disturbed your afternoon nap," Tubby said as I stepped out of the building. Two guys from the insurance office on the first floor were looking out the window. I glanced up and saw Louie still standing in front of our window. Next to our window, two women draped in green plastic with bits of tinfoil in their hair were looking out the beauty parlor window. Two hairdressers stood behind them, shaking their heads.

"Hey, Tub, err, umm, Mr. Gustafson. You might feel more comfortable up in my office, and we could discuss whatever it is that—"

"Silenco! You moron. That pool of petulance you refer to as your office? Not a chance. You were supposed to get back to me yesterday. Unless I'm mistaken, I haven't heard a damn thing. I need an update, now, damn it."

"Sorry sir, I've been just a little busy, and—"

"Watch the tone, Haskell. Watch the damn tone," Tubby shouted.

"I was thinking it might make more sense if we weren't yelling at one another across the street when I gave you an update, sir," I said and stepped off the curb.

I hadn't taken two steps toward Tubby when he shouted through the megaphone, "Hold your position, Haskell. Hold your position you bacteria-infested virus carrier." He grabbed the megaphone from Fat Freddy and shouted, "Frederick, shoot to kill if he continues." Fat Freddy appeared momentarily dazed from the megaphone pointed six inches from his face. Tubby backed up onto the sidewalk, all the while keeping a wary eye on me. "Stop that fool if he takes one more step, Frederick."

Fat Freddy pulled a pistol halfway out of his pocket.

I looked up and down the street, hoping someone, somewhere, had called the police.

"I can assure you, sir, that within the next twenty-four hours, the individual you have expressed an interest in will most likely be taking up residence compliments of the City of Saint Paul."

That seemed to calm Tubby down, at least for the moment. "I'll expect," he shouted, then brought the megaphone up to his face shield. "I'll expect a full report by this time tomorrow. God help you if you're the least bit late." He turned to Fat Freddy standing next to him and shouted into the megaphone, "Get me out of here before his vile germs cross the street."

Freddy jumped, and his eyes seemed to cross. He shook his head in an effort to regain some semblance of balance as he pulled open the rear door on the Escalade. Tubby slid into and across the back seat. Freddy hurried around the front of the Escalade and climbed in behind the wheel. Once he started the car, Tubby lowered the window and shouted into the megaphone, "I'll expect to hear from you in twenty-four hours, Haskell. Do you hear me, Haskell? Twenty-four hours," he continued to shout as the Escalade sped up the street and turned onto the freeway entrance ramp.

I glanced up and down the street. At least a half-dozen different people were standing in their front yards, watching as the Escalade disappeared from sight. Once Tubby was gone, they turned and looked at me. I glanced up to the second floor. Louie was nowhere to be seen, and now the two women with tinfoil in their hair were shaking their heads.

"Well, if that doesn't make your day memorable, I don't know what will," Louie said when I stepped back into the office. "That was beyond crazy."

"What an idiot. What was I supposed to do? Broadcast it up and down the street that the police are planning an early morning raid on Tommy Benedetti and his thugs? I'm telling you, Tubby is getting crazier by the day. The guy is an absolute nutcase."

"You won't get any argument from me. You up for one at The Spot?" Louie asked.

"Thanks, Louie. I'd love to, but I'm going to drop Morton off at home and then check in on Heidi. I want to make sure she's doing all right with the ventilator I hooked up."

"Probably a good idea. I'll see you in the morning," Louie said.

When I grabbed Morton's leash, he immediately hurried over and sat next to me, pretending to be trained.

Thirty-nine

Morton and I headed home. I pulled into the driveway, let him out of the back seat, and we went for a twenty-minute walk. We only passed four people on our walk, and everyone smiled and kept their social distance. Once home, I filled Morton's water dish, tossed him a biscuit, and then headed over to Heidi's.

I pulled my mask and gloves on. Once inside I stepped into the surgical gown and headed for Heidi's bedroom. The face mask was just as I left it, and she seemed to be breathing much better. She didn't so much as move or cough as I watched her. I went into the kitchen, emptied the dishwasher, and checked on Heidi again. Satisfied that she was okay, I pulled off the surgical gown and went out to my car. I sent Nora a text message that everything seemed okay and had maybe even improved slightly. I drove over to Davanni's and ordered a BBQ chicken pizza. I thought about stopping over at Candi's then quickly decided against it. With tomorrow's supposedly early morning raids, she had more than enough going on without me trying to get her into bed. Besides, maybe she and Turner were 'resting up.'

I took the pizza back to Heidi's and parked in her garage. Since it was a nice warm evening, I sat on her front steps and started in on the pizza. I had just taken a bite of the last piece when someone called "Dev?"

I looked over, and Nora was standing on her front porch. She waved and headed toward me.

"Hi, Nora. Hey, perfect timing, I'm on the last piece so I don't have to share."

Fortunately, she laughed and asked, "Everything okay with Heidi?"

"Oh, yeah, I set her up on that sleep apnea ventilator, and I wanted to check and make sure everything was all right. I watched her for maybe an hour this afternoon after I hooked the thing up, and she seemed good, maybe even a little better. She seemed to be taking slightly deeper breaths. I checked on her maybe thirty minutes ago, and she was the same, so I guess that's positive."

Nora nodded. "She's at that point where she's either going to begin to improve, or there's going to be a rapid decline."

"Well, I think she's improving, but I'm keeping my fingers crossed."

"Let me go in and check on her. I'm wondering if you would mind spending the night here. Just to make sure the mask and ventilator aren't causing a problem. If she's doing okay, she may begin to come out of it in the next twenty-four to forty-eight hours."

"Yeah, I can stay here, if you think it would help."

"Not so much help as just a safety precaution. I don't expect any problems," Nora said.

"Yeah, sure. I'll hang around."

"Oh, thanks, Dev. Let me go suit up, and I'll check on her." She went into her house and was back five minutes later, all gowned up. I unlocked the door for her, and she said, "You stay out here. I'm just going to do a quick check. Be back in a couple of minutes," she said and closed the door behind her.

Nora was back out, maybe ten minutes later. "She's doing just fine, and I'd say there's a definite improvement. That mask and ventilator seem to be making all the difference in the world. Good move on your part. Let me just get rid of this PPE, and I'll join you."

She was back twenty minutes later. She brought her own lawn chair along with what looked like a grilled cheese sandwich and two ice cream bars, one of which she handed to me. She talked about her days working at the hospital. It was interesting and, at times, heartbreaking. I had the sense she hadn't told many people, or maybe anyone, about her experience. Once she started, it just all came out. She cried, she laughed, she shook her head, and in the end said, "Oh, man, sorry to go on like that. I didn't mean to."

"Nora, you're fighting a war every day, and you and your workmates are doing the best you can with what you have. You're doing a hell of a job, and you're saving lives. Stay focused on that."

She nodded but didn't say anything. After a few minutes, she said, "Well, I'd better start to get ready for work. I'll stop and check on Heidi on my way down to the hospital."

Forty

I was upstairs in Heidi's guest room watching tv when I heard Nora call my name.

"Dev? Hello. Are you up there?"

"Yeah, Nora, everything okay?" I said, hurrying out of the room and downstairs.

"Yeah, just checking in on our patient. She's doing fine. You're here for the night?"

"Yeah, I'll be up for a few more hours, and I'll check her before I go to bed. Do you want me to check on her in the middle of the night?"

"Umm, don't set an alarm or anything. If you're up, you can peek in, but otherwise, check on her when you get up. I'll be stopping in a little after nine tomorrow morning. If you're not up, I'm not going to wake you."

"I'll probably be out of here around six in the morning. I've got my dog, Morton, at home, and if I wait until nine, I'll be coming home to a not nice surprise."

"Will he be okay tonight?"

"Yeah, he should be just fine." I didn't feel the need to tell her it wouldn't be the first time Morton spent a night on his own.

"Okay, well, wishing you a safe and quiet night," she said.

"And you too, hang in there, Nora, and thanks, you're doing a great job."

"Thanks, Dev. Yeah, we are."

I watched <u>Get Shorty</u> for the umpteenth time. I checked on Heidi a little after eleven and went to bed. My phone rang at 3:00. "Hello," I groaned.

That seemed to bring a laugh from the voice on the other end. "Hi Dev, Delton Lange. We're getting ready to move out. The Feds are hitting the Benedetti house out in Mahtomedi in an hour. If you still want to warn his soon to be ex-wife, now would be the time."

I cleared my throat and said, "Thank you, Delton. But I decided not to do that. Will you be joining them?"

"Yeah, with the understanding I'm simply an observer. I'll be hitting Thomas Avenue at seven this morning with the SWAT team."

"And you're hitting The Market House too?"

"Yes, we'll have a team going in there but not until later in the morning. We've got it scheduled for nine."

"You stay safe, Delton. If you're not going to Thomas Avenue until seven, would you mind if I tagged along? Strictly as an observer, I won't get in your way."

He seemed to think about that for a moment and said, "I don't have a problem with that, as long as you do just that, observe."

"Where are you meeting?"

"One block away on Edmund Street. We'll be meeting at a quarter after six."

"I'll see you there," I said, and he disconnected. As long as I was awake, I pulled on my jeans and went downstairs to check on Heidi. She was breathing deeply and regularly.

I was about to head back upstairs when I heard something in the kitchen. As I walked into the kitchen, I saw a shadow at the back door. The upper portion of the door had nine panes of glass, three panes across, and three panes high. A white lace curtain hung over the glass. I walked along the kitchen counter, stood in front of the refrigerator, and peeked around the corner.

The motion detector light was on, and someone was definitely at the back door. The door shook again, this time a little more forcefully as the doorknob turned slightly. Suddenly, there was a slow scratching across the pane of glass in the lower right-hand corner. I didn't have a gun with me. I pulled a carving knife out of the rack on the counter and quickly stepped across to the exterior wall.

With my back against the wall, I watched as the scratching continued. Once it stopped, I waited. There was a sudden snap as a circular piece of glass landed on the black doormat. A hole appeared where the pane of glass had been just a moment ago. A second or two after that, a forearm with a skull tattoo and the numbers 666 reached in, Melvin Cummings.

I jumped, grabbed the forearm and pulled hard. Cummings slammed into the back door. I sliced the knife across his wrist, and blood immediately squirted up, across the door and the kitchen wall. Cummings screamed as I jammed the carving knife into the skull tattoo and let go. He stumbled off the back steps, ran across Nora's front yard, and disappeared.

I was barefoot and decided trying to follow probably wouldn't be the wisest choice. I debated calling Delton Lange with the SWAT team and decided against it. Instead, I phoned 911 and reported an attempted break-in. I mentioned that I had stabbed the guy, and there was blood. The dispatcher asked if I was safe, then asked my name, the address, and said he was sending a squad car. Although I never saw the vehicle, I told the dispatcher the burglar fled in a gray SUV, license number EMA 268. I placed the carving knife in the kitchen sink and hurried upstairs to put on my t-shirt. Maybe three minutes later, I heard the siren.

As the squad car was coming down the street, I walked out the front door wearing my face mask and gloves. I waved at the squad car, and it pulled over. As soon as the cops climbed out of the car, I told them I was caring for a COVID19 patient. I then went on to explain what had happened, describing Cummings skull tattoo but not mentioning his name.

At the mention of a COVID19 patient, they didn't seem all that eager to get too close.

Forty-one

The police followed me around the side of the house to the kitchen door. They wore face masks and gloves. They took a number of pictures of the back door and the hole that had been cut in the class. One of them placed the circular piece of glass as well as the carving knife in evidence bags and recorded my statements. The entire process took no more than thirty minutes. Along the way, they were joined, briefly, by four more cops in two separate cars. They all left before four in the morning.

I relocked the back door and checked on Heidi. She was breathing regularly and, by all appearances, normally. I took a legal pad from a drawer in her desk and removed the back cardboard sheet. I cut the cardboard to fit the damaged windowpane and taped the cardboard in place. At least it would keep the bugs out. I attempted to clean the blood off the wall and door with a spray bottle of anti-bacterial cleaner and paper towels. My effort only served to spread the bloodstain more evenly across the wall and woodwork.

I went back upstairs, set the alarm on my phone for five in the morning then slept fitfully in increments of a few minutes for the next half-hour. At five, I slipped on my surgical gown, shoes, gloves, and mask and checked on Heidi. I sprayed more anti-bacterial spray over the blood on the wall and lightened the stain slightly. I left Nora a note explaining the stain and the cardboard and went home.

I showered and changed clothes then woke Morton and let him out the back door. I filled his food and water dishes and let him back inside. He did not seem all that happy. He headed for his pillow in the corner of the kitchen, curled up, and was asleep in about sixty seconds. I locked up and headed over to Edmund Avenue. There were two squad cars and two flat-black Humvee's parked one behind the other. A number of guys were standing around in black helmets and protective vests, knee and elbow pads. They were all wearing blue latex gloves and white face masks. SWAT in yellow letters was on the back of everyone's protective vest.

Delton Lange and another guy were going over what looked like a map spread out on the hood of one of the Humvee's.

As I climbed out of my car, one of the police officers approached and put his hand up, signaling not to proceed any further. "I'm sorry, sir. We're in the middle of an operation, and I'm going to ask you to get back in your car and—"

"I'm here to see officer Delton Lange. He's expecting me. I've been inside 458 Thomas Avenue, your intended target for this morning."

He nodded and said, "Wait here one minute." He turned and hurried over to Lange. A moment later, Lange looked up and motioned me toward him.

I slipped my .38 in the back of my belt, pulled on my mask and gloves, and hurried over. "Thanks, Delton," I said and glanced at what I thought had been a map spread out on the hood of the Humvee. It was actually a floor plan of Tony Benedetti's apartment. I noticed the closets in the bedrooms weren't indicated, and I pointed and mentioned that fact.

"Good to know," Lange said. "Anything else? What about furniture?"

"Very little furniture and what's there is, well, it's pretty bad. This is his bedroom, mattress on the floor in this corner. He keeps a pistol underneath a pillow. Two piles of clothes on the floor here, just outside the bedroom. The kitchen has a freestanding cabinet here, a refrigerator here, and a window. The living room has a couch against this wall. A leg missing on this corner of the couch, and it's held up by two bricks. A tv sits here against the wall on an empty half-barrel. This closet in the bedroom has a bunch of clothes on the floor and a football jersey hanging on a hanger. Bathroom has a toilet, sink, and tub, no shower."

"Is there a rear exit out of the unit?" the guy in the helmet asked.

"Not that I saw. There's just this one entrance, and it's almost directly across the hall from the entrance to the other apartment on the second floor. This staircase leads up to the third floor. It was originally an attic, and now is the fifth apartment. There's two apartments on the first floor. I don't know anything about them."

"Who's in this third apartment, the one opposite Benedetti's?" Lange asked.

"A woman. Her name is Joyce, don't know the last name. She doesn't like Benedetti and told me she hadn't seen him in four or five days, and that was two days ago. She's got a key to Benedetti's place. If you can get it from her, it might be a safer way to get in. I might have an update on another one of these guys."

"Oh?"

I went on to tell them about a guy attempting to break into Heidi's. How I cut him up pretty bad, and I suspected it might be Melvin Cummings.

"And he was bleeding?"

"Yeah, quite a bit. I stabbed him in his right forearm. The cops took the knife as evidence. They tracked a trail of blood out to the street where it disappeared, so he must have hopped in a car."

"We'll look for Cummings when we hit his sisters place in The Market House," Lange said. "There's no rear entrance to the building shown on this floor plan. Are you aware of one?"

I shook my head and said, "No, and nothing in my memory suggests there is one, but I wasn't looking for that when I was inside. So, there could be, and I just never saw it."

Lange checked his watch and said, "I'm going to send the two police officers through this property to watch the rear of 458 Thomas. We'll approach from either end of the street. Haskell, I'm riding in this vehicle. You'll follow me. When we stop at the final point before we go in, you're to stay in that position until you get the all-clear. I don't want you in the way or getting hurt. Understand?"

"Sounds good to me," I said. Lange took a step into the street, raised his right hand, and moved it around in a circle. Everyone hurried into their respective vehicles, and I ran to my car.

I followed Lange's Humvee around the block. We stopped at the corner and waited for maybe three minutes. Lange was probably doing a final communications check and giving last-minute instructions. Suddenly, both Humvees took off and converged on 458 Thomas. The doors flew open, and eight men hurried across the front lawn, taking up positions against the house on either side of the front door.

Two men were suddenly running toward the building, one carrying a battering ram. A moment later, the front door was open, and everyone charged in. I sat behind the wheel of my car, waiting. It seemed to take forever, but it was really just a matter of a few minutes. A guy suddenly stepped outside onto the front stoop and waved me forward.

I sped down the street and hurried out of my car. I was so anxious I left my car running and had to stop, open the driver's door, climb back in, turn off my car, pull my keys out of the ignition, and then hurry into the house.

I ran up the stairs and down the hallway. Joyce was standing in her doorway wearing a motley gray, terry-cloth bathrobe and a pair of fuzzy triangular shaped slippers designed to look like pizza slices, yellow with red areas supposed to represent sausage.

"Hi, Joyce," I said and hurried into Tony Benedetti's apartment. I noticed the key from Joyce was hanging from the lock. Two cops were in the kitchen, chuckling over the dead mouse in the trap next to the stove. I peeked into the bedroom, and another cop was in the process of placing the Colt .45 Defender from beneath the pillow into a plastic evidence bag.

I stepped into the spare bedroom as Delton Lange was in the process of dragging the black plastic trash bag out of the closet and onto the carpet. "Bingo," he said and grinned. "Look familiar?" He let go of the trash bag, and it tipped over, spilling out bundles of counterfeit hundred-dollar bills wrapped with a rubber band around them. There weren't any notes written with a Sharpie.

"This is great," I said. "Any sign of Tony Benedetti?"

Lange shook his head. "No, unfortunately, and by the look of things, I'd say your assessment of him being gone for maybe a week appears to be correct."

"I noticed the woman across the hall, Joyce, was up and watching. She could give you some background information on this guy. Like I said, she wasn't too fond of him."

"Yeah, she was more than happy to give us the key. This worked out better than we could have hoped. The icing on the cake would have been getting Benedetti, but this will do for the moment. With any luck, we'll meet his acquaintance at the Market House in a couple of hours. You going to join us?"

"I wouldn't think of missing it," I said.

Photographs were taken, and the evidence sent back to the police station in a secure van. Joyce was interviewed, and then everyone piled back in the vehicles and I followed them into downtown.

Forty-two

The Humvees pulled into the parking lot next to CHS Field, where the St. Paul Saints play baseball. Four police squad cars suddenly joined us. The parking lot was just a block away and out of sight from the Market House building.

While I sat in my car, someone from the Market House was going over another floor plan spread out on the hood of the Humvee and explaining things to Lange.

After maybe fifteen minutes, Lange strolled over to me and said, "Haskell, I want you to remain here. We'll be going in the front entry, and we'll have a team of people covering the rear of the building. We've got someone letting us in, so it should be short and sweet. I want you to remain here; in fact, pull over there to a proper parking place," he said and pointed to a parking spot next to a black Prius. "I'll send you a text when it's safe for you to enter. I'll have someone stationed at the front door. Any questions?"

"No, sir."

"Right answer," he said and smiled. A moment later, the Humvees and the squad cars headed down the street. As the Humvees crossed the intersection and pulled in front of The Market House, the squad cars turned at the corner and headed down the street to the back of the building. Just like before, the doors on both Humvees flew open, and everyone hurried out and into the building. My cellphone was resting on my lap, waiting for the signal from Lange.

I waited and waited and then waited some more. After the better part of a half-hour, a one-word text message came across the screen. *'OKAY.'* I hurried out of my car and ran down the street. An EMT vehicle was parked out front behind one of the Humvees.

Two officers were standing in front of the security door. As I approached, one of them said, "I'm sorry, sir, but at the moment we have to deny entry. We're checking on a problem, and hopefully, it won't be too long."

"I just received a text message from Delton Lange, telling me to head up to the fifth floor."

"You're Hassle, the private investigator?"

"Yes," I said, seeing no point in correcting him.

"Okay. You can go on up. They're in unit five-twelve."

I hurried through the security door and got onto the elevator. Coco Cummings' place was off to the right and down the hall. I had just stepped off the elevator when three cops standing in the hall suddenly stepped aside. Two EMTs wheeled a gurney out the door of the unit and turned in my direction. "Hold that elevator," one of EMTs shouted. I stepped back in between the doors just as they began to close, and they quickly reopened. I pushed the stop button on the elevator and then stepped out of the way as they began to angle the gurney onto the elevator.

There were two IV bags hanging from a stand attached to the gurney. An oxygen mask covered the better part of the victims' face, but I could still recognize Melvin Cummings. His right forearm was covered with blood-soaked bandages, and he had a tourniquet wrapped around the upper portion of his arm. I stared as the doors closed behind them, and they began their descent.

I shook my head to get back to where I was and headed down the hallway toward Coco's unit. The cops stopped talking and watched as I approached. Fortunately, one of them recognized me, nodded, and stepped aside to let me in. What was left of the front door was wide open. There was a large hole where the doorknob used to be. It looked like someone had fired a bowling ball at it.

I stepped into a small unit with a view of the gray brick building just across the street. The living room was small and narrow, with a couch facing the window and a small end table between the couch and a chair. A coffee table was positioned in front of the couch. An empty pizza box and an almost empty bottle of Smirnoff vodka sat on the coffee table. The carpet between the couch and the coffee table was blood stained, and I guessed that was where Melvin Cummings had spent the past few hours.

"Get your damn hands off of me. I want to call my lawyer, now!" a woman shrieked. I turned and watched as Coco Cummings stepped out of the bedroom. She was barefoot with her hands cuffed behind her back. She wore a pair of tight-fitting jeans. The zipper was pulled down, the waist unbuttoned, and her sleeveless blouse was unbuttoned. For a half-second, I thought about taking a picture of her implants for Gina Benedetti.

Coco was escorted by a female cop who had hold of her right arm and was pulling her along. Behind them, another female cop followed, carrying a pair of pink running shoes, Officer Lin Nguyen.

I'd had some memorable past experience with Officer Nguyen. I smiled and said, "Good morning, Lin."

She smiled politely and said, "I'm afraid you'll have to come back at another time, Mr. Haskell. Coco is going to be tied up for the rest of the day."

"Did you have an appointment, honey?" Coco called as they escorted her out into the hall.

"You know her?" Lange asked, stepping out of the bedroom.

"Coco? No, really, I don't. She must have me confused with someone else," I said.

Lange looked at me but didn't comment.

"Please, tell me Tommy Benedetti is around here somewhere," I said.

"Sorry to say, there's no sign of him. Well, other than clothes hanging in the closet. A shaving razor and boxers in the bathroom. Maybe he had a change of heart and went home to his wife.”

“She didn’t seem like much of a fan. I think he would have been safer staying here.”

“Did you give her a call after I phoned you earlier this morning?”

“No, I decided not to, and now, with him not showing up here, I’m glad I didn’t call her this morning,” I said. Lange seemed to study me for a moment but didn’t make a comment.

“Did you find anything of interest?” I asked.

“We’re just starting to look around. Have you heard anything from your friend, Agent Mangle?”

“No, I haven’t,” I said, shaking my head.

Lange glanced at his watch. “Well, they followed their schedule and entered the Benedetti home right around four this morning. Everything went well, but no one was home.” He stared for a moment but didn’t say anything.

I thought it would be a cold day in hell before Benedetti returned home and an even colder day before Gina would let him in the house. But then, she and the boys were at her sister’s house.

“Well, I think I’m going to head home and try to catch up on my sack time,” I said. “You’ll keep me posted if you find anything of interest or if Benedetti shows up looking for his trash bag?”

Lange chuckled at that and said, "Oh, if only it would be that easy. Anything happens I'll give you a call. You do the same."

"I will. Hey Delton, thanks for letting me tag along this morning."

"Thank you for the information," Lange said and watched me as I left.

I took the elevator down to the ground floor, hoping I might meet up with Officer Lin Nguyen. No such luck as I stepped out of the elevator and looked around. I walked back to my car and drove home.

Morton met me as I stepped inside and I let him out the back door. Surprisingly, no mess in the house. After twenty minutes, I coaxed him into the car with a dog biscuit, and we drove to the office.

Forty-three

As I pulled behind Louie's car, a text message from Nora came in. *'Much improved. Heidi is breathing deeply. Had short conversation. Back asleep. I'm going to bed.'*

I replied, *'Thanks'* and added a thumbs-up Emoji.

Louie was just packing up his briefcase when we stepped into the office. Morton headed for the rawhide chew resting on his pillow. "You heading down to the courthouse?" I asked.

"No, detox center. Interviewing a new client. She was brought in two nights ago. Belligerent with her arresting officers."

"Always a good move," I said.

"Apparently, they arrested her as she was pounding on the door of the liquor store. Imagine, the store had the audacity to be closed, not that they would have sold to her anyway."

"Gee, she sounds charming."

"We'll see. How was your morning?" Louie asked, closing his briefcase and heading toward the door.

"Interesting. I'll tell you when you've got more time. It gets a little involved." He nodded and closed the door behind him. I watched out the window as he crossed the street and climbed into his car. I phoned Candi Mangle as Louie drove up the street.

"Well, and how are you this morning, Mr. Haskell?"

"More importantly, how are you, Candi? Did you go to the Benedetti house this morning?"

"Oh, yeah, bright and early. Well, actually, it wasn't bright; in fact, it was still dark, but it was definitely early. We're still here as a matter of fact."

"Was Tommy there?"

"Unfortunately, no, he wasn't. As a matter of fact, no one was here. The place was empty," she said and let that last comment hang out there for a moment. "I understand you were with the Saint Paul Police. How did that go?"

"Did you talk with Delton Lange?"

She chuckled and said, "As a matter of fact, I did."

"Did he tell you about the trash bag?"

"Oh yeah, and he told me about getting Coco Cummings and her brother in their second raid. He sounded very happy."

"Yeah, Coco and Melvin Cummings and a trash bag in Tony Benedetti's place filled with bundles of counterfeit hundred-dollar bills."

"That's what Lange said. Apparently, this Melvin Cummings wasn't in the best of shape," Candi said and then waited, maybe hoping for some inside information.

"The EMTs were rolling him onto the elevator by the time I got up there. Lange kept me out of both places until they were all clear, so I missed out on any action."

"Lucky you. Any idea where Tommy Benedetti might be?"

"I wish I knew. But I have no idea. I'm not aware of any office he had. God, he's in arrears on his mortgage and behind on the property taxes. For all I know, he could be sleeping in a city park," I said, wondering at the same time where, exactly, he could be.

"Well, should you hear anything, I'd appreciate a call."

"Candi, if I find out where Tommy Benedetti is, you'll be the first person I call."

"I going to hold you to that, Dev. Talk to you later," she said and hung up.

I walked over to The Spot. The place was open, but Mike was the only one in there. He was wearing latex gloves and busily placing beer bottles into a cooler behind the bar. He wasn't wearing a mask. He peeked over the bar as I walked in and said, "Having one of those days, Dev? You coming over for some liquid courage?"

"Surprisingly, no. But I am having a phone problem. Mind if I make a call on the bar phone?"

"Long as it's local, help yourself," he said as he opened another box and began removing bottles.

I pulled out my cell, brought up Gina Benedetti's number, and punched it in on the bar phone.

"Hello?" she answered after the second ring.

"Gina, it's Dev Haskell."

"Oh, how come the number came through as un-known?"

"I'm not calling on my phone. I'm at a business across the street. Just checking in. Are you guys doing all right?"

"Yes, we're fine. The boys are on their iPads, oblivious to everything going on around them." She lowered her voice and asked. "Have you heard anything?"

"They went into your house early this morning. I know they're still in there searching and probably will be for the better part of the day."

"Searching for what?"

"Anything and everything. Weapons, cancelled checks, business files, whatever they come across that might be of interest. I'll drive by later today and see if I can learn anything. I think it would be best if you spent another night at your sisters."

"You think it will take that long?"

"It might. Like I said, I'll drive by and check it out. I'll see if there's any damage to the front entry," I said, remembering Delton Lange told me there wasn't any. "If there is, hopefully, we can get it repaired before you're back with the boys. They don't need to see their home torn apart."

"Thanks, Dev. I appreciate all you've done for me, for us. Especially convincing me to get out of there last night."

"Not a problem. You hear anything from Tommy?"

"No, and I wish he'd call because I would love to give him a piece of my mind right about now."

"There'll be plenty of time to do that. Let's focus on getting you resettled first. I'll phone you after I've taken a look." We said our good-byes, and I hung up.

"Everything okay?" Mike asked as he stood up. He reached down, picked up three empty beer boxes, and placed them on the bar.

"Yeah, a friend going through a tough time."

"God, I tell you, the world today," he said and shook his head. "Get you something? It's on the house."

"Thanks, I'd love to, but I better not. I've got a lot on my plate today."

"Okay, watch yourself," he said and began to knock down the cardboard boxes.

I walked out of The Spot, climbed into my car, and headed over to Heidi's. I parked in front, pulled on my mask and gloves, and let myself in. I slipped into the surgical gown and made my way to Heidi's bedroom. As I opened the door and stepped in, she pulled the apnea mask off and, in a hoarse voice, said, "Dev?"

"Oh my God, Heidi, how are you feeling?"

"I've been better," she said and coughed.

I noticed her water glass was empty. "Let me get you some water. I'll be right back."

She nodded and pulled the apnea mask back on as I left. I hurried out to the kitchen, put her glass in the dishwasher, and took two glasses out of the cabinet. I filled one with water, the other with orange juice from the re-frigerator, and hurried back into her bedroom.

Her eyes were closed, and I set both glasses on the bedside table. "Heidi," I called softly. She moved her shoulders slightly, wrinkled her nose, and took a couple of deep breaths. I watched her sleeping for a few minutes before I left. I grabbed a tape measure from a drawer in the kitchen and measured the glass panel in the back door that had to be replaced.

I peeked in on Heidi again. She seemed to be in a deep sleep and breathing much better. I hung my surgical gown by the door and went out to my car. Force of habit, I glanced up and down the street looking for a gray SUV and fortunately didn't see one. I climbed behind the wheel, tossed my mask and gloves in the plastic bag, and drove over to Frattallone's hardware store on Grand Avenue.

There were a dozen parking places behind the building. I knew they had a mandatory mask and glove rule for everyone entering, so I pulled on a new mask, slipped the gloves on, and headed for the side door.

I explained the type of glass I needed to the guy inside the door and gave him the measurements. He said it would take just a couple of minutes and then directed me to the aisle with the window caulk. I was in and out of the hardware store in under twelve minutes for less than ten bucks.

I let myself back in Heidi's and peeked in on her sleeping soundly. I removed the remnants of broken glass from the door, inserted the new panel, and caulked the area around it. I checked on Heidi once more. She seemed fine, so I hung up my surgical gown, and went out to my car.

I debated going back to the office, but I had a problem to deal with. I drove over to Tubby Gustafson's house. I thought it better to deal with Tubby now rather than wait for him to get even crazier, if that was possible.

Forty-four

I pulled in front of the iron gates at the entrance to his brick mansion. I got out of my car and pressed the button on the intercom.

The green light flashed on, and a grumpy voice growled, "Yeah?"

"Hi, my name is Dev Haskell. Tub, err, Mr. Gustafson came to my office yesterday and asked me to stop by today."

There was an audible click. A long minute later, the iron gate groaned open. So much for positive social interaction. I pulled into the parking area and approached the front door wearing my mask and surgical gloves. The two thugs were in the shade, leaning against the front of the house. As I got out of the car, they moved about ten feet apart. Both of them had a pistol shoved into the front of their belt.

The larger of the two was holding the metal detector wand, and I stopped a couple of feet from him with my arms extended out to the side. I'd left my gun in the car and held the car keys in my right hand. He waved the wand over me twice and then nodded to his partner, who opened the door for me.

I stepped into the entryway as the door closed behind me. The same guy who was here at my last visit sat in a chair working a crossword puzzle. If it was the same puzzle he hadn't progressed very far.

He frowned at me like I was interrupting some important conversation. He stood, tossed the crossword on the chair, and said. "Turn around, arms out." He patted me down, then said, "This way."

I followed him across the large entry, past the dreadful painting of Tubby holding a bunch of papers and attempting to look respectable. Just when I thought we might be heading to Tubby's office at the end of the hall, he stopped and opened the small door beneath the staircase. "You remember what to do?"

"Gee, let me think, umm, press the button," I said.

"Wiseass," he grumbled. As soon as I stepped into the small room, he slammed the door and clicked the lock into place. I jumped and banged my head on the angled ceiling from the staircase rising overhead. I pressed the button on the computer, and the musical tone sounded as I settled into the chair. A moment later, Tubby Gustafson's face exploded onto the screen. He was wearing a black face mask with the impression of a skull and appeared even more frightening than the usual Tubby image.

He was seated at his desk with his elbows resting on the arms of his desk chair. He was shirtless or possibly even worse; thankfully, I couldn't tell. Both his hands extended off to the side. The two Asian women were sitting on either side of him, apparently working on his manicure.

"What is it you need this time, Haskell? I'm in the middle of my workout," Tubby said.

"You asked me to stop by today, sir, and here I am," I said and smiled.

He shook his head and growled, "Actually, you half-wit, what I told you was, I wanted a full report on the arrest of Tommy Benedetti."

"Unfortunately, sir, to the best of my knowledge, he hasn't been arrested yet. I can tell you that—"

"Hasn't been arrested? Exactly what, in God's name, are they waiting for?"

"Well, sir, they have to find him first. And that seems to be a bit of a problem right now."

"My God, I think I could find him in about sixty seconds."

"If you know where he might be, I would be glad to pass on that information to the police. They raided his brother's apartment, Tony Benedetti, and Coco Cumming's apartment, the woman he was supposed to be living with. They raided his home out in Mahtomedi, too. They just haven't been able to find him."

"Mmm-mmm, they need to check his friend, DeCulo," Tubby said. "He might be sleeping in the back of that stretch limousine. So, what, exactly, is the status of his investment in this LeMax Fund your friend is involved in."

"Well, the status is, there is no investment. The money Benedetti gave her was determined to be counterfeit. All the money has been confiscated by federal authorities. I know they raided his home, but I'm unaware of anything being found there. The police did find a large black trash bag filled with more counterfeit money in Tony Benedetti's apartment.

"My friend contracted the virus, so she's literally been out of it for the past week. She's unaware of the counterfeit funds being confiscated or the warrants out for the arrest of Tommy Benedetti."

"Interesting," Tubby said. "So, if Benedetti's investment has been confiscated, I would guess that the LeMax Fund might be getting a little desperate for investment."

"They may in time, sir, but like I said, my friend is unaware of any of this happening. She's only now showing the beginnings of a recovery from the virus, and I would guess it will be a few more weeks before she's able to return to work."

"You see, Haskell, that's one of your many problems. Hard-working, successful people don't think like you do. They get out and accomplish things. They get things done, and they're successful for exactly that reason. You, on the other hand, remain oblivious to what is involved with the term success. Are you aware of any success, Haskell?"

"I think I've heard about it, yes, sir."

"Think you heard about it, honest to God." He examined the nails on his right hand, nodded, and said, "You may begin." The woman set her nail file on the edge of his desk and began to massage Tubby's hairy shoulder and upper arm. "Well, once again, Haskell, you never fail to disappoint. Against my better judgment, I expect to hear from you tomorrow. Now get out," he shouted those last three words then turned off his computer, and my screen went blank.

I got out of my chair and tried the doorknob. It was locked. I knocked on the door then called, "Hello?" a number of times before the door finally opened. "Thanks," I said as I headed toward the front door. "I'll be back again tomorrow."

I nodded goodbye to the two thugs in the shade leaning against the front of the house and walked over to my car. I climbed in, started the car, and drove around the circular drive to the front gate. The gate began to open as I approached. I only had to wait a few seconds before I drove out the entrance and pulled onto the street. I drove two blocks and pulled over once I was out of sight of Tubby's mansion. I took my phone out and called Gina Benedetti.

"Hi, Gina. It's Dev again."

"I thought you weren't going to call me on your phone?"

"Oh, damn it, I forgot. Shit. Okay, quick question for you. Victor DeCulo, how well does Tommy know him?"

"Victor, oh, wow, they see each other just about every day. They've been doing that for at least the twenty plus years I've known Tommy. They were just about inseparable. They'd have lunch together almost every day. If I wanted to find Tommy, I'd call Victor. Not that he always told the truth, but it got the word to Tommy I was looking for his worthless ass."

"Okay, thanks, that's what I wanted to know."

"Anything else?"

"No, that's it."

"Nice chatting, Dev. Don't forget to use a different phone next time you call," she said and hung up.

I called Candi Mangle.

"Dev, twice in one day. Missing me?" was how she answered.

"Hi, Candi. Hey, I just left Tubby Gustafson's place and—"

"Oh my, but you do get around."

"He's had more than a passing interest in this Tommy Benedetti situation. He was asking me about Benedetti, wondered if he'd been arrested."

"Let me guess. You told him we couldn't find him. Honest to God, Dev. Did you ever think that an individual like Tubby Gustafson possibly doesn't need to be kept up to date on what we're doing?"

"I got news for you, Candi. A guy like Tubby probably knew what the results were going to be today before we even began. But he made an interesting comment I wanted to pass on."

"Such as?"

"When I mentioned Tommy Benedetti, he said Benedetti is sleeping in the back of that stretch limousine."

"Dev, that was probably a figure of speech."

"Well, Benedetti has seen Victor DeCulo, the guy who owns the limo, just about every day for the past maybe twenty or so years. They've been pals since they were kids. You might want to check it out."

"I'll put it on my *to-do* list, Dev," sounding like it was the last thing she intended to do. "Anything else?"

"No, just trying to keep you up to date."

Forty-five

I went back to the office and accomplished absolutely nothing between worrying about Heidi and where in the hell Tommy Benedetti was. I left Louie a note. Morton and I left the office a little early and headed home. I took Morton for a long walk. Fortunately, the sidewalks were relatively empty. I got him settled in for the night after sweetening the deal with a couple of dog biscuits before I headed over to Heidi's.

I gowned up and tiptoed in to check on her. She was sitting in bed with three pillows propped up behind her. She had the apnea mask off and resting next to her. The ventilator was still going, and the tv was on some news station. She looked at me in the surgical gown and mask as I stepped into the room.

"Well, look at you, all dressed up," she said in a barky voice and followed up with a cough.

"Hey, how are you doing, Heidi?"

"Well, I'm awake and still tired."

"Oh, it's so good to see you up."

"Yeah, such as it is. Any chance of getting some water?"

I grabbed her water glass and said, "Back in just a minute." I hurried out of the room and into the kitchen. I put her glass in the dishwasher, filled a new one, and brought it back to her.

"What do you say to getting some food in you? You haven't eaten much, if anything, for the last few days. We need to get some nutritious things going in your system."

"Thanks, Dev, but if you're thinking of cooking me a pizza or a cheeseburger, I really don't think that's going to help just now."

"No, I was thinking more along the lines of some chicken noodle soup. How does that sound?"

"Oh, that sounds wonderful. Yeah, I could go for that."

"Okay, you stay right there, and I'll bring it to you. Anything else you want?"

"Are there some oranges in the refrigerator?"

"I'll look. Do you need any help getting into the bathroom?"

She smiled and said, "Thanks for asking, but I've already been."

"How are the legs?"

"Sore. I vaguely remember having muscle cramps, and my chest and shoulders are sore as well."

"Maybe I can give you a back rub later. We'll see how you do with the soup. Let me get going on that," I said and went back into the kitchen. Thankfully, there were four cans of chicken noodle soup in the cupboard next to a can of artichoke hearts. God only knew what she planned to do with artichokes. I dumped the soup into a pan and turned on the stove. There was a packet of ciabatta rolls in the freezer. I took one out, cut it in half, and placed it in the toaster. I brought the soup and the roll in to her a few minutes later.

"Mmm-mmm, you're a good cook," she said after a couple of spoonfuls of soup. "God, how long have I been out of it? Everything seems so foggy. I remember we had dinner at Chez Charles. Was that two nights ago?"

I shook my head and said, "No, more like a week ago."

"A week?" she said, coughed, and then took a spoonful of soup.

"Yeah, a lot's been going on since then. You eat and let me fill you in." I gave her a virus update that the country was well over a hundred and thirty thousand deaths. "The states have been more or less on their own. Fortunately, Governor Walz has been doing a good job here. For some states, it's not going all that well. You want a business update?"

"Oh, God," she said and went into a coughing jag that sounded like it would really hurt. "The—" She started coughing again.

"Don't say anything, Heidi. Just listen to what's been going on."

She looked like she was going to object, which launched her into more coughing.

"Heidi, do not talk. Just eat that soup and listen. Okay?"

She nodded and slurped a spoonful of soup.

I brought her up to date as far as Tommy Benedetti and the counterfeit money. I told her about Candi Mangle with the FBI, George Turner with the Secret Service, and Delton Lange with the police. I told her about the early morning raids and the arrest of just about everyone except Tommy Benedetti. I mentioned the trash bag full of counterfeit bills from Tony Benedetti's apartment. I didn't mention Melvin Cummings attempting to break in the other night. "So that's about where you stand. You're out free and clear from that so-called investment Benedetti forced you to take."

She looked like she was going to say something. "Don't talk, Heidi. Finish up that soup and maybe go back to sleep. Nora O'Rourke has been terrific and has been checking on you twice a day. I've been checking on you twice a day, too. I can't tell you how happy I am to have you on the road to recovery." She looked like she was going to say something. "No, don't say anything. Just finish that soup. Let me check in the refrigerator and see if you have any oranges. I'll be back in a minute."

I hurried into the kitchen and opened the fridge. There were three oranges in there. I took one, peeled it, and put the slices on a plate. I brought the plate back into the bedroom. "Okay, here we—" She was asleep. I set the plate on the bedside table and picked up the empty soup bowl. I brought the soup bowl and the ciabatta slices into the kitchen. I went back and turned off the tv using the remote then carefully placed the apnea mask on her face.

Her eyes opened for a brief moment. She adjusted the mask and went back to sleep. I sent Nora a text message giving her an update. I locked up, climbed in my car, and headed out to the Benedetti house.

I pulled to a stop outside the gate and looked in. There were five cars in the paved parking area. They all looked like government vehicles, gray or black, with no whitewalls on the tires. Two of the vehicles had federal government license plates. The door to the house was closed, and nothing I could see seemed to suggest damage. So that was a good thing.

One of the garage doors on the three-car garage was open. Two guys with their shirt sleeves rolled up to their elbows were in there going through what looked like a recycling bin. I was about to pull away when Candi Mangle stepped out of the house.

She was dressed in black slacks and an untucked white blouse. She wore what looked like leopard skin flats on her feet. She opened the rear door on one of the cars and tossed something inside.

I lowered the driver's window and called, "Candi."

As she looked up, one of the guys in the garage stepped out to see who yelled. "It's okay, Bob. He's out of my office," she said and waved me forward. I climbed out of the car.

"Just couldn't stay away?" she asked as I approached.

"Checking in. Any luck?"

She shook her head. "Not really. Some general bits and pieces, credit card statements, phone records, although I don't expect them to reveal anything. They were just in a file, not hidden."

"Well, his wife Gina told me he hasn't been living here for the last ten months, so I'm guessing any important records, things he needed or wanted to hide, he probably took with him. Wherever that is."

"We're going through the place top to bottom. We've got enough with the counterfeiting to charge him and put him away. It would just be nice to shut down the entire enterprise, so he has nothing to come back to if he ever gets out. You want to come in and take a look?"

"Yeah, sure, if that's okay. How'd you get in here anyway?" I went on to describe the bowling ball hole in the door at Coco Cumming's place.

"We had someone watching the place starting last evening. They never saw any activity. We rang the doorbell a number of times. One of the guys is pretty adept at picking locks. We got in, the alarm was off, and the place was empty. Come on in, and you can see for yourself."

I followed her into the house. Once inside, we stood in a small entry area. Winter coats hung in a closet with bifold doors that were pulled open. There were four steps leading down to a lower level. Six steps led up to a kitchen and what looked like a combination dining area and living room. The upper and lower levels appeared to look out the back of the house and onto a large lawn and White Bear lake. A hallway went off to the right, toward what I guessed would be bedrooms. Two guys were going through cabinets in the lower level. Another guy was seated at a desk in front of a computer. Two more guys were up in the living room. They were in the process of tipping over a couch and waving a wand of some sort over the thing.

"What are they looking for?" I asked.

"Just about anything. In the old days, we would have slit the cushions and the back. Now we get an image. It's faster and more efficient," Candi said.

"I could use one of those at home to help me find my car keys."

"You look like you've never been here before," Candi said.

"I haven't, at least never inside. I spoke to Gina Benedetti outside twice, but only for a couple of minutes and never got in here. I never made it into the garage either."

"Well, so far, you didn't miss much. Lovely home, of a sort, just none of the criminal evidence we were hoping to find." We chatted for maybe five minutes, never leaving the entry area.

"You think you'll finish up today?" I asked.

Candi nodded and said, "Probably the next hour or so. We've got a list of phone numbers and some other items, but as I said, nothing we were hoping for." She held out her hand, signaling it was time for me to leave.

"Keep me posted if you find anything. Oh, and don't forget, Tubby Gustafson thought Benedetti might be sleeping in DeCulo's stretch limo."

She nodded, looked unimpressed, and didn't say anything.

"Hey, Candi?" someone called from the lower level, and she ushered me out the door.

Forty-Six

I went back to the office and basically twiddled my thumbs for an hour then headed over to Heidi's. She was asleep with the mask on. I got her a fresh glass of water and drove home. I got Morton more or less settled in for the night then drove over to Brandon and Tracy's and took up my position on the bench across the street.

I sat out there until it was dark, waited another thirty minutes as the mosquitos lowered my blood level before I finally went home. I watched a movie and slept fitfully because tomorrow I was supposed to meet with Tracy Kelly. I had absolutely nothing concrete to tell her, other than my suspicions about Brandon maybe being gay. I would hasten to add that they were merely suspicions. I'd be armed with the non-incriminating handful of photos taken at 'Going My Way,' proving beyond a doubt that I'd done a horse shit investigation.

Morning came all too soon. I was up before my alarm. I showered, shaved, and went downstairs and turned on my computer. I heard Morton jump off the bed maybe an hour later. I let him outside, had another cup of coffee, and let him back in. We were down at the office before Louie. I put on a fresh pot of coffee and then watched out the window as Louie parked behind my car. As the stairs began to creak with his ascent, I filled his coffee mug and set it on the picnic table.

"Mumph," he said by way of a greeting and dropped into his chair. After a few minutes and maybe half a mug of coffee, he asked, "How'd things go yesterday?"

I gave him the rundown. I told him about the search of Tony Benedetti's apartment and the trash bag of counterfeit currency. I described Coco Cumming's arrest and Melvin Cummings being wheeled out by EMTs. I mentioned Heidi's continued improvement and finished up with the search of Benedetti's home.

"Sounds to me like you had one hell of a day. Anything on Tommy Benedetti?"

"Vanished. Seems to have disappeared into thin air. I forgot to mention I paid a visit to Tubby Gustafson yesterday. He seemed to think Benedetti might be sleeping in the stretch limo."

Louie seemed to think about that for a moment, then nodded and said, "That may not be as farfetched as it sounds. Did you pass that on to the police?"

"I told Candi Mangle about it. She didn't react one way or the other."

Louie drained his mug and got up to refill it. "Maybe tell that cop who went through the apartment and arrested Coco."

"Delton Lange, yeah, that's a good idea. I'll give Candi twenty-four hours to act on it. If she doesn't, I'll call Delton. It just sounds so crazy."

"Which is exactly why it might be true," Louie said.

My phone rang. Tracy Kelly, the call I'd been dreading. "Hi Tracy, I was just about to call you," I lied.

"Are you still able to meet today, Dev?"

I wanted to tell her I didn't have any information. Instead, I bit my tongue and said, "I sure am. You name the time and place, and I'll be there."

"How about same as before, the Japanese Garden over at Como Park? I'll bring lunch. Do you like sushi?"

"Tracy, why don't I bring lunch? I can—"

"Oh, no, you've already done more than enough work."

Oh, God, I thought, can it get any worse?

"I'll bring lunch, Dev. I make my own sushi. You'll love it, and it's such a lovely day. We can social distance. The sushi and the garden will put me in a relaxing mood for your report."

"All right," I said, doomed to failure. "What time works best for you?"

"If you don't mind, I'd like to avoid the noontime visitors to the garden. Would a quarter after one be too late?"

"No, that works for me. I'll see you then."

"Oh, wonderful. I'm so looking forward to meeting you and hearing what you've found out. I've been a basket case over all this."

"Not to worry. I'll see you in a couple of hours," I said, and she disconnected.

Louie stared at me for a moment and said, "You're not looking too happy. Who died?"

"Oh, man, my case from hell. I maybe have some so-so information on her husband. I emphasize the word maybe. Nothing proof positive, but the little I have suggests he might be gay. Maybe having an affair with a young blonde guy. Honest to God, I just want to scream."

"So just tell her the truth. Between this whole Benedetti affair and Heidi ending up with the virus, you haven't been able to concentrate, haven't had the time. Tell her you'll refund her money, or you'll start over, whatever she would prefer."

"Yeah. I suppose, but it's going to suck, big time."

"Look at it this way, Dev. If this is the worst thing that you'll have to deal with in the next month, you've gotten off pretty easy. No one is dead. Heidi is on the road to recovery. Benedetti is pretty much out of the picture. It's all good. Just tell her the truth. She'll understand."

"I suppose, but this is still going to suck."

"Dev, take a chill pill and relax. Explain the situation. She seems nice enough. She'll probably want to help you calm down."

"God." I checked the time on my phone. I had three hours before I had to tell Tracy that I didn't have any news. I basically sat at my desk and stared out the window. I didn't even get my binoculars out to check the apartment across the street. What was the point? Besides, the way the day was shaping up all the shades would be pulled anyway.

On the one hand, the minutes seemed to drag. On the other hand, all too soon, it was suddenly time to leave and meet Tracy.

Forty-Seven

I headed over to Como Park. Wouldn't you know, I made it through just about every stoplight along the way. I suddenly found myself pulling into the parking lot for the Japanese Garden. There were only two other cars in the parking lot, so I was able to park almost next to the garden. I walked down the asphalt path to the entrance.

The garden is peaceful, tranquil, and lovely. Large rocks, a gorgeous stone walk, bonsai plantings, a little water pond with Koi fish and flowering lily pads. There's a little stream flowing downhill over rocks emitting a calming little splash. It really was lovely and, at the moment, totally lost on me. I sat on a bench and felt sorry for myself, dreading the moment when Tracy would show up.

An elderly woman sat on the far side of the pond with her legs crossed appearing to meditate. All I could think about was the disappointment I was going to be for Tracy.

A mom with two young boys walked into the garden. The boys looked like brothers, maybe six and eight. The smaller of the two made a move to push his older brother into the pond, which earned a cross word from mom. They all turned on their heels and headed right back out to their car.

A tanned looking guy with a white face mask strolled in a minute or two later. He was muscular, dressed in shorts, a black t-shirt, and had a black backpack slung over his shoulder. An image of a bat in the gay pride rainbow colors was emblazoned across the front of his t-shirt. His hair was shaved on the sides and black and curly on the top. He followed the path around the pool. He strolled past the woman meditating and was about to pass me, but instead of walking past, he stopped. "Mr. Haskell?" he said in a soft voice. He wiggled his shoulders as he raised his right hand and basically flopped it in my general direction.

I didn't recognize him, and right now, I wasn't in the mood for a friendly catch-up conversation with someone. "Yeah," I said, not sounding all that nice.

He smiled, extended a hand, and said, "Hi, I'm Tracy Kelly. It's nice to finally meet you."

I sat and stared.

"Mr. Haskell?"

"Oh, Tracy, sorry about that. I was, umm, meditating and was in an inner place. Nice to meet you. Very nice to meet you. Please, call me Dev."

He set the backpack down next to me and then took a seat on the opposite end of the bench. "Oh, say, listen," again with the hand flop. "I absolutely love it here. It's so relaxing. It's like a secret little place, right here in the middle of the city. Never more than two or three people around, quiet, private. I like to think of it as mine." He shrugged his shoulders and grinned.

"Yeah, it's very lovely," I said, steering away from why we were meeting. I was trying to get my head around the fact that Tracy was a guy. It suddenly made sense that his husband, Brandon Lovelace, would end up at 'Going My Way.' "You were down in Chicago?"

He smiled and said, "Yes, Evanston, actually. My parents own some buildings, and my mother was transferring the titles to us children. I'm the only one not in the business. But they still needed my signature."

"Everything go okay?"

He smiled. "Oh, yes, we all get along well, very well. I'll have to go on a diet for the next two months, water and salads, but it was nice to catch up. Listen, before we eat, can we get the bad news over with? I'm good. I'm in a place where I can accept whatever you've found out, and I'll just deal with it. So please, just tell me where things stand."

I was still trying to get my head around the thought that I'd completely misread a major fact in the investigation. "Okay, first of all, Tracy," I pulled my wallet from my pocket, reached in, and pulled out three hundred-dollar bills. I handed the bills to him and said, "Let me return these to you. Due to circumstances beyond my control, I haven't been able to be as diligent as I would like in relation to your investigation." I went on and gave him a summation of Tommy Benedetti's idiocy and Heidi's virus. I may have elaborated my interaction in both cases.

"Oh, Dev, I'm so sorry. I want to give you a big hug, but with social distancing…"

"Thanks, Tracy, not to worry, in both instances, things are heading toward a positive conclusion. I was able to conduct some investigation into Brandon." I went on to tell him about time spent on the bench across the street, running along the River Boulevard, watching outside the Northwestern Building, and last, but not least, the incident at 'Going My Way.'

When I mentioned the bar, Tracy sat back with his mouth open and just stared. He suddenly looked deflated.

"I'm sorry to be the one to tell you this, Tracy. I mean, I'm always hoping I can tell clients their suspicions are unfounded."

"But we go there. In fact, it's where we had our first date. How could he? Why?" He looked over at me with watery eyes, about to cry. "Who is he seeing? Who was he with?"

"Well, that gets a little complicated. Certainly, the one guy was at your place a couple of nights. I—"

"Our home? He actually carried on his affair in our home?"

"Yeah, sorry to say, and then they met on another night at 'Going My Way.' That's where the third guy joined them. They all seemed to be *enjoying* each other's company. I have some pictures if—"

"No, no," he said, and a tear rolled down his cheek. "I knew something was up. Oh, I just knew it. I just had a sense there was something going on. But he gets so damn private sometimes, and he doesn't tell me. Oh," he said and began to sob.

"I'm sorry, Tracy. I wish there was something else I could tell you. I just hate giving this kind of news to—"

"Let me see the pictures. I want to see them."

"It's just the three of them in the bar, hugging at the table."

"Let me see them," he said. "Chances are I know who it is, probably that slut Bishop. He's always had a thing for Brandon, I could tell. I just knew it."

I pulled my cellphone out and brought up the images from the other night. "Here you go. I can print these images and get them to you a little later today if you want."

Tracy sniffled, wiped away another set of tears, and took my cellphone. He looked at the first image, looked at me, and then back at my cellphone. He moved to the next image and the one after that.

"Bishop wasn't the name I came up with," I said. "I ran a check on the blonde guy's license plate. He drives a blue BMW. His name is—"

"Stop," Tracy said and laughed. I wasn't sure if he was completely losing it or if the pictures just confirmed his worst suspicions. "Oh, this is great," he said and laughed some more. He turned and looked at me, brushed at the tears running down both cheeks, and said, "His name is Dylan Finch."

"Yeah, that's right. You know this guy?"

"Oh, yeah. He's Brandon's nephew. Dylan's father died in a car crash, oh God, must be twenty years ago. Brandon's been his surrogate father ever since. He's a wonderful kid. Well, not a kid anymore. Now I get it. Dylan is in the process of coming out of the closet. He was in a relationship with this other guy, Danny Andersen. Brandon's been giving the two of them advice for the past three or four months, ever since Dylan first told us. Oh, God," he laughed and held the phone to his chest. "Oh, thank God, hilarious."

"Yeah, so I knew it didn't seem right, didn't seem like an affair on the side," I said, trying to cover myself.

"Oh, Dev, you made my day. I can't thank you enough." He laughed again and brushed more tears from his cheeks. "Oh, god, this is hilarious. Oh, all right. Let's eat. I'm suddenly starving." With that, he opened his backpack and brought out two long rolls of sushi wrapped in cellophane. "I made these this morning. We'll start with this one. It's a California roll, crab and avocado. This other one is a Philadelphia roll, smoked salmon, cucumber, cream cheese," he said and smiled. He brought out two paper cups and then a bottle of chilled saki. He glanced around, quickly filled the glasses, and then returned the bottle to the backpack.

We sat and ate sushi, drank saki, and Tracy couldn't stop laughing. Eventually, the sushi was devoured and it was time to leave. We walked out of the Japanese Garden together. Tracy was parked two spots away from me in a black Prius. Unfortunately, there was a gray SUV parked between our cars.

Forty-eight

As we approached, both front doors on the SUV swung open. Tommy Benedetti and Victor DeCulo stepped out of the car.

"Hey, Tracy, umm, I'm going to talk to these two guys. You better take off."

"What? Dev, I still want to give that money back to you. You can't believe how happy I am that—"

"Hey Tracy, you better go," I nodded toward Benedetti and the other thug coming from the gray SUV. Benedetti was dressed in a wrinkly gray suit, a white shirt with a food stain on the pocket, and no tie. He looked like he'd slept in the outfit for more than just one night. He needed a shave. As an accessory to his suit, he held a pistol in his right hand.

"Hold on, Tommy. My friend was just leaving. Go on, Tracy. Get out of here. I'll give you a call and—"

"No, Dev. I wanna help you. I'm not leaving you. Not after what you did for me."

When Benedetti heard his voice, he laughed. "So, Haskell, all of a sudden, you're batting for the other side. Go on. Get the hell out of here while you still can, you limp wristed—"

"I'm staying with Dev, and I suggest you two gentlemen make other plans. Your behavior is uncalled for."

Benedetti looked at DeCulo and shook his head. DeCulo took a step forward just as Tracy spun and delivered a roundhouse kick to the guy's chin. DeCulo's eyes rolled up in the back of his head, and he dropped to the ground.

Benedetti began to raise his pistol as Tracy gave him a quick jab in the throat. Benedetti dropped the pistol, his mouth opened, his tongue hung out, and he wrapped both hands around his neck. His face was scarlet. Tracy gave him a solid kick in the crotch. As he bent over, Tracy grabbed him by the ears and brought a knee up into his face then gently lowered him to the ground. It all happened in about just a few seconds.

"Whoa, where did you learn that stuff?"

"As a kid. My dad knew I was different from my brothers, and he sent me to martial arts school when I was ten. Been involved ever since, for the last twenty-some years. You know these two guys?"

"I know him, or actually, about him," I said, pointing to Benedetti. "Cops are looking for him. Probably be a good idea if we got out of here. I'll phone the police on the way."

Tracy nodded and said, "Do me a favor and email me those images, will you?"

"I'd be happy to, Tracy. Glad it worked out."

I watched as he backed out of his parking place and left. I pulled some Kleenex from my glove compartment and picked up Benedetti's pistol from the ground. I tossed it on the passenger seat and started my car. Benedetti was in a fetal position. DeCulo was up on all fours bleeding from his nose and mouth. I backed up past the two of them then tooted my horn and drove out of the parking lot.

I stopped at a Walmart on the way back to the office. I went inside, purchased a flip-top burner phone for fifteen bucks, and called 911 from the Walmart parking lot.

"911. What's your emergency?"

"Umm, I was just leaving the Japanese Garden in Como Park, and there were two guys fighting in the parking lot. They were hitting each other. I think one of them had a gun," I said, looking at Benedetti's pistol on my passenger seat.

"We've already dispatched officers, and they are en route," the dispatcher said.

I disconnected and snapped the top off the phone. I pulled my car over to the trash bins alongside the building, tossed the two pieces of cellphone into two different bins, and headed back to the office.

Forty-nine

Morton was the only one in the office when I got back. The coffee pot was empty so I turned off the burner. I hooked my phone up to the computer, downloaded the images from 'Going My Way,' and emailed them to Tracy. I thought about taking the rest of the day off then remembered I was supposed to report to Tubby Gustafson.

I drove home and let Morton out into the backyard so he could enjoy the afternoon. I drove over to Tubby's and pressed the intercom at the front gate.

"Yeah," came the not so friendly response.

"Oh, hi. Dev Haskell to see Mr. Gustafson at his request. I have an update for him on an individual."

The intercom clicked, and I waited, then waited some more. Finally, the iron gate began to roll back. I hopped in my car and drove up the circular drive. I pulled in next to a dark blue Mercedes. As I got out of my car, one of the thugs at the front door shouted, "Just wait in your car. The boss is meeting with someone for a couple of minutes." I settled back in behind the wheel and waited.

I checked my watch at a quarter after, at half-past, and at a quarter to. Eventually, there was a knock on my window that woke me up. "He can see you now," the thug who'd told me to stay in my car said. I followed him up to the front door, and the two of them put me through the search process with the metal detector wand.

Once they were finished, the guy with the wand said, "Take a seat over there." He pointed to a black metal chair in the shape of a butterfly. The thing was splattered with bird droppings.

"Really? You want me to sit here? With all that bird—"

"Just get your dumb ass over there before I make you lick the thing clean," he said. He stood about six-five, muscular, with tattooed arms and a chain tattooed around his neck. I decided it might be best if I stood over by the chair and quickly headed in that direction. I stood next to the butterfly chair for just a minute or two before the front door opened and a guy stepped out of Tubby's mansion.

He looked about six-one, maybe mid-fifties with slicked-back black hair, a pencil mustache, and dark beady eyes. He wore a black silk suit and, with the red scar along his jawline, looked like something out of a Godfather movie.

"How's it going fellas?" he said, as he smiled at the two thugs, and headed for the dark blue Mercedes.

"Fine, Mr. Griffin," the guy who'd called me dumb ass not five minutes ago said.

"Have a nice rest of the day, sir," the other thug called to him.

Once he backed the Mercedes out of the parking spot and headed toward the gate, the 'Have a nice rest of the day' guy opened the front door and said, "Let's go. Get in here, dip shit."

I hurried inside the mansion, and they pulled the door closed behind me. The guy who was usually attempting to work a crossword puzzle was reading a comic book today. He looked up for a moment then went back to reading until he finished the page before he stood and said, "Arms out."

He searched me then led me to the small room beneath the staircase. As we walked across the entry, I noticed three AR-15s and three thirty-round magazines lying at the base of the staircase. Once I was locked in the room, I sat down. An empty crystal glass rested on the table. Apparently, Mr. Griffin had received a little better service than I was used to.

I pushed the button on the computer. Tubby burst across the screen a moment later, actually dressed and seated at his desk. He was wearing a black mask with a Superman logo, but it was pulled down onto his chins. The two massage women didn't appear to be in the room. A crystal glass matching the empty one in front of me rested on Tubby's desk. There was a small amount of brown liquid in the glass. I guessed it wasn't tea.

"Let's hear it, Haskell. I haven't got all day."

"Thank you for seeing me, sir."

"Get to the point," Tubby said, shaking his head.

"Just an update, sir. I heard a rumor that Tommy Benedetti and some other guy were involved in an altercation over at the Japanese Garden in Como Park. Apparently, it did not go well for them."

"Who did you hear this from?"

"A friend of mine was driving past and saw the police there."

"I see. Is this friend able to recognize Benedetti on sight?"

I didn't expect that question. "I think so, sir, because he called me and mentioned the counterfeit currency and the arrest of people involved with Benedetti. I know the Federal authorities searched his home out in Mahtomedi, and they arrested the woman he was supposed to be living with and her brother. I—"

"Old news Haskell, old news. Did you mention to your police friends that Benedetti was sleeping in the stretch limo?"

"I mentioned it to a person with the FBI, sir."

Tubby shook his head. "Not what I asked."

"Oh, umm, I was planning to tell the police, sir."

"Might be best for all involved to wait until tomorrow. How is your friend doing? The woman with the virus."

"Oh, she seems to be on the mend, slowly but surely."

"Amazing, she's survived your so-called care. What did you say her name was?"

"Heidi."

"She have a last name, Haskell?"

"Bauer, Heidi Bauer," I said, wondering where this was going.

"Anything else to report?"

"No, sir, I—" Tubby reached for his glass, and the screen suddenly went blank. I waited a couple of minutes just in case he came back on, but he didn't. I knocked on the door and said, "Okay. I'm finished. Hello. Hello? Anyone out there? I'm all finished in here. Is anyone—"

"Will you relax?" the guy said as he opened the door. He held the comic book in his hand. I think he was on the same page he'd been attempting to read when I first came in. I hurried out of the room and made my way to the front door. Along the way, I noticed the AR-15s and the thirty-round magazines were gone. "Thank you," I said to the two idiots standing out front as I walked past.

"Get your ass out of here," one of them replied. So much for trying to be nice. I climbed in my car and drove to the front gate, waited for a half-minute as the gate slowly opened, and fled the scene.

I drove over to Heidi's to check on her. As I opened the front door, I could hear music coming from her bedroom, and I gowned up. Heidi was sitting in bed watching tv. She was wearing a t-shirt, her hair was brushed, and it looked like her nails had recently been done.

"Hi, Dev," she said, giving me a quick look before refocusing on the tv. Some woman in a blue see-through outfit was dancing with two guys. At the moment, they were lifting her up above their shoulders.

"Oh, sorry, am I interrupting?"

"Dancing with the Stars. I've seen this one before. It's really good."

I couldn't imagine. There was a plate on the bedside table with a crust of toast and remnants of what looked like grape jelly. An empty bowl held a spoon and two noodles, no doubt chicken noodle soup. At least she appeared to be eating. "Can I get you anything?"

She continued to stare at the tv. The two guys were tossing the woman back and forth at the moment." Orange juice, if there's any left. Maybe take that plate, the bowl, and the glasses into the kitchen. Take one of the Weight Watcher meals out of the freezer." Heidi was definitely getting back to normal.

I carried the dishes out to the dishwasher, loaded them, added soap, and turned the thing on. An empty soup can, a half-loaf of bread, and the jelly jar were on the counter. I put them away then pulled out the carton of orange juice and emptied it into a glass. It filled the glass not quite halfway. There were a half-dozen Weight Watcher's meals stacked in her freezer. I took the one off the top of the stack and set it on the kitchen counter.

I brought the orange juice back to her room and said, "I'm going to run to the grocery store for you. Anything special you want or need?"

"Bring me my notebook from the office and a pen, so I can make you a list."

Yeah, she was definitely getting back to normal.

Epilogue

I woke the following morning to the news that two men were found shot to death in the back of a stretch limo that had been parked in a garage over on University Ave. Names were being withheld pending notification of family. Not that I had to wait. Victor DeCulo's limousine service was located on University, and I was willing to bet that he and Tommy Benedetti were the victims. That was confirmed twenty-four hours later, along with the information that they had been shot multiple times, not three or four times, but more like a hundred. I remembered the three AR-15s and the magazines resting at the bottom of Tubby's staircase and was pretty sure what had happened. Aaron LaZelle, my pal in homicide, told me later that the bodies were literally in pieces.

Arnold Benedetti, Tommy's uncle, was arrested, and his printing company, Inkoholic, was shut down. Delton Lane and George Turner had gone through the place and found evidence. At age seventy-eight, if Arnold was sentenced to more than twenty-four months, there was a good chance he'd never get out.

Gina Benedetti and her sons left town for California a few days later. I had phoned her as they were getting ready to board a plane out to LA. We had a quick conversation where she told me she'd signed paperwork turning the house back to the bank just the day before. Apparently, Tommy had a fairly substantial life insurance policy so it sounded like she and the boys would be okay. I told her to stay in touch just before she rang off, but I'd be surprised if I ever heard from her again.

Four days later Tony Benedetti was listed as one of eleven deaths that day from the virus. In an odd way the news of 'only' eleven deaths was celebrated as a decline.

Heidi continued to improve, and after a couple of weeks, she was back to about ninety-eight percent. I'd been over and repainted her kitchen wall. She was still tired and taking a nap every day, but the naps were short. She was back working at least half-days. She had expected the LeMax Fund to be facing hard times, but apparently, at the last minute, some investor had shown up, so all was good.

I phoned my take-out order into Carmelo's, picked it up a half-hour later, and drove over to Heidi's. She had the wine chilling in an ice bucket and the kitchen counter set for two. A Waterford crystal wine glass was placed on either side of the ice bucket.

Heidi was wearing tight black slacks, a white silk blouse, and a diamond pendant. I set the meals on the end of the kitchen counter. "Heidi, this is the best I've seen you looking in weeks."

"Oh, thanks. I think I'm finally back to normal. Heck of a way to lose eight pounds. Open the wine, Dev, and let's make a toast."

I twisted off the cap and filled the crystal wine glasses with chilled Sauvignon Blanc. I handed a glass to Heidi and raised my glass. "To your recovery, thank God. You had us worried there for a while," I said.

"Oh, boy, talk about a lesson. I have nothing to complain about. Let me tell you. To good health, Dev," she said, raising her glass. "Nothing else matters as long as we have that." We clinked glasses, took a sip, and Heidi set her glass down. "I'll tell you that virus was like the worst hangover I've ever had, times a thousand. Oh, awful, just awful."

"And," I said, raising my glass again, "you mentioned you found a new investor, and the LeMax Fund is good to go."

She grinned and clinked glasses with me, took a small sip, and set her glass on the counter. I pulled the bottle from the bucket and refilled my glass. I was about to top up Heidi's, but she said, "I'm okay for right now, Dev."

"Okay, no pressure. So, how did you find this investor?"

Oh, that's the funny thing. Well, one of them, he actually found me. He phoned me about two weeks ago. I put him off just because I was still pretty exhausted and taking long naps every day. He phoned again last week, and we met down at the office. Interesting guy, he even mentioned you."

"Me?"

"Yeah, he said he read something about you, or someone mentioned you to him. I can't remember. Anyway, things are about to take off," she said and grinned.

"What does he do?"

"To tell you the truth, I'm not really sure. He looks like he walked out of some old movie."

"I'm not following," I said.

"Oh, you know, dark slicked-back hair. He's tall, maybe a little taller than you. Black eyes, you literally can't see the pupil in his eyes. He's got this just thin line for a mustache. What do they call that, a pen mustache?"

"A pencil mustache."

"Oh, yeah, that's it, and then a deep red scar along his jawline." As she said that, she ran her hand along the length of her jawbone.

The light suddenly went on in my head. "Mr. Griffin," I said, remembering the guy I'd seen leaving Tubby Gustafson's.

"Yeah, that's right. You know him? Brutus Griffin?"

I shook my head, "No, just saw him once, and he made an impression. Drives a dark blue Mercedes. He actually knows Tubby Gustafson."

"The criminal?"

"Yeah."

"Well, he paid with a certified check, Dev. He was an absolute gentleman. Besides, I know you, and people that are aware of that are still friends of mine." She pushed her glass toward the bucket, smiled, and said, "I'm thinking we should go into the bedroom and celebrate my recovery."

The End

Thank you for taking the time to read **Cash Up Front.** If you enjoyed the read and would like to leave a review it really, really helps. I'm indie published. Thank you.

Don't miss this sample of **Dream House,** the next book in the Dev Haskell series.

Sneak Peek

Dream House

Second Edition

MIKE FARICY

Prologue

The mechanic stepped back and said, "You're good to go, Mr. Wazinski. We changed the oil and filled your window washer fluid. Tires are fine, air conditioner works. We installed a new lock on the driver's door and a new ignition. I've got two keys in the office. Come on in, and we can settle up. Looks like whoever tried to steal your truck was ready to take off. They had it all set to hot wire. Good thing you caught 'em when you did."

Ken flashed his sparkling white teeth and said, "You just can't make it up. Wouldn't that just piss you off? I'm about to drive half-way across the country, and some idiot decides to steal my truck just as I'm getting ready to leave."

"Yeah, the world's full of 'em. Come on. We'll get you settled up and on your way."

Ken followed him through one of the work bays at the gas station and into a rear office. "Here's the list of work we did. Oh yeah, and we put a padlock on that door to the back. You don't want some idiot getting into the back of the truck. They'll have you emptied out before you know it. Now is this going to be credit card or cash?"

"I'll be running it on my business credit card," Wazinski said as he pulled the card out of his wallet.

"That's fine. Now, we add on a one-and-a-half percent charge to all credit card payments."

"I don't blame you. Surprised it's not more. Here you go," Wazinski said and handed him the credit card.

Jerry looked at the card. "Able Manufacturing? You're over in Compton, right?"

Wazinski gave a slight nod and said, "That's one of our locations. We're all over California. Say, I should probably get going. I've got a lot of miles ahead of me."

"Oh yeah, sure." Jerry ran the credit card and handed Ken the keys. "Okay, you're good to go. Safe journey. Been a pleasure meeting you."

"Thanks, appreciate the quick service. I'm going to mention you to all my friends, and I'll see if the company can get in touch. We got a fleet of trucks, and there's always something that needs to be taken care of."

"Thanks. If you do that, I'm sure we could work something out, make it worth your while."

"I'll get on it," Wazinski said. He headed out to the parking area and climbed in the truck.

The mechanic stepped back from the raised hood and wiped his hands on the rag draped over the radiator. "What is with that dude? His eyes were all squinty, that forehead, the cheeks, the lips. Was he in some major accident?"

"You got me. Strange duck, that's for sure. You look inside that truck?"

"Yeah, full of boxes. I'd guess he came out here to be a movie star, and after waiting tables for ten years, decided to head back to wherever home is. I'll be finished with this one in about fifteen minutes if you want to give them a call," the mechanic said and bent down under the hood.

Wazinski checked the mirrors, and waited for two woman to walk past before he pulled onto the street. Three blocks away, he stopped at the light. A homeless man held out his baseball cap and looked hopeful.

Wazinski flashed his sparkling white teeth and rolled down the window.

"God bless you, sir," the homeless man said. His eyes were bloodshot, and he was missing his front teeth.

Ken dropped the Able Manufacturing credit card into the hat and got a questioning look in response.

"Good for only one day," he said, laughed as the light turned green, and he drove off.

One

ouie pulled his Ford Fiesta to the curb in front of the police impound lot. The thing was a faded orange color and hadn't been washed since the day he bought it back in 2016. It shuddered for a painful five seconds when he turned the engine off. "Dev, you sure you don't want me to wait for you?"

"No, thanks Louie, but I don't know how long this is gonna take."

"I thought you said you had the winning bid?"

"Not exactly, I had the highest online bid as of ten o'clock this morning. But the auction starts in twenty minutes, and there are lots of guys like those two who are probably here every month bidding on cars." I nodded at the two guys heading into the office. One wore a navy-blue sport coat and jeans, and the other had a white shirt with a button-down collar and dress slacks. I was wearing cut-offs, a faded t-shirt, and was armed with a cashier's check for two-thousand-seven-hundred-and-fifty dollars.

"You got your check?" Louie asked as a red BMW parked across the street from us. A guy in a grey suit hopped out and headed inside the building.

"Yeah, certified, I just hope some regular attendee doesn't outbid me. I've never been to a police auction before."

"Well, it's basically cars that have been confiscated in an arrest or left on the side of the road. Who knows, all these folks might be here to bid on the same fancy car. Look, I got some cash," Louie said, pulling out his wallet. He reached in, pulled out some bills, and handed them to me.

"Oh, Louie, I can't take—"

"Come on, man. Take it. I know you're good for it. Just in case some jerk tries to go ten bucks over your bid."

I took the bills and counted them, three twenties, a ten, a five and a bunch of ones. "Oh, thanks, Louie. Eighty-seven bucks. Much appreciated."

"My pleasure. Now you give me a call if you need a lift after this."

"Well, hopefully, I'll be driving back to the office within the next ninety minutes. It's the third lot on the list."

"Better hurry in there. I'll see you back at the office, Dev."

I shouted a thanks as I climbed out. Louie's car emitted a dark cloud of exhaust as it sprang to life. He gave a wave and pulled away from the curb.

"There's one for you to bid on, Jack," some guy said to his friend eyeing Louie's Ford Fiesta.

"I don't think so," the friend chuckled. They crossed the street laughing and headed into the building as Louie disappeared around the corner.

I followed them inside, up a flight of stairs, took a right, followed the arrow marked 'AUCTION,' and went down another flight of stairs. Two women in shorts, t-shirts, and baseball caps sat at a table at the edge of a large parking lot filled with cars and a few trucks.

"We'll need a driver's license, proof of insurance, and five dollars for the bid card," one of them said to me. I pulled my license out of my wallet and handed it to her. I had the insurance papers in my back pocket and laid them on the table next to the license. I tossed Louie's five-dollar bill on top of the insurance papers.

She typed my name, address, and insurance info into the computer. "Okay, you're good to go, Mr. Haskell. Good luck," she said a minute later and handed me a cardboard card with the number one-fifty-one on it along with my driver's license and insurance papers.

I wandered into the center of the lot. Over two hundred cars and trucks were parked, one next to the other. Vehicles abandoned in the April blizzard that dumped twelve inches on the city. Stolen vehicles no one had bothered to claim. Vehicles parked too long in one spot that were eventually towed, and apparently, no one missed them. They all had a number written on the front windshield in yellow marker.

I glanced at number three, the vehicle I would hopefully get. I didn't go near the car for fear of attracting attention. I wandered through the lot, looking at various cars until a loud, high-pitched squeak sounded over a loudspeaker followed by a voice that said, "Good morning, ladies and gentlemen. We want to thank you all for coming. Before we get started, the four portable units at the back of the lot will be serving as our restrooms today. All vehicles are sold as-is. All sales are final and must be paid with either a certified check or cash by four o'clock this afternoon. Now, if you'll gather round, we'll begin in just a minute."

It was more like ten minutes, but eventually, the auction started. The first lot was a 2014 Mercedes C-class, blue with a crack running across the entire base of the windshield. Bidding began at twelve-five and ended at an even fifteen hundred. The next vehicle was a 2011 Toyota Camry with a major dent in the driver's door. Four bids were given, and the vehicle sold for forty-nine hundred.

The next car up was the one I'd bid on. "Let's move on to lot number three," the auctioneer said. "It's a two thousand nine Ford Crown Victoria Police Interceptor. Black, with a hundred and sixty-nine thousand miles on it. Bidding will begin at two-thousand-seven-hundred-and-fifty dollars." The auctioneer raised his voice on the word fifty, and I could feel my heart pounding in my ears.

He waited a moment and repeated, "Lot number three. A two thousand nine Ford Crown Victoria Police

Interceptor. Black, with a hundred and sixty-nine thousand miles on it. Do I have a bid? A two thousand nine Ford Crown Victoria. We're starting at two-thousand-seven-hundred-and-fifty dollars. Do I have a bid? Going once, going twice, sold for two-thousand-seven-hundred-and-fifty dollars. Lot number four, a two thousand thirteen Chevrolet Traverse. White, with one hundred and twenty-two thousand miles…

I drowned the rest of the auction out and hurried over to the table with the two women in t-shirts. There were still people just coming into the auction, and I had to wait in line behind four people before I could pay. I gave them my check and had to wait for another hour before the auctioneer took a break, and I could drive my Crown Victoria out of the lot. Thankfully, it started on the first try.

TWO

I stopped at Rooster's Bar-B-Que just up the street from the office. I got two pulled pork bar-b-que sandwiches for Louie and me and a bone for Morton. Morton met me at the door as I stepped into the office. Louie slowly opened his eyes and sat up in his desk chair.

"I hope you haven't had lunch already," I said, as I placed the Rooster's bag on his picnic table desk.

"Mmm, no, this is perfect. I can use a little break."

I decided not to mention he'd been asleep. I set a Styrofoam sandwich container down in front of him and settled in behind my desk. The bar-b-que smell permeated the office once we lifted the lids on our carryout containers. Morton gave me an orgasmic look as he rubbed his head on the pork bone and seemed to settle even deeper onto his pillow.

There was no talking for the next few minutes as we attacked the bar-b-que. Eventually, Louie swallowed his most recent mouthful and said, "So, if you're back already, either you got the car, or someone outbid you. Which one is it?"

"I got it. It's parked out on the street, right behind yours. Before I forget, let me return this cash to you. I still owe you twenty-five bucks."

"Not a problem. So you got the car. Great," he said, standing and stepping over to the front window. "Let me just take a look and— Dev, are you kidding me? You can't be serious. That black Crown Vic? That's the car you bought?"

"Yeah, and no one else bid against me."

Louie shook his head. "There's a surprise. Really, that black Crown Vic?"

"Yeah. Why are there two out there?" I made a show of pulling my binoculars out of a desk drawer and scanning the street.

"You bought that Crown Vic?"

"Yeah. You like it?" Along with being black, it had tires with absolutely no whitewall. There was a moveable spotlight mounted just above the sideview mirror on the driver's side. The front of the car featured two large rubber bumpers running from the front bumper up to the top of the chrome grill, designed to push stalled vehicles.

"I don't know. It would just seem to me, given the business you're in, that maybe you might have thought of something a bit more understated."

"What do you mean, understated?"

"You know, for when you're supposed to be keeping a quiet eye on someone or something. When you're supposed to watch someone sneak in or out of an office or from someone's house. How many times a year does someone ask you to take photographs of a significant other they suspect of dabbling? Do you ever attempt to follow someone unobserved? Ever think about blending into a crowd?"

"Mmm, yeah. I guess I didn't really consider any of that. I was more focused on the fact that it's bulletproof, and I was so blown away by the speedometer. It can do up to a hundred and twenty-nine miles per hour and goes from zero to sixty in five seconds. A pal from the department motor pool turned me onto this one going up for auction. They did a whole revamp of the engine, everything from new battery to spark plugs and new fuel filters, added a new fuel pump. They checked the ignition, rotated the tires."

"After they did all that work they put it up for auction for two grand?"

"Two-thousand-seven-hundred-and-fifty," I corrected.

"Okay," Louie said, settling back in behind his picnic table and finishing the last half of his sandwich. He ran a finger through the bar-b-que sauce left in the container and licked it a couple of times. A half-hour later, he stuffed his laptop in his computer bag and headed toward the door. "I've got a court appearance at three, but I should be back after that, hopefully. You up for The Spot later today?"

"Yeah, I can do that. I'll buy."

Louie smiled. "Yeah, you're right. You will. See you over there," he said and headed out the door.

I tossed the Styrofoam containers in my wastebasket, picked up the binoculars, and scanned the apartment building across the street. A woman in one of the units was busy preparing something in the kitchen. Unfortunately, she was dressed. I returned the binoculars to my desk drawer and glanced out the window. A pink Mercedes convertible with a two-seat black interior parked behind my Crown Vic. The left rear taillight appeared to be broken, which didn't come as a surprise. I watched a busty blonde slide out from behind the wheel, Barbie Dahl. The last time I saw her was out in Vegas, where she'd dumped me for Goose Gander's brother, Kenny. She was still gorgeous, and I presumed still certifiable.

She waited for a car to pass, but the guy slowed down and stopped so she could cross in front of him. As she walked past, he lowered the driver's window, shouted some comment I couldn't hear, and gave a whistle that I did hear. Barbie smiled, gave him a sexy little wave, and entered the building. A moment later, I heard her on the stairs.

I quickly pulled my wastebasket behind my desk and Googled the police department on my computer. The site came up on my computer screen just as she opened the door, smiled, and gave a sexy little knock on the door frame.

She wore an extremely short, pink plaid schoolgirl skirt, thigh-high white nylon stockings, white stiletto heels, and a pink, short-sleeve tie top. Her gorgeous blonde hair hung a good four inches below her shoulders, and her enhanced attributes appeared to have gone another round or two in the enlargement department. She smiled and slowly turned from left to right as if on stage, giving me a hundred-and-eighty-degree view as she stood in the doorway. "Miss me, darling?"

Three

Morton was suddenly off his pillow. He hurried over and shoved his nose beneath her schoolgirl skirt. "Wow. Barbie, long time no see. To what do I owe the pleasure?""Mmm, Martin, I see you haven't changed." She gave a sexy little shrug as she spoke but didn't push him away.

"Actually, his name is Morton. When did you get back in town? Last I knew, you were out in Las Vegas living it up in the Barbie Suite. Are you just back visiting?"

"All good things must come to an end. Are you going to invite me in?"

"Oh, yeah, please, please, come on in and have a seat. Can I get you something? I think there might be some coffee left, or maybe you'd like a beer?"

"No, thank you, Dev. I'm just fine." She gave a little sideways glance, suggesting my offer sounded crazy. As she sat down, she crossed her legs. Unfortunately, my desk limited the view. "So, how have you been, big boy?"

"Who, me? Well, I've been pretty good. You know me, I remain the most boring guy in town. So, you never said, are you just back for a visit?"

She shook her head. "No, as a matter of fact, I moved back almost two weeks ago. I bought a townhouse out in the burbs. After working in Vegas, I went out to California for awhile and made some movies. I toured the country on a promo tour dancing." I had the feeling the term XXX might be in there right before the word 'movies'. "I came back because I want to follow my true vocation."

"Your vocation? What are you planning to do, Barbie?"

"Hospital work."

"Really? You thinking of going to nursing school or trying to get into med school?"

"Don't be silly. I've built a following all across the country. I'm planning on opening up a Barbie hospital."

"A Barbie hospital?"

"Yeah, you know, Barbie has an ambulance and a hospital playset, and so I figure the next logical thing is for me to open up a Barbie hospital, except I'm going to call it the Dream House. I'll repair the various dolls, replace hair, maybe an arm or a leg."

"The Dream House?"

"Yeah. The market's ripe, and I've got over two million followers."

"Two million followers?"

"Yeah, between Facebook, Twitter, and my Podcasts."

"You do Podcasts?"

"Oh, yeah, Barbie Podcasts. I do them weekly. I've got a number of virtual Barbie backgrounds I use. My fans just love them. It would only seem logical that they'd all want to refresh their dolls. Don't you think?"

"I, umm, guess I never quite thought of it like that. Good for you, go for it."

"Well, thank you. Now, there just seems to be one little problem."

Here it comes, I thought. I figured she was about to ask me for money. I learned my lesson four years ago when we were out in Vegas. No way, not a cent. "So, you've got a little problem?"

"Yes, Ken's missing, and he's driving a truck filled with my entire Barbie collection."

"Wait a minute. You mean Kenny Gander, the IT guy from Vegas. He was, or is, my friend Goose's brother. He's missing?"

"Oh, I haven't seen either one of those two in years. No, this is my Ken, Ken Carson Wazinski. Although he's in the process of getting his name changed, I'm sure you can understand why."

I nodded and had no idea what she was talking about. "So, this Ken Carson guy is missing?"

"Yes. I flew back here from L.A. after I purchased the townhouse. I had my car and all my furniture shipped, and everything was delivered on time. But I didn't want to risk having anything happen to my Barbie collection. It's been appraised for between one-point-five and two-point-five million dollars."

"Of course," I said and nodded.

"Anyway, Ken graciously offered to drive it out here. We loaded everything in the truck. Packed it carefully, secured it so things wouldn't be bouncing around on the cross-country trip, and now he's nowhere to be found. I can't reach him on his cell phone. I'm not getting any responses to my text messages or my emails. It's like he's simply vanished."

"Did you ever think he just might be in an area where he's unable to get internet service? You know somewhere in the mountains or the middle of Nebraska."

"It's been over eight days."

"Hmm, do you know the route he was planning to take?"

"The route? More or less. L.A. to Vegas going up into Utah. From there, he would drive across Colorado and Nebraska and come up through Iowa and into Minnesota. He figured five days at the very most, you know driving a truck and all."

"So he's a day or two late. Maybe he had to stop for a repair or—"

"But I haven't been able to contact him since he left L.A. Certainly he would have stopped somewhere along the way and called me. I'm really worried something may have happened to my Barbie collection. Oh, yeah, and I guess Ken too," she added as an afterthought and not sounding all that convincing.

"Do you know who he rented the truck from?"

"He didn't rent it. He borrowed it."

"Do you know who he borrowed it from?"

"No, I don't. I can't locate him. I've called the highway patrol in all seven states, and they all say the same thing. They need more information."

"I don't suppose you have the license number of the truck."

"No, I don't. To be honest, at the time, I never even thought about it. He paid for the taxi to take me to the airport, said he would be leaving in a couple of days, and that's the last time I saw or talked to him. I'm worried about my collection. It's almost every Barbie item I own."

"Is your collection insured?"

"That was one of the benefits of having Ken drive everything up here, so I wouldn't have to pay insurance."

I took out a pen, pulled the bag from Rooster's out of the waste basket, and asked, "What's Ken's phone number?"

"She pulled her cellphone from her pink purse and moved her thumbs at lightning speed until she arrived at Ken's number. I found it interesting she didn't know it off the top of her head. I wrote the number on the Rooster's bag along with Ken's full name, Barbie's address, phone number, and email address. I opened a desk drawer, pulled out two business cards, and handed them to her. "Let me do a little checking, and I'll get back to you. Did you have any of Ken's personal items packed in the truck that brought your furniture and things?"

She nodded and said, "I've got maybe a half-dozen boxes and two suitcases with some clothes."

"Okay, I'll get on this right away. I'll call you in a couple of hours. Don't worry. We'll find him."

She pushed the chair back, stood, and slowly leaned over my desk. Her pink, short-sleeve tie top left nothing to my imagination. She gave me a lingering kiss on the lips, slowly stood and said, "Mmm, I really missed you. Don't forget to call me, Dev."

With that, she picked her purse up off the floor and sashayed out of the office. I watched out the window as she strutted across the street. Some guy drove down the street and tooted his horn as she climbed into the pink Mercedes. A moment later, she drove up the street and disappeared.

Four

I punched in the phone number Barbie had given me for Ken. The phone rang a number of times, before it dropped me into voicemail without having to listen to a recorded message. Once the beep sounded, I said, "Hi Ken, my name is Dev Haskell. I'm a friend of Barbie's. Just calling to make sure everything is all right. She was worried about you and stopped by my office. Please give me a call, so we know everything is okay, or in the event you need some assistance, we can get moving on that. Thanks, my number is six-five-one, blah, blah, blah. Looking forward to hearing from you."

Next, I Googled Ken Wazinski, and a message immediately popped up, 'There are no results matching your search.' I came up blank on a half-dozen other searches and called Aaron LaZelle, my pal heading up the homicide division in the St. Paul police department. I ended up leaving a message. "Hi Aaron, this is Dev. Would you give me a call when you have a minute? I'm trying to find a guy, and I'm drawing a bunch of blanks."

I brought up a Google map of routes from Los Angles to the twin cites. There were basically two, one of which listed all the states Barbie had mentioned. I

Googled state by state car accidents but only came up with legal firms looking for clients. Iowa looked like it had a site that listed accidents by date and county, but when I filled in the information, I got the notice that the site had been out of service since 2015 with no restart date available. No wonder Barbie was having a hard time finding this guy.

It was about half-past four when I heard the stairs creaking, and a moment later, a red-faced Louie opened the door and collapsed in his chair behind the picnic table. I knew better than to ask him a question at the moment. A couple of minutes passed before he said, "Oh, man. I wish there was an elevator I could take in this place."

"Yeah, I know what you mean. Climbing all the way up to the second floor can be a lot of work," I said.

Louie looked at me for a moment but didn't say anything.

"Everything go okay at your court hearing?" I asked.

"Yeah, other than they were running behind schedule. We weren't even called until almost half-past three. But in the end, we got what we wanted."

"Charges dropped?"

"If only. No, nothing quite that good, but a suspended sentence with charges expunged from her record after twenty-four months as long as there's not another incident."

"Will your client be able to do that?"

"Yeah, I think so. She's a grade school teacher. Got in a fender bender that actually wasn't her fault. Unfortunately, the cops happened to show up. She'd been drinking and blew over the legal limit. Cost her twelve hundred in repairs, a five hundred dollar fine, and she'll be in a risk insurance category for the next seven years. Even with the charges dropped, it's going to cost her eleven to twelve hundred bucks over the next seven years. Anything happen in your life?"

"Well," I said and proceeded to give him my Barbie update.

Louie just shook his head as I described her situation, what she looked like, and the fact that I had found absolutely nothing on her close personal friend Ken. "So let me get this straight. She still thinks she's the real-life Barbie. She's ended up with some fruit cake who's going to change his given name, whatever the hell it is, to Ken Carson. She does Barbie podcasts and is going to open up a Barbie Hospital and call it the Doll House, or Dream House, or something. Does that pretty well sum things up?

I nodded. "Yeah, pretty much. Don't forget, this Ken character is missing in action."

"Oh yeah. How could I forget? Barbie can't seem to find Ken. I'm thinking it sounds like he maybe absconded with all her Barbie stuff. What'd she say that junk was worth? The dolls and all the other crap?"

"She wasn't that specific. What she actually said is the stuff has been appraised at between one-point-five and two-point five million."

"Maybe it is. I'm certainly the wrong guy to ask about it," Louie said. "Could be this Ken character, or whatever his name really is, took that appraisal for hundreds of thousands to heart and headed somewhere else with her Barbie collection. Nowadays, with eBay and the like, he could be selling that stuff all day, every day, and it would be damn near impossible to stop him."

"God, I never even thought of eBay," I said. I Googled eBay and entered 'Barbie Dolls.' The site had fifty items per page, and I don't know how many pages. The first item on the page was Flash Dance Barbie for a hundred and seventy-five bucks, and the second item was Barbie the Rose for seventy-five dollars. "This is crazy. There are people out there paying this kind of money for these things?"

"Collectors, Dev. Is it that much different from collecting stamps or coins?"

"I don't know. It's just, oh man. Check this out."

"What is it?" Louie asked.

"There's two pictures of Ken, the doll. I completely forgot that was the guy doll Barbie was having an affair with. Interesting, they're only going for twenty-four bucks. I'll bet that's why I couldn't find him online. His name isn't really Ken. She told me he was changing his name, but I figured it would just be his last name. Oh man, if he's changing his name, I wonder if he's done any plastic surgery to make him look like the dolls."

"I'm guessing they're handsome," Louie said.

"Actually, they kind of look like the guy you'd want to punch in the nose just because. One of those privileged jerks everyone thinks the world of. If he looks anything like these things, no wonder we can't find him. The first guy who saw him probably just beat the crap out of him."

"Maybe ask your pal Barbie if she's got a picture of him. Just for starters. You could always put something online. You know, a missing Ken doll report." Louie laughed. "You know it would be interesting to do that. Just to see if you got a bunch of women replying saying the picture looks just like their Ken doll."

"Actually, Louie, that's not a bad idea. Hang on." I punched in Barbie's number. She answered on the third ring. "Hi Barbie, it's Dev."

"Did you find Ken already?"

"No, at least not yet, but I'm chasing down some leads. You said you have some items of his at your place?"

"Yeah, a couple of suitcases and some boxes."

"I'm just about to go into a meeting. Once that's over, I'd like to head out to your place, if that's okay, and go through those things. Might be an hour or two before I get there."

She seemed to think about that for a long moment.

"Barbie, you still there?"

"Yeah, umm, I guess that would be okay if you think it would speed things up."

"You're at the address you gave me in Oak Park Heights?"

"Yes, my townhouse."

"Okay, I'll see you in ninety minutes or so," I said and hung up.

"You've still got a meeting this afternoon?" Louie asked.

"Yeah, with you. Remember, I'm buying over at The Spot."

To be continued...

Books by Mike Faricy
Crime Fiction Firsts

A boxset of the first four books in four crime fiction series:

Russian Roulette; Dev Haskell series
Welcome; Jack Dillon Dublin Tales series
Corridor Man; Corridor Man series
Reduced Ransom! Hot Shot series

The following titles comprise the Dev Haskell series:

Russian Roulette: Case 1
Mr. Swirlee: Case 2
Bite Me: Case 3
Bombshell: Case 4
Tutti Frutti: Case 5
Last Shot: Case 6
Ting-A-Ling: Case 7
Crickett: Case 8
Bulldog: Case 9
Double Trouble: Case 10
Yellow Ribbon: Case 11
Dog Gone: Case 12
Scam Man: Case 13
Foiled: Case 14
What Happens in Vegas… Case 15
Art Hound: Case 16
The Office: Case 17

Star Struck: Case 18
International Incident: Case 19
Guest From Hell: Case 20
Art Attack: Case 21
Mystery Man: Case 22
Bow-Wow Rescue: Case 23
Cold Case: Case 24
Cash Up Front: Case 25
Dream House: Case 26
Alley Katz: Case 27
The Big Gamble: Case 28
Bad to the Bone: Case 29
Silencio!: Case 30
Surprise, Surprise: Case 31
Hit & Run: Case 32
Suspect Santa: Case 33
P.I. Apprentice: Case 34
Rebel Without a Clue: Case 35

The following titles are Dev Haskell novellas:
Dollhouse
The Dance
Pixie
Fore!
Twinkle Toes
(*a Dev Haskell short story*)

The following are Dev Haskell Boxsets:
Dev Haskell Boxset 1-3
Dev Haskell Boxset 4-6
Dev Haskell Boxset 7-9
Dev Haskell Boxset 10-12
Dev Haskell Boxset 13-15
Dev Haskell Boxset 16-18
Dev Haskell Boxset 19-21
Dev Haskell Boxset 22-24
Dev Haskell Boxset 25-27
Dev Haskell Boxset 28-30
Dev Haskell Boxset 1-7
Dev Haskell Boxset 8-14
Dev Haskell Boxset 15-19
Dev Haskell Boxset 20-24
Dev Haskell Boxset 25-29

The following titles comprise the Jack Dillon Dublin Tales series:
Welcome
Jack Dillon Dublin Tale 1
Sweet Dreams
Jack Dillon Dublin Tale 2
Mirror Mirror
Jack Dillon Dublin Tale 3
Silver Bullet
Jack Dillon Dublin Tale 4
Fair City Blues
Jack Dillon Dublin Tale 5

Spade Work
Jack Dillon Dublin Tale 6
Madeline Missing
Jack Dillon Dublin Tale 7
Mistaken Identity
Jack Dillon Dublin Tale 8
Picture Perfect
Jack Dillon Dublin Tale 9
Dublin Moon
Jack Dillon Dublin Tale 10
Mystery Woman
Jack Dillon Dublin Tale 11
Second Chance
Jack Dillon Dublin Tale 12
Payback Brother
Jack Dillon Dublin Tale 13
The Heist
Jack Dillon Dublin Tale 14
Jewels To Kill For
Jack Dillon Dublin Tale 15
Retirement Scheme
Jack Dillon Dublin Tale 16
The Collector
Jack Dillon Dublin Tale 17

Jack Dillon Dublin Tales Boxsets:
Jack Dillon Dublin Tales 1-3
Jack Dillon Dublin Tales 4-6
Jack Dillon Dublin Tales 1-5

Jack Dillon Dublin Tales 1-7
Jack Dillon Dublin Tales 6-10

The following titles comprise the Hotshot series;
Reduced Ransom! Second Edition
Finders Keepers! Second Edition
Bankers Hours Second Edition
Chow Down Second Edition
Moonlight Dance Academy Second Edition
Irish Dukes (Fight Card Series)
written under the pseudonym Jack Tunney

The following titles comprise the Corridor Man series:
Corridor Man
Corridor Man 2: Opportunity knocks
Corridor Man 3: The Dungeon
Corridor Man 4: Dead End
Corridor Man 5: Finger
Corridor Man 6: Exit Strategy
Corridor Man 7: Trunk Music
Corridor Man 8: Birthday Boy
Corridor Man 9: Boss Man
Corridor Man 10: Bye Bye Bobby

Corridor Man novellas:
Corridor Man: Valentine
Corridor Man: Auditor
Corridor Man: Howling

Corridor Man: Spa Day

The following are Corridor Man Boxsets:
Corridor Man Boxset 1-3
Corridor Man Boxset 1-5
Corridor Man Boxset 6-9

All books are available on Amazon.com
Thank you!

Contact the author:
- Email: mikefaricyauthor@gmail.com
- Twitter: @Mikefaricybooks
- Facebook: Mike Faricy Author
- Website: http://www.mikefaricybooks.com

Published by

MJF Publishing

Mike Faricy • 338